Until HARRY

ALSO BY L.A. CASEY

SLATER BROTHERS SERIES

DOMINIC

BRONAGH

ALEC

KEELA

KANE

AIDEEN

RYDER

STAND-ALONE NOVELS

FROZEN

Until HARRY

L.A. CASEY

Montlake Romance

This is a work of fiction. Names, characters, organisations, places, events, and incidents are either products of the author's imagination or are used fictitiously.

Published by Montlake Romance Publishing, Seattle
www.apub.com

ISBN-13: 9781503936607
ISBN-10: 1503936600

Cover design by Ryan Young

Printed in the United States of America

To all of my angels up in heaven – I'll see you later

CHAPTER ONE

Day one in York

Lane,

I'm writing you this letter because I think there is a better chance you will open it and read it, instead of just deleting it like I know you do to my emails. I'm not going to sugar-coat anything or talk pleasantries. I'm getting straight to the point. I'm sorry to tell you this through a lousy piece of paper, but Uncle Harry passed away this morning. You need *to come home and say goodbye. Mum and Nanny aren't dealing well with Harry's death. None of us are. We miss you terribly, and right now we need you. We all do. The funeral is on Saturday. Please, come home. Please.*

—Lochlan

I pushed my glasses up the bridge of my nose as I reread the letter from my brother for the millionth time since I received it two days ago. It stated two things. One, my uncle passed away. My godfather and dear friend was gone. And two, I had to go home.

I wasn't jumping for joy about either fact.

I looked up from the worn paper Lochlan's letter was scribbled upon and gazed out the window of the train I was sitting inside. The Yorkshire countryside passed me by, and in seconds I was lost in the green beauty of it. Unfortunately, the glamour of the never-ending dreamlike view wasn't enough to mask the pain in my chest. The horrendous agony quickly brought me back to the present, and it screamed that I couldn't run from it.

Not this time, Lane, a sour voice in my mind hissed. *You can't escape this.*

Nothing beautiful to the naked eye or soothing to the delicate ear could erase the inevitable reality I would soon have to face head on. I shifted in my seat as my stomach roiled at the thought of what the next few days entailed.

Why did this have to happen? I glumly wondered.

I felt guilty that I momentarily wished I were back in my New York apartment instead of travelling to my home town of York, England. I then felt shamefaced about pondering why my uncle's death had to land me in such a horrible situation when what I should have been thinking of is why God had to take him away in the first place.

My priorities, as usual, were messed up.

I had difficulty swallowing a lump that formed in my throat. After I took a couple of deep breaths to relax myself, I took my phone out from my coat pocket and opened up my emails. My lip twitched as I scrolled through them. There were hundreds upon hundreds of messages from my Uncle Harry that I never got around to deleting and I was glad of it. He was the only person from back home who I talked to daily. Actually, he was the only person from home that I still spoke to at all. I could escape everyone else, but not my Uncle Harry.

He was a pain in the arse, but I wouldn't trade him for the world. He was my truest and most trusted friend, and now he was gone.

I had questioned what was wrong when he never emailed me on Tuesday morning. We spoke over Skype the previous afternoon, and he was perfectly fine. We had a routine; I woke up to an email from him every morning, and we would chat back and forth until I spoke to him over Skype during my lunch break at work. When it was 2 p.m. in New York, it was 7 p.m. in York. Uncle Harry went to bed around 9 p.m., so we always spoke beforehand.

I immediately called his phone on Tuesday morning when I didn't receive an email from him, but his house phone just rang until his answering machine picked up. I left a brief message asking him to ring me as soon as he could, and when he didn't, dread filled me. I was terribly apprehensive and I couldn't call my parents to check in on him because I'd deleted their phone numbers years ago – my brothers' too.

The only number I knew by heart was my uncle's because he had had the same number for as long as I could remember.

When Wednesday morning came and he *still* hadn't contacted me, I decided to go online and get the number to Lilly's Café on Pavement Street. My grandmother owned the business, but she was also on my do-not-speak-to list, just like my parents and siblings, so we weren't close.

Not like we used to be before I moved away.

That glitch aside, I figured if I had to ring someone to check on my uncle, it would be my nanny. She was stubborn as hell, but she was the only member of my family that could be reasoned with. Scarcely.

I didn't have Internet in my apartment – which was shocking considering I was a freelance editor – because the signal strength in my area was very poor. I availed myself of the free Wi-Fi at the local Starbucks whenever I needed it. I got dressed that Wednesday morning, with the intention of heading to Starbucks for the use of said free Wi-Fi to contact my nanny.

I met my postman on the bottom floor of my apartment complex on my way out, and he handed me a single letter. There were urgent stickers all over it, as well as stickers for next-day delivery. It had been sent the day before. The return address was from my brother, so I immediately ripped it open.

Reading that godforsaken letter was the second time in my life that my heart broke into a million pieces. The devastation that dwelt within me was a familiar emotion, but this time it was due to a completely different person, in relation to an entirely different situation. Once more I was overtaken by the kind of sadness that seeps into your bones rather than explodes in a cascade of tears. The misery that I felt filled me from head to toe, and I couldn't escape from it.

I tried, though. I tried to think about something else as I booked a flight to London. I tried to think of something else as I landed in Heathrow Airport and took the Heathrow Express train to Paddington Station. I tried to think of anything but my Uncle Harry's face, and I did well until I got a taxi from Paddington Station to King's Cross Station and got on the final train in my journey to York. After I stepped foot in Coach B – it was the quiet carriage – my Uncle Harry's voice broke through every single thought I fabricated to cover him up. His voice stuck with me, and I found both comfort and sorrow in that.

I was pulled from my thoughts when the train came to a sudden stop. I blinked my eyes a couple of times and looked out the window. I was no longer looking at the countryside; I was staring at the busy platform of my final stop. York.

Welcome home, Lane.

After exhaling a deep breath, I nervously got to my feet and shoved my phone back into my coat pocket before grabbing my small suitcase from the storage compartment above my head. I was walking along the platform a few minutes later, pulling my suitcase behind me. I got a taxi from the station to the Holiday Inn, a small hotel roughly ten minutes away from my parents' house, and checked into the hotel, settling into my small but cosy room. I was freshening up when my phone pinged. At the sight of my brother's name, I groaned.

Lochlan was looking for confirmation that I was coming home for my uncle's funeral. I didn't blame him for checking in – I'd never replied to his letter. I just read it and acted by booking the next flight out of New York.

I'm here, I thumbed out. *Where is he laid out?*

I swallowed the bile that rose up my throat as I impatiently waited for his reply. I had so many questions, but I didn't want any answers. I wanted to know why my uncle was dead when he had been perfectly healthy. I wanted to know why he had been living Monday night and was dead Tuesday morning. But if I got the answers my mind sought, then it would be like I was accepting that my uncle was gone, and I just wasn't ready to do that yet.

I jumped when my phone pinged with a new email.

Mum and Dad's house. We're all here.

A lump formed in my throat. It made sense that my uncle would be at my parents' house; my uncle adored my mother, and she cherished him in return. She was his little sister, his partner in crime and his twin.

I rubbed my eyes when they began to sting.

I'll be there in 20 minutes.

I grabbed a pair of black fitted jeans, black ankle boots, a black long-sleeve T-shirt and a grey blazer. When I was dressed, I turned to the full-length mirror and stared at myself. I looked the same as I always had, but noticed the subtle differences others would see when they looked at me. My chocolate-brown hair was longer now, almost to my waist. My breasts were fuller, and hips were a little wider, giving a curve to my body that now showed me as woman, and not a girl. My porcelain skin had a splash of light freckles, and my emerald-green eyes were still hidden behind the glasses that sat atop the bridge of my nose.

I adjusted my blazer and blinked. I didn't know why, but I didn't want to dress down to see my family for the first time in six years. I wanted to look put together, even though inside I was falling apart.

I plaited my hair back into a French braid to keep it out of my face, and didn't bother with make-up, because seeing my uncle would open a floodgate of emotions, so it would get ruined anyway. I picked up a pale blue scarf from the bed and wrapped it around my neck before grabbing my phone and key card.

As my parents' house was close by, I decided to walk. It wasn't raining out, for once, but being the middle of October, it was already pitch-black by 6 p.m. and starting to get *really* cold. I folded my arms across my chest and kept my head down as I scurried past my nanny's café. It was closed as expected. I saw no lights on out of the corner of my eye, but just in case, I kept my gaze averted.

The walk to my parents' place was quicker than I remembered, and before I knew it, I stood in front of the door of the house I grew up in. I blinked as I took in my childhood home. It was mildly adorned with some Halloween decorations – reminding me of the upcoming holiday – but that aside, it looked the exact same as the last time I'd seen it six years ago, just like nothing changed . . . or happened.

You can do this, I told myself.

I repeated the thought over and over in my mind as I lifted my hand in the air and prepared to knock on the darkly varnished door. I didn't get the chance, though, because the door suddenly opened, revealing a pair of women in their mid-twenties who were exiting the house. I had no idea who they were and found myself staring.

"Oh, I'm sorry," the woman with platinum-blonde hair said on a gasp before composing herself. "Can I help you?"

Who is she? I wondered, *and why is she asking if she can help me?*

"No, thank you," I replied civilly. "Can I get by you?"

The woman didn't move, and the brunette next to her folded her arms across her chest and stepped closer to her friend. I glanced to her, then back to the blonde. It looked like they were trying to keep me out of the house.

"Who are you?" the blonde asked.

Her tone wasn't rude, just curious.

I impatiently tapped my foot against the ground and counted to five before answering. "I'm Lane. This is my parents' house. Can I *please* get by you?"

"Lane?" the blonde woman gasped.

She spoke as if she knew me, but I didn't recognise her. I nodded to her question, and it caused both of the women to widen their eyes and instantly separate, forming a passage between them. I thanked them, stepped between them and entered my parents' house. I took a nervous breath and walked across the hallway and towards the parlour.

I glanced over my shoulder when the blonde and brunette rushed by me and headed down the hallway in the direction of the kitchen. I looked away from them and back to the parlour door. I knew my uncle would be in there; it was where my Aunt Teresa had been laid out after she'd died many years ago.

I reached for the handle of the door and gently pushed it open with my fingertip. The scent of jasmine filled my nostrils and wrapped around me like a blanket. I inhaled a deep breath and let the comfort of the familiar scent surround me. My gaze was downcast, but out of the corner of my eye I could see the legs of the stand that the coffin was lying on. I slowly walked over to it and lingered for a moment. Before I froze up altogether, I moved around to the right side of the coffin and sucked in a breath when I lifted my head and my eyes landed on him.

I slapped my hand over my mouth when a sob escaped. He was really there – it wasn't some sort of sick joke. . . My uncle was really dead. The sight of him brought back a sudden memory of talking to him over Skype a few years ago, and it played havoc on my heart.

"Lane, darling, please talk to me," my uncle pleaded. "You aren't happy. I can see it in you."

"I'm fine, Uncle Harry," I sighed. "It's just taking me longer to settle in here than I thought it would."

My uncle dead-panned, "You moved to the city four years ago."

"So?" I grunted. "It's a different country. It's still a lot for me to get used to."

"Are you sure?" my uncle pressed. "Maybe you should talk to your nanny – she's very good in situations when you're sad."

An alarm went off in my head.

"Nuh-uh, I don't think so. I don't want to speak to the Irish Oprah. She'll just nit-pick and I don't want that. You know she will talk me into getting on a plane and coming home. She has a gift, and I'm not letting her sway me."

"Then tell me what's going on – please?" he pleaded. "I can sense something is off with you. Did something happen?"

"I'm. Fine," I assured him, then decided to put him out of his misery. "I just had a bit of a weak moment and thought about doing something silly, that's all."

"Explain," my uncle almost growled. "Now."

I gnawed on my lower lip and brought the volume of my voice way down so the other customers in Starbucks couldn't hear me. "I had a dream about him last night, and I woke up in a cold sweat. For a second, for a split second, I thought about taking some pills. Before you freak out and demand I come home, know that I know it was a very serious thought, and I've booked a session with a therapist to talk about it."

"Lane," said my uncle firmly.

"I'm fine – I just want to talk to a therapist about it."

My uncle blinked. "It may help if you talk to Ka—"

"No." I cut my uncle off. "I can't."

"Lane—"

"No, Uncle Harry, I don't want to see or speak to him. Please. I can't."

My uncle grumbled. "Okay. Fine."

I groaned. "You do this at least once a week. When will you give up on getting me to talk to him?"

"When I'm dead and buried."

"Don't talk like that." I wagged my finger at him. "You aren't going anywhere."

"Uncle Harry," I whimpered as I was pulled from my memory and brought back to the present. I moved closer to the coffin, my stomach brushing against the wood. "I'm . . . I'm *so* sorry I wasn't here."

Remorse filled me, and in that moment I was sick with myself. I hadn't been here for him when he needed me most. I'd put my own selfish needs above a man who had done nothing but love me all of my life.

A soft cry came from behind me, then I felt arms wrap around my body. I had no idea who was comforting me. I could smell the aftershave he wore, which cloaked around me just like his arms did. I placed my hands on top of the hands that rested on my stomach.

"It's okay, my love."

Daddy.

I burst into tears and, turning into my father's embrace, I wrapped my arms around his waist. My father held me and swayed us from side to side until my sobs became sniffles. After a few minutes I turned and looked back to my uncle. I placed my hand on top of his head, squeezing my eyes shut when I found it was ice-cold to the touch.

I reopened my eyes and looked at his handsome face.

"I'm sorry," I repeated, leaning over and kissing his soft cheek. I then gently pressed my forehead to the side of his head. "I'm *so* sorry."

I let everything go and cried and cried and cried.

I had wept when I read Lochlan's letter, but it was nothing compared to the emotion upon seeing my uncle. I was just short of wailing in sorrow. I was heartbroken, and the more I looked at my wonderful uncle, the more destroyed and empty I felt inside.

"How was your flight?" a voice asked from the parlour doorway.

I didn't need to look to know it was the voice of my brother Layton. I hadn't heard his voice in close to a year, but it was still the same. It was just a little huskier, probably from his bad habit of smoking. That wasn't surprising, though. He was twenty-nine now and had smoked for as long as I could remember.

"Long," I replied to Layton without looking away from my uncle.

My father stayed behind me, holding me tightly. I was aware that the close contact was probably going to change after my uncle was buried in the cemetery tomorrow, but I didn't linger on it. I didn't see eye to eye with my parents, my nanny or my brothers, but right now I wasn't thinking of our differences; I was thinking of my Uncle Harry.

"Where is your suitcase?"

I tensed a little at the sound of my mother's voice, then murmured, "At the Holiday Inn."

I heard a snarl. "You're staying in the hotel, and not *here*?"

I exhaled a tired breath. "Don't do this now, Lochlan. Please."

He didn't listen.

"You're *not* staying in a poxy hotel—"

"Lochlan." Layton's stern voice cut our brother off. "We'll discuss it *later*."

Silence.

I closed my eyes when I heard the pounding footsteps of Lochlan as he stormed out of the room and down the hallway into the sitting room, slamming the door behind him. I wasn't surprised that he walked away. Lochlan might be the temperamental brother, but Layton's word was law. He was the only person who got through to Lochlan when he stepped over the line. I tried not to let my brother, or his outburst, bother me, so I focused completely on my uncle.

"I was waiting for your email," I crooned to him and waited for his reply, even though I knew it would never come.

My father squeezed me. "It was sudden, sweetheart."

I felt ill.

"How did it happen?" I asked the dreaded question that was on my mind from the minute I'd read Lochlan's letter two days ago.

"A heart attack," my father exhaled. "He felt no pain. It happened in his sleep."

A heart attack, I silently repeated. *That's what took my uncle.*

I gnawed on my lower lip as I glanced at his attire. I couldn't help but grin as I took in the thick fleece jumper that I'd knitted him when I was sixteen. He'd loved it, and no matter how many times I'd told him to bin it, he'd refused. He'd said it was the best present he had ever received, which caused me to feel bad for him because it was downright disgusting-looking. I couldn't knit to save my life.

My nanny forced the unholy task of knitting upon me during the summer I turned sixteen. I was *more* than awful at it, but my nanny didn't care. She made me do it every weekend with her and her friends, who combined had three hundred plus years on me. If my nanny heard me say that, she would whack me. I inwardly giggled to myself at the silent jab and shook my head good-naturedly.

"Him and that bloody jumper," I muttered.

Soft chuckles filled the parlour then, and it helped take some of the hurt and tension away for a few fleeting moments.

When I was ready, I took a steady breath, then turned to look at the faces I hadn't seen in the flesh for six years. The first person I saw was my mother. She looked older than her fifty-four years, but no doubt my uncle's passing had added to the lines on her still beautiful face. My nanny, who was next to my mother, still looked the same as she had the day I left. My second brother was different. He was muscular . . . *very* muscular. He'd been overweight the last time I'd seen him, but that wasn't the case anymore.

"Jesus, Lay, did someone buy you a gym membership?" I asked, stunned.

My father burst into laughter behind me while my mother and nanny covered their mouths and tried to muffle their giggles. My brother smirked at me, but his aqua-blue eyes shone brightly.

"I couldn't be the fat twin forever, now could I?" he asked, tongue-in-cheek.

I playfully grinned. "I guess not. You look great."

Layton winked. "You too, sis."

My lip quirked for a moment, then I turned and looked at my father. His handsome face was the same, just hairier and fuller. His entire body was fuller.

I blinked. "While Layton hit the gym, you hit the pub and chippy. Huh?"

My father gently clipped me around the ear. "Cheeky brat. I'll have you know a few layers of fat never hurt anyone. It keeps me warm on these cold winter nights."

"I'm teasing," I chortled, and hugged him.

I liked that he was fuller; there was more of him to snuggle.

My brother, mother and nanny were in a fit of laughter at my teasing, and it took them a few moments to calm themselves. My nanny walked towards me when she was at ease and pulled me into her warm embrace.

"Hello, me darlin'," she crooned.

I closed my eyes and gave her a tight squeeze as I got lost in her soothing voice. My nanny was from Crumlin in Dublin, Ireland. Her accent was thick as ever – even though she had lived in England the past fifty years, she never lost her Irish brogue and I loved that about her.

I smiled affectionately. "Hey, Nanny."

When my nanny let go of me, Layton was right there, gathering me up in his thick, muscled arms. I yelped a little when he lifted me clean off the floor and held me in mid-air like I weighed nothing.

"Can't breathe," I playfully wheezed.

My brother set me down and snorted, "Little terror."

I teasingly grinned, then lost it and replaced it with a bright smile for my mother when she approached me. I was expecting her to smile at me and possibly be a little teary, but I definitely didn't expect her to burst into tears as she hugged me, which is exactly what she did.

"Welcome home, baby," she wept. "I've missed you *so* much."

I folded my arms around her small body and squeezed. "I've missed you too, Mum."

That was the God's honest truth. I did miss her. We didn't agree on my living away from home, but she was still my mother, and I loved her dearly. She held onto me for a long time as she cried. She kept pulling back from our hug, looking at my face, then throwing her arms back around me and squeezing me as tightly as she possibly could. It was like she couldn't believe I stood in front of her. That made me both happy and sad. Happy because she was happy to see me, and sad because it was my fault that she rarely got a chance to see me in the first place.

You have your reasons, I reminded myself.

I stroked her back. "It's okay, Mum."

Nothing was okay, but it felt right to say it.

When we eventually separated, I looked from my family to my uncle and frowned. "I guess the only person left for me to greet is Lochlan."

A throat cleared from behind me. "Not quite."

Oh, no, I silently pleaded. *Please, God, no.*

I felt my eyes widen as his voice encircled me like a warm blanket. No matter how many years went by, I would know his voice even if it were a whisper. I slowly turned, but I froze when I saw him standing in the doorway of the parlour, leaning against the panel with his hands jammed into the front pockets of his jeans.

His eyes, my mind whispered. *What's wrong with his eyes?*

There were many things that I loved about the man before me, but his eyes were by far my favourite. They were the first things I looked at whenever I saw him. There was always a mischievous glint in his whisky-coloured eyes that only I could see because I looked hard enough. It was a glint that told me his soul was alive and thriving, but what I saw now caused me to shiver.

There was no glint, gleam or light of any sort in his eyes. They were dead and reflected the clouded grey skies that often hung over York. They were as captivating as they were haunting.

Even though I moved thousands of miles away to escape him, every day for the past six years I woke up seeing those hazel eyes and fell asleep hearing that soothing voice. I couldn't shake him whether I was half a world away or in the next room.

I lived and breathed Kale Hunt, and it was killing me.

"Kale," I managed to whisper as I stared at the first man to ever break my heart.

He gazed at me, then with no trace of emotion he robotically blinked and nodded in greeting. "Welcome home, Laney Baby."

CHAPTER TWO

Six years old (twenty years ago)

Lane? Where are you?"

I placed my hands over my ears and squeezed my eyes shut and tried to contain my sobs, but couldn't. They racked through my body because my head hurt so bad. Rubbing it didn't make the pain go away and only worsened the throb.

I opened my eyes when an arm slid under my knees, then another slipped around my back. I yelped when I was suddenly lifted up into the air, and instinctively latched my arms around the neck of the person who lifted me up. I looked at the person's face, and when bright hazel eyes shone back at me, I cried.

"Kale!"

Kale Hunt was my best friend in the whole wide world. If anyone could make me feel better when I was hurting so bad, it was Kale. He was always the one to take my tears away and put a smile on my face.

I buried my face into the crook of his neck and sobbed like my world was ending. Kale walked over to a desk in my classroom. He sat me on his lap, and hugged my body to his. He rocked me from side to side until I was calm enough to sit up without snotting and blubbering everywhere.

I looked to Kale when he handed me some tissue from his pocket. After wiping my nose and face clear of tears and snot, I blew my nose and sniffled before crumpling the used tissue.

"What happened to you?" Kale asked me, his concern laced through his words.

I continued to sniffle but remained silent and still. I didn't want to tell him because I would get in big trouble, and he would probably shout at me. I didn't want to be shouted at.

"Lane?" Kale pressed when I turned my gaze from his. "What. Happened?"

I felt my lower lip wobble, and he sighed.

"I'm not mad at you," he softly assured me, "but you *need* to tell me what happened. Anna O'Leary came and told me that you ran in here from the yard and that something happened. Tell me what. Please."

"I . . . I was playing skipping with Anna O'Leary and Ally Day when Jordan Hummings took our rope and ran away." I lowered my head until my chin touched my chest. "I chased after him and tried to get it back, but Jordan fell and said it was my fault, so he punched me in my head and now it *really* hurts."

Kale's hold on me tightened.

"Jordan Hummings?" he growled. "The boy in *my* class?"

I slowly nodded.

That's why I was so scared; Jordan was a big boy like Kale.

"He *hit* you?" Kale asked, his voice a snarl.

I began to cry again when Kale's anger became evident. He quickly lost the livid look on his face and just as quickly put his arms back around me. He hushed me, said sweet things to me and that he was going to make everything better.

I believed him.

"Come with me," he said, and stood up, then settled my feet on the floor. "My playtime is over in a few minutes, so I have to do this quick."

Kale was in big boy classes, and I didn't like it. He had to be in big boy classes, though, because he was nine years old and had to learn big boy things . . . like maths. When I start year 2 classes next year, Kale and I will have the same yard time and can play together all the time. He told me so.

"Where are we going?" I asked Kale as he threaded his fingers through mine.

He grunted in response as he led me out of my classroom and down the long corridor to the exit door that opened up to the playground.

"I'm going to fix what happened to you," he said as he pushed the door open and stepped through it.

I gripped his hand tightly as we walked around loads of children who were playing chase, hopscotch and skipping. We stopped at the girls who were skipping in the spot I'd been skipping on a while ago.

"Hey, girls, have either of you seen Jordan Hummings?" Kale asked.

I didn't know who they were, but they were older than me. They might have even been in Kale's class because they both smiled wide at him when he spoke to them. I narrowed my eyes at them and pressed closer to Kale's side. I didn't like that way they were looking at him. They looked a little *too* happy to see him.

"Hey, Kale." The girl with the bright red hair and lightly freckled skin beamed. "I did actually. He's gone behind the prefabs with his friends. I'm not sure why, though."

Kale smiled to the redhead. "Thanks, Drew."

Drew's smile touched her ears. It was that big.

"Anytime," she replied, tucking a piece of her luscious hair behind her ear, a coy smile on her lips.

I didn't like Drew; I didn't like her at all.

I tugged on Kale's hand when he didn't move. He was just standing there, looking at this Drew girl with a weird, goofy look on his face, and it made me mad.

"Kale!" I snapped.

He jumped a little, then looked down at me and blinked as if he'd forgotten I was there.

"She is *so* cute – is she your sister?"

Kale looked away from me and back to Drew when she spoke.

"Lane? She's actually my best friend. I'm really close with her brothers and family. She *is* pretty much my sister."

The look of admiration Drew shot Kale really ticked me off.

"Wow. That's *really* cute, Kale," Drew said, and lifted her right hand to her shining red hair, twisting her fingers around the end of it.

I wanted to chop the hair off her head. She touched it way too much.

"It-it is?" Kale stuttered, then had to clear his throat because it made a funny noise.

Drew nodded. "Yep. I think it's really cool that you look out for her."

Kale acted differently then. He shrugged his shoulders like what Drew said was no big deal and then untangled his hand from mine so he could leisurely drop it over my shoulder. "Well, you know. Someone's gotta look after her. She's six but she's really small for her age. She's only a kid."

I frowned up at Kale and decided I didn't like how different he was around this Drew girl and her friend with blonde hair who did nothing but stand and stare at him since the moment he'd asked where Jordan was.

Jordan.

At the reminder of why Kale was even talking to these girls, I tugged on his hand to get his attention, and when he looked down at me I said, "Jordan."

Kale blinked, then shook his head clear and set his jaw.

He looked back to Drew. "You said Jordan went behind the prefabs, right?"

Drew bobbed her head up and down. "Uh-huh."

Kale winked. "Thanks, beautiful."

He turned to me then and said, "Stay here with Drew. I'll be right back."

With that said, he walked around me and headed in the direction of the prefabs. I was on the verge of tears because he'd done something wrong. He'd called Drew beautiful, but that had to be wrong because he said *I* was the only beautiful girl in the world. Just me. He always told me that.

"Did you hear that?" Drew squeaked to her friend and clapped her hands together like a seal at the zoo. "He called me beautiful. *Beautiful!*"

Drew's friend jumped up and down and squealed. I resisted putting my fingers in my ears to block out the horrible noise.

"I did," Drew's friend said as she too clapped her hands together like a seal. "I *so* did. Oh, my God! He *so* likes you! Did you see how he couldn't stop staring? You're so bloody lucky, Drew – he is gorgeous!"

I didn't want to stand there and listen to Drew and her friend as they gushed over Kale, so I ran after him. I heard Drew call for me, but I didn't turn around to answer her. In fact, I mentally stuck my tongue out at her.

Take that, Drew.

I spotted Kale's back as he disappeared around the back of the prefabs, so I ran my fastest after him. I got to the back of the prefabs at the same time a hand clamped down on my shoulder.

"Hold your horses – Kale said you have to stay with *me*." I looked over my shoulder and stared up at Drew, who was looking down at me with furrowed brows. Her chest rose and fell rapidly like my own as we both tried to catch our breath.

She lifted her gaze and looked straight ahead. Her mouth formed into the shape of an O before she flung her hand over her mouth and screeched. I jumped with fright and snapped my head forward, but like Drew, I too screeched when I saw what she had.

Kale was in a fight – with *three* boys.

"Kale!" I cried when one of the boys kicked him in the side of his belly.

I tried to rush forward to help him, but arms folded around me from behind.

"Stop!" Drew's voice hissed in my ear. "You'll get hurt!"

I didn't care; I had to help Kale before *he* got hurt.

"Leave him alone!" I screamed at the boys. "Stop it, *please*!"

The noises of punches and slaps filled my ears, and just as I was about to scream again, one of the boys on top of Kale suddenly yelped in pain after receiving a kick between the legs. He fell backwards onto the ground and held both hands between his legs. He didn't get back up and try to hit Kale again; he stayed down and began to cry in pain.

A few seconds later a second boy fell back off Kale, holding his nose, and he began to cry too, and like the boy next to him, he stayed on the ground and held onto his face as blood began to seep through the fingers he had pressed over his nose.

I didn't know why, but I held tightly onto Drew's arms as she bent down and picked me up. She held me to her and tried to turn so I couldn't see what was happening, but I turned my head just enough to see that the last boy to fight Kale was Jordan Hummings. The boy who stole my skipping rope and punched me in the back of my head.

Kale was on top of Jordan. Both of them had blood on them, but Jordan had a lot more on him than Kale did, and he was crying.

Kale was not. Jordan lifted his hands and tried to push Kale off, but Kale knocked his hands to the side and grabbed him by the collar of his school uniform and held him in place.

"If you *ever*," Kale bellowed down into his face, "touch my family again, I'll fucking *kill* you!"

I gasped. Kale said a bad word, a *really* bad word. He was going to be in *so* much trouble when his mummy and daddy found out.

"I didn't touch *anyone*!" Jordan wailed, his hands desperately trying to break Kale's hold on him.

"You did!" Kale bellowed, grasping Jordan's collar with his other hand. "You hit Lane! She is only a little girl. She is only *six*, and you punched her in the head!"

Drew gasped at Kale's announcement and held me to her, rubbing her hand up and down my back. I hated that it comforted me and helped slow my tears. I hated that I was holding onto her, and I hated that it made me feel better. I didn't want to need Drew to help me, because Kale had said she was beautiful.

"Drew, what are you doing back – *hey*!" When the voice of an adult bellowed from behind us, I gasped and pressed my face against Drew's shoulder.

I was frozen with fear as a grown man rushed past Drew and myself and shot over to Kale and Jordan. He pulled Kale off Jordan first and held him to one side, and then he reached down and pulled Jordan up to his feet. Jordan was crying, and so were his two friends who were still on the ground. Kale was the only boy not crying. He was just glaring hard at Jordan and had his hands balled into fists as his chest rose and fell swiftly.

Now that Kale stood up and faced me, I could see his face, and I didn't like what I saw. He had a little cut over his eyebrow. A trickle of blood ran down from said eyebrow and stopped halfway down his cheek. Both of his eyes were red, a little swollen, and his lips were stained with the blood that was smeared across his mouth. I could see blood stained his teeth too, because he had his mouth open as he was breathing heavily.

Now that things weren't as loud, my whimpers could be heard. Kale turned his head in my direction, and his entire demeanour changed.

"It's okay, Lane," he assured me, giving me a wink. "I'm okay, I promise."

"Liar!" I cried. "You're bleeding! Look at all the blood. You're probably *dying*!"

The thought of that turned my stomach.

"What the hell happened here?" the man who was holding Kale and Jordan snapped.

I gasped. The man said a bad word too.

"He punched Lane in the back of the head!" Kale stated, throwing his accusation in Jordan's face.

The man looked at me, then looked to Kale, Jordan and the two boys still crying on the ground. He shook his head and walked forward, pulling both Kale and Jordan with him.

"Everyone to the principal's office," he ordered. *"Now!"*

The fear that settled inside me was enough to make me want to pass out. Drew set me down on the ground and took my hand as we walked ahead of Kale, Jordan and the man who'd stopped the fight. He called for the other two boys to get up and follow or he'd come back for them.

"Yes, sir," both of them rasped.

Sir.

The man was a teacher in the school, and he was bringing us to the principal's office. We were in *so* much trouble.

The next while passed by in a blur. I had to sit in the waiting room to the principal's office with Kale, Jordan and the two other boys as our parents were called. Drew was sent to class because she'd had no direct involvement in what had happened other than witnessing the fight. She told the teacher what happened and was sent on her way.

I kept my head down, even though the "sir" who stopped the fight told me that I had nothing to worry about and that I wasn't in a bit of trouble. That made me feel better, but I still felt horrible that Kale was going to get in trouble because of me.

The waiting room to the principal's office was quiet one minute and then loud the next as our parents arrived. I could hear my father and Kale's arguing with multiple grown-up male voices from somewhere outside. I then heard our mothers' voices trying to calm things down; other female voices did the same thing.

I ran to my mother when she entered the waiting room, and I sobbed as she lifted me up into the air and held me to her chest. I felt a hand press against my back, then lips brushing against the side of my head.

"Lane?" my father's voice murmured.

I looked to him, my vision blurred from my tears.

"Are you okay?" he asked, his voice filled with concern.

I shook my head. "Jordan punched my head, and it *really* hurts."

My father's jaw set as he looked over his shoulder. "Deal with your kid before I do."

Arguing started again, and the teacher who had stopped the fight entered the waiting room and had to intervene to calm everyone down. Jordan's mother was kneeling in front of him and pointing her finger at him as she told him off. His father stood next to them and glared down at Jordan, with his arms folded across his chest.

I swallowed when I spotted Kale's parents. His daddy was next to him, checking his face; his mummy was worried as she fussed over him too, even though Kale tried to tell her he was fine. He didn't look fine; his red and slightly swollen eyes were now blue as bruises formed on them. There was a dark bruise forming around the cut on his eyebrow and on his busted lip too. It had to hurt him, but he grinned and winked at me whenever he caught me staring.

I had to go into the principal's office with my parents and tell him what happened. I did exactly that, and when I was finished, I had to sit in the waiting room with my parents as Kale, Jordan and Jordan's two friends all went into the principal's office with their parents. We waited for ages then, and sometimes there were raised voices, and sometimes there was crying. I knew neither came from Kale. He never cried. *Ever.* Not even when his grandmother died last year.

I was playing the game "I spy" with my daddy when Kale and his parents re-entered the waiting room. I jumped up and ran over to Kale at full speed, making him and our parents laugh. I wrapped my arms around his waist and pressed my head against his stomach as I squeezed him. He placed a hand on my shoulder and gently rubbed the back of my head with the other.

"You okay?" he asked me.

Now I am, I silently said to myself.

I looked up at him and nodded.

"I love you," I said, making our mothers sigh and our fathers chuckle.

Kale snickered. "I love you too, Laney Baby."

I pressed my face into his stomach as I smiled. He was the best friend ever.

"What did the principal say?" my father asked Kale's as we all exited the waiting room and headed out of the school.

My mum whispered that we were allowed to go home, and I thought it was really cool, because I didn't want to go back to my class anyway.

"He understood Kale was upset and felt the need to defend Lane, but violence wasn't the way to go about it. Kale is suspended for two days, but Jordan and his friends got a week."

I frowned. "What's 'spended' mean?" I asked, my head tilting to the side.

Kale laughed and slung his arm over my shoulder. He leaned down and whispered, "It means I get to stay in bed all day while you have to go to school."

What?

I gasped. "No fair! I want to be spended too!"

Kale's rich laughter filled the corridor we walked down, but he stopped when a door further down opened up and out stepped Drew with her stupid pretty red hair. Kale's arm tensed around me, but he grinned when Drew's gaze fell on him.

"Kale!" Drew squeaked when she spotted him, and she ran all the way down the corridor to reach him.

She really ran *all* the way.

I stepped to the side when she crashed into him and gave him a big hug. I glared hard at her and stepped back until my back pressed against my daddy's legs. I looked up at him and noticed he was sharing a grin with Kale's daddy and shaking his head. Our mummies were also smiling and shaking their heads as they observed Drew and Kale.

I don't get it, I thought. *Why are they happy?*

"Hey, Drew," Kale murmured into her hair as he inhaled.

I was disgusted. He sniffed her hair. I *saw* him sniff it!

Drew pulled back from the hug. "I'm *so* happy you're okay, I was worried about you."

"You were worried about *me*?" Kale asked, his voice disbelieving.

"Of course," Drew said, nodding. "Are you suspended?"

Kale shrugged, seemingly not caring. "Two days."

I frowned. He was acting like it was no big deal.

Drew's mouth formed into the shape of an O. "For defending your sister? That's *so* stupid."

"Tell me about it," Kale chuckled, scratching the back of his neck.

Drew blushed then when she noticed my parents and Kale's were watching the exchange. "Well, I'll be in every day. I can get notes for you and mark chapters you will miss," she said, and flushed so much her entire head turned the colour of a tomato. "I can bring them to you after school every day so you don't fall behind."

Kale's face was red too, but he remained silent. I wanted to kick him and say no to Drew for him, but I couldn't. I couldn't do a thing. I was so angry, but I had no idea why.

"That'd be great . . . Drew, is it?" Kale's mummy said after Kale still hadn't replied to her.

Drew looked at Kale's mummy and nodded, smiling shyly. "Yes, my name is Drew."

"Pretty name." Kale's mummy smiled.

Drew's face flushed some more, and she murmured, "Thank you."

She then cleared her throat and looked down to her hands. I only then noticed she was carrying a sheet of paper with a bunch of different words on it.

"I've got to get this photocopied for my teacher, so I better go, but I'll keep one for you, Kale, and make extra notes. I'll bring them to you today after school – is that okay?" Drew asked, her eyes hopeful.

"Yes," Kale instantly replied, then cleared his throat. "I mean, yeah, sure, that'd be cool. Whatever."

Kale's daddy and mine began to snort, and it caused Kale to tense up.

"Okay, great. I know where you live, so I'll see you later." She leaned in and kissed Kale's cheek.

She *kissed* it!

She flicked her eyes to me then and said, "I hope you're okay too, Lane."

She said bye to us all then and, walking around us, went on her way down the hallway. Kale didn't move, so his daddy shoved him forward and laughed. "Smooth, son. *Real* smooth."

Kale was still red in the face but playfully shoved his daddy back. "Shut up," he mumbled, a smile tugging at his lips.

I glowered at the exchange, and my mummy noticed. She nudged Kale's mummy, and both of them looked at me and smiled. They were weird like that, always smiling at me when I was looking at Kale. It freaked me out, but I never said anything because they were old, and I wanted them to be happy.

"Kale," Kale's mummy murmured, and jerked her head in my direction.

Kale looked at me and blinked when he saw my expression.

"Why're you angry?" he asked, frowning.

I didn't know why I was angry other than that Drew annoyed me, but I didn't want to tell him that.

"My head hurts," I replied.

I wasn't lying; it did hurt, just not as much as my chest suddenly did.

Kale walked over to me and slung his arm back around my shoulder. "We can watch films with our mums and eat ice cream when we go home. Will that help?"

I forgot about everything.

My sore head.

My aching chest.

Drew.

Kale calling her beautiful, smiling at her and acting so differently around her.

I focused on thoughts of playing with Kale and watching films for the rest of the day. I leaned into him and smiled, making everyone chuckle. He knew my response was a silent whopping *yes*.

"Come on then, let's go." He beamed and removed his arm from around my shoulder only to reach down and grasp my hand with his. "We have films to watch, Laney Baby."

I held onto Kale's hand tightly and smiled with delight as we left our school. I loved spending time with him, and I loved when he called me Laney Baby. I loved everything about Kale, and I knew that I always would.

He was my best friend, my best not-really big brother and my best protector. He was my best everything. He was *mine*.

CHAPTER THREE

Day one in York

My heart was pounding against my chest, and my hands got sticky with sweat.

He called me Laney Baby, my mind whispered. *Kale Hunt is standing in front of me in the flesh, and he called me Laney Baby.*

I felt like I was thrust back into my early years when things were okay with us, when things weren't . . . arduous. I forced that knowledge to the very back of my mind and willed myself to calm down. I refused to appear as flustered and unprepared for this meeting as I truly was. I knew coming back here heightened the possibilities of running into Kale; I just hadn't realised it would happen ten minutes after I stepped foot through my parents' front door.

"How are you?" I asked after a long stretch of silence, my voice formal.

Kale's lips thinned to a line. "I'm good, kid. You?"

Kid. I wanted to growl that I wasn't a damn kid any more, but I didn't. I somehow kept my composure.

"I've" – I glanced at my uncle's coffin, then back to Kale – "been better."

He frowned and nodded in understanding. "It's good to have you home."

Was it? a voice in my head taunted.

"Thanks," I replied, then lied through my teeth. "It's good to be back."

It wasn't good to be back.

It was absolute torture standing here and acting like I wasn't hurting all over again. Like my heart didn't kick into overdrive at the mere sight of him, like my palms didn't itch as they ached to touch him, like my knees didn't shake to keep from walking to him, like shivers didn't dance up and down my spine upon hearing his husky voice, like my lips didn't want to fucking *devour* his until there was nothing left in existence but the two of us.

It's only for a few days, I quickly reminded myself. *You can do this.*

I remained mute as my family suggested we go into the sitting room so we could "talk". I went with them because I needed to be away from my uncle for a few moments to gather my thoughts. I was devastated over him, and ripped apart at seeing Kale, and if I didn't leave the room soon and refocus, I feared I would have a nervous breakdown.

I was the last to enter the sitting room, so I sat on the lounge chair across from everyone else on the huge L-shaped sofa where Lochlan already sat, scowling at me. I pretended not to notice him, even though I was hyper aware of his gaze on me.

My brothers, like my mum and uncle, were fraternal twins, and they had a similar close bond, though they were the polar opposites of one another. Lochlan was temperamental, whereas Layton was calm-headed; their differences balanced them out. I greatly appreciated Layton when Lochlan got angry with me because the thing about my brother was that I could never ignore him when he was mad with me, mainly because he never let me get away with anything, which apparently had followed us into adulthood.

Everyone sat on that sofa with my pissed-off brother except Layton. He slid onto the lounge chair next to me and put his arm around me. I smiled because he was big with muscle, and his sharing the chair with me just squashed my body into his. I didn't complain, though, I loved the closeness. I had missed this. I had missed him.

Layton was the true peacekeeper in our family, and the only reason I didn't see eye-to-eye with him was because he didn't like me living abroad. He feared for my safety and thought it was cruel of me to disregard my family's concern for me. He made it clear how much he would miss me when I was away and how much he flat-out hated that I chose to live so far away, but unlike Lochlan, he brooded in the comfort of his own mind after I made it clear I couldn't come back home. Layton suffered in silence, and he took his silence seriously, which is why we never spoke after I left, unless I was wishing a family member a happy birthday or merry Christmas.

Things were rosy right now because I was home, and my family were glad to see me, but it didn't change the fact that we had problems. There was a reason I'd only spoken to my uncle. He was the only person who didn't threaten me or guilt me into coming home; everyone else did with no remorse.

They didn't understand that I *needed* to be away from home. They knew *why* I needed to be away – they just didn't *get* why. My decision to leave abruptly ended day-to-day communications between us. It sucked not speaking to them. I missed them terribly, but I was just as stubborn as my family and fought their anger and hurt with my own. It resulted in a barrier of silence that only my uncle's death had been able to break through.

I leaned my head back against Layton's shoulder and hummed with content when he leaned his head on mine. "God," I murmured, "I missed you, Lay."

He kissed the crown of my head. "Missed you too, darling."

I snuggled into him and listened to everyone as they spoke about mundane things. I made a point not to look at Kale, who was on the far end of the sofa, well away from me. I didn't need to look at him to know he was there, though. I could feel his presence. I was always aware of when he was close by; it was like my body had a sixth sense designed specifically for him.

I glanced to the sitting room door when the blonde woman and her brunette friend I met upon entering my parents' house walked by and out of the house, closing the door behind them.

"Who are they?" I inquired, finding it bizarre that two strangers were just walking around the house like it was nobody's business.

Layton turned his head and said, "Samantha Wright is the brunette, and Ally Day is the blonde."

I knew the second girl's name – I was sure I did. I thought about it for a minute, and then like the snap of my fingers, the name clicked in my head. I blinked and stared around the room dumbly.

"Ally Day?" I quizzed. "The Ally Day who convinced me, along with her evil friend, that I was fat and ugly when I was younger . . . *that* Ally Day?"

Everyone froze as they looked at me.

"People change, Lane," Layton murmured, making sure to keep his arm tightly around me, like he was afraid I would bolt. "She's not the mean girl she was when she was a kid."

Was that supposed to be comforting? I angrily thought.

I swallowed the sudden lump that formed in my throat. "You didn't suffer like I did because of her and Anna O'Leary," I said, fighting to keep composure. "I was self-conscious for a long time because of those two. Do you know how many times I wished

I looked like anyone other than myself just so I could feel like a regular girl?"

I was met with silence, so I balled my hands into fists as annoyance filled me.

"Why the hell was she even here?" I snapped, feeling exasperated they would even let her into the house after the hurt she caused me.

My nanny sighed. "She works for me, in the café."

Stunned speechless, I could not get past my incredulity over what I was hearing.

"Lane," my nanny prompted when I stared at her blankly, blinking. "Are you okay?"

I couldn't respond to that in a way that wouldn't have her smacking me around the head.

"So you're recruiting staff from the forces of evil?" I asked, staring icily. "Nice, Nanny, *real* nice."

My nanny brooded in silence, and it gave me some much-needed time to think. I couldn't believe I didn't recognise Ally at first. The last time I'd seen her was when we left secondary school nearly a decade ago. I heard she'd moved to London, but she was obviously back in York and working in my nanny's café of all places!

I loved that café, and now it would forever feel tainted to me.

"Do I know the brunette?" I questioned, my jaw set.

"Yeah," Lochlan answered me with a snarky tone. "She was in your school year, but you never hung around with her. She works in Nanny's café too. They are our *friends*."

I couldn't remember a Samantha Wright, so I didn't dwell on her; instead, I focused on Ally bloody Day.

"I just can't believe you're all friendly with Ally Day. Do you invite Anna O'Leary over for tea on the weekends too?" I sarcastically asked.

My father clucked his tongue at me. "You sound like a child, Lane."

He was right; I was being bratty and rude. It was uncalled for and not needed, but I was hurt they could just forget what Ally had done to me. They'd seen first-hand what I'd gone through because of her; I didn't understand how they could just get over that.

I glowered at him. "Good thing you only have to put up with me for a few days then, isn't it?"

It was a low blow, throwing my departure in his face when I'd just arrived, but I couldn't help it. It slipped out before I could stop myself.

"What do you mean a *few days*?" my mother snapped, speaking for the first time since we embraced in the parlour. "When are you leaving?"

I avoided direct eye contact with her as I softly muttered, "Sunday night."

"Lane!" my family bellowed in unison.

I guess we're over pleasantries.

"I *have* to go back," I countered, trying to defend myself. "I have to work!"

"You're a freelance editor," Lochlan growled, barely able to hold his sitting position on the sofa. "Once you have Internet access, you're solid to work wherever you are!"

I couldn't think of anything to say in response because he was right, so I remained quiet.

"Lane," my nanny said. "Kitchen. Now."

I watched as my nanny got up and walked out of the sitting room, her body tensing with each step she took. "Crap," I grumbled as I got to my feet and followed her into the kitchen, my eyes cast downward. I felt like I was little again, and she was about to tell me off.

I entered the kitchen and saw she was already seated at the kitchen table, so I walked over and sat across from her. I clasped my hands together on the surface of the table in front of me and stared down at them with intent.

"You're me granddaughter, and I love ye with all me heart," my nanny started, "but sometimes I want ta just whack ye with a common-sense stick right across that beautiful head of yours."

Trust my nanny to keep things real.

"I'm sorry," I said, hoping it would dampen her burning temper.

"Sorry isn't good enough," she clipped, then lowered her voice. "Me baby died, Lane. Your uncle *died* . . . and ye just want ta up and leave a day after we put 'im to rest? That's not me grandbaby – *she* wouldn't do that."

Your grandbaby died a long time ago, a cruel voice in my head taunted.

Burning pain filled my chest. I glanced up to my nanny before quickly looking away from her aged but still graceful face. I saw my Uncle Harry when I looked at her; they shared the same aqua-blue eyes, high cheekbones and button nose. My brothers and I had inherited the very same features too.

"I can't stay here," I murmured, and took another glimpse up at her. "You know why."

My nanny shook her head, disappointment crossing her features. "That's not good enough, and ye bloody well know it," she remarked. "Ye have ta act like the twenty-six-year-old woman ye are and push your issues with Kale ta the side and focus on Harry. *He* doesn't deserve ta be pushed aside, Lane. *You* of all people know that."

I felt horrible as I let what my nanny said sink in. I really did deserve to be whacked around with a common-sense stick. How could I have ever thought my leaving right away would be a good idea for anybody? My family would be heartbroken, and so would I.

I couldn't be here and remain sane, but I couldn't leave either without losing my mind, so close after my uncle's death. I didn't win either way, but the latter meant my conscience would be clear.

"I'll . . . you're right," I acknowledged. "Uncle Harry deserves more than a brush-off. I'll stay longer. I'll help with whatever needs helping. I promise."

My nanny reached over and took my hands in hers, rubbing her fingertips back and forth over my knuckles.

"Ye can help me and your ma clear out his house after we meet with his solicitor on Monday," she said, sighing. "We have so much ta sort through, but we have ta hear the contents of Harry's will before we can start a clean-out."

I blinked, dumbly. "Uncle Harry had a will?"

My nanny nodded. "Yeah, we all have a will, silly."

I don't, I thought.

My nanny snorted at my facial expression. "By 'all' I mean Harry, your parents, and me . . . because we're old and can kick it at any given time."

"Nanny!" I choked. "Don't talk like that. You aren't going anywhere."

I hoped not, anyway. My heart couldn't handle it if anyone else were to die.

My nanny smiled lovingly at me as she reached out and brushed her fingertips over my knuckles once more. She did this to me often when I was younger to relax me, and it seemed to still have a calming effect on me. It was nice to know that hadn't changed.

I remained silent for a few moments, but when I looked back at my nanny, I saw she was gazing at me. "What is it?" I inquired.

She blinked and without missing a beat she said, "I want ye home every Christmas."

Not a question. Not a request. A demand.

I sat motionless. "Nanny—"

"I don't want an excuse," she said sternly. "I want your word ye will come home every Christmas. I can't go on with me granddaughter being on the other side of the world and never seein' 'er. Me heart can't take the pain and longin' anymore."

I gasped in dismay. "Oh, God! Is *your* heart okay?" I asked, terrified.

"Me heart is fine," she assured me, "but it won't be in the future unless ye come back home every Christmas."

I stared at my nanny for a moment, and then I flat out glared at her. "Are you – are you *guilting* me into coming home every Christmas by threatening that you could have a *heart attack*?"

She tried to guilt me with her old age before, when she wanted me to come home from New York, and when that didn't work, she stopped speaking to me. It seemed she was upping the ante. I didn't know whether to be furious or impressed.

My nanny looked to her nails and shrugged. "I wouldn't say threatenin' ye exactly. I'm just sayin' if ye continue to stay away from your family and I have a heart attack and die, it would be your fault."

She's doing it again, I told myself. *The whole convincing thing.*

"Nanny!"

"I know it's awful that it could happen," she said, bobbing her head up and down in agreement.

The twisted old bat!

"I can't believe you," I crossly stated. "I don't even know how to respond to something like that."

My nanny devilishly smiled. "Say ye'll come home every Christmas."

I am related to a bloody con artist.

I huffed. "You can't be serious."

"I'm dead serious," she countered, all traces of humour fleeing from her face.

We had a ten-second stare-down before I threw my hands up in the air. "Fine!" I groaned in defeat. "I'll be home for Christmas."

"Every year?" she questioned.

I grunted. "Every. Year."

"Ye promise?" she pressed.

I gritted my teeth. "I promise."

She gleefully clapped her hands together. "I'm so happy ye decided this."

Yeah. Decided.

"I feel like I've just been hustled," I mumbled, and shook my head. "You'd convince the Devil that he was God."

When I looked back up to my nanny, her lip was quirked. "What now?" I warily asked.

She shrugged. "Nothin'."

It wasn't "nothing"; she was grinning at me, and that meant something.

"Are you sure?" I pried.

My nanny nodded, but said nothing.

Bloody woman, I thought.

We both turned our heads and glanced at the kitchen door when my father, brothers and Kale walked in, talking about ordering takeaway from the local chippy because none of them felt like cooking. I didn't realise how hungry I was until food was mentioned. I couldn't even remember the last time I ate anything.

An hour and a half later and I was still sitting at the kitchen table, but now I had a belly full of chicken, chips and *at least* a litre bottle of Coke. I was so full I felt like I was going to burst. When we were finished, we all went into the sitting room and sat down so we could digest our food in comfort.

"So, when are you going back to New York?" Lochlan asked me after a few minutes of mindless chatter.

I noticed he said "New York" and not "home".

I didn't look at him, Layton *or* Kale as I said, "I don't know yet, but not soon. I'm going to help Mum and Nanny with Harry's house after we hear his will on Monday."

I made a mental note that I needed to change my flights home and extend my stay at the Inn.

Lochlan said nothing.

Layton cleared his throat. "Well, that's great."

Yeah. Great.

I nodded. "Yeah."

I felt Lochlan's gaze back on me. "How long are you going to stay away when you go back this time? Ten years? Twenty? Or just come back when one of us dies?"

I didn't even flinch at his jab.

"Loch," Layton pressed, "don't start with her – not tonight. She just got home, for fuck's sake."

I appreciated Layton shutting down Lochlan before he had a chance to have a go at me, but I looked up to my brother's intense gaze, and instead of remaining silent, I said, "I'll be back for the holidays."

Lochlan blinked at my reply, clearly stunned speechless at my response. So were Kale and Layton, who looked at me with wide eyes and gaping mouths. They were shocked. I noticed, in Kale, it was the first real emotion I had seen him express since I arrived. The old Kale would usually tell me a story from the emotions constantly displayed on his face, but not this poker-faced Kale.

What happened to you? I wondered.

"Christmas?" Layton murmured after a moment, his eyes unblinking.

I shrugged, trying to downplay how much of a big deal they thought it was. I mean, it *was* a big deal, but I didn't want them to act like it was.

"Yeah. Nanny made me promise to come home every year for Christmas." I shook my head in annoyance. "She said missing me was pushing her in the direction of a heart attack, and if she died, it'd be *my* fault."

Things were silent for a moment, and then male laughter filled the sitting room. I focused on Kale when he laughed, and I felt dejected when his laughter didn't reach his eyes and seemed forced.

I pushed my observations aside and grunted. "It's *not* funny; she placed the ultimate guilt trip on me. We're burying Harry tomorrow, and she decides to throw *this* curve ball at me? The bloody vixen."

The light-hearted laughter continued, and I fought off the smile that twitched at the corner of my mouth.

"That's genius, you have to give it to her," Kale said.

I hated that he was speaking to me; things would have been so much easier if he left me alone. It would hurt, it would damn well hurt, if he ignored me, but that hurt would be nothing compared to the pain I felt right now. I didn't get how he could chat to me like he didn't ruin me.

Goodbye, Laney Baby, his voice echoed in my mind.

I forced away the memory that tried to creep its way into focus. I cleared my throat and didn't look directly at him as I replied, "She'd agree with you. She's pretty pleased with herself right now."

Kale snorted, and I hated myself for thinking the sound was cute.

I swallowed the hurt I felt and looked down to my leg when it vibrated and continued to vibrate. I reached into the front pocket of my jeans, took out my ringing iPhone and saw "Roman" flashing across the screen.

Fuck, I cringed. *I forgot all about Roman, he was going to kill me.*

"Excuse me for a few minutes," I said to the lads, then stood up and quickly stepped out into the hallway, closing the sitting room door behind me.

"Hey, Ro, what's up?" I said, keeping my voice low.

The gasp that came through my receiver was dramatic and expected. "'Hey, Ro, what's up?' Are you fucking *serious* right now, Lane?" Roman, my very-high-maintenance friend, bellowed at me. "That's all I get?"

I pushed a few strands of hair that escaped my plait out of my face. "I'm sorry, okay? The past few days have been crazy. I should have told you I was going to be gone for a few days."

His hiss was audible. "Don't talk like you're taking a quick vacay down to Cali for the weekend, Lane! You're in England. E–n–g–l–a–n–d."

I couldn't help the snort that erupted from me. "I am aware I'm in England – and how to spell it, Ro. I was born here, you know?"

"Lane!" he growled. "I'm freaking out here. I'm out of my mind with worry for you. You up and leave the country without even texting me. No email. No note. *Nothing.* You could have died! I wouldn't have known a thing if your landlord hadn't told me where you were. I was going to call the freaking cops and report you missing!"

I winced and then frowned when guilt flooded me. Roman Grace was pretty much my closest – no, make that my *only* friend. We met five and a half years ago in a café in downtown Manhattan when he spotted me reading a steamy romance, and we instantly clicked over our love for Mr Grey.

I had been living in New York six months at that point, and I'm embarrassed to say I had hardly experienced the city. I became closed off when I moved, and I never had enough courage to explore. I liked New York, but I wouldn't say that when I was there I was living; I merely existed in a city that never sleeps.

I was a shade of grey on a canvas of colour.

Roman helped brighten things up for me. He gave me somewhat of a social life through his own, but even with his vibrant self, I wasn't happy. I wasn't sad either. I was just . . . numb. I was content with working and reading book after book in my spare time, but after I met Roman, he made sure to rectify that problem. He took me to bars, clubs and plays. He even introduced me to his book club and made me an official member. Sure, I was the only straight female when I was with Roman and his friends, but it was refreshing. *He* was refreshing. He brought something new to my introverted life, and I adored him for it.

"I'm so sorry, Ro. I swear that when I got a handle on shit, I was going to ring you. I only got here a few hours ago. Getting through the airport was a nightmare."

Roman let out an exasperated breath. "I don't care about the airport – I care about *you*. How are you, honey? Your landlord mentioned why you had to leave in such haste. I'm *so* sorry about your uncle. I know how close you were to him."

I looked down at my feet. "I'm fine," I whispered.

"That line may work on your family, but I know you better than that, and I call it bullshit," Roman said in a matter-of-fact tone.

I was glad when a chuckle left my mouth. "Okay, I'm *not* fine, but I'm not falling apart. Not right now anyway."

Roman was silent for a moment. "Have you seen him?"

I glanced at the closed parlour door where my uncle was with my mother and nanny as they fussed over him. I heard their low murmurs as I pressed my back against the hallway wall. I adjusted my glasses when they slipped down my nose and said, "Yeah, I saw him. He looks great. Just like he's sleeping."

Roman sucked in a gulp of air. "I meant *Kale*."

I froze at the mention of his name and glanced at the sitting room doorway. I relaxed when nothing happened. He was still in there with my brothers. I shook my head and mentally bitch-slapped Roman for bringing him up. He dragged Kale, and our history, out of me one very drunken night two years ago. He knows everything that happened between us.

Every. Single. Thing.

"Yeah, I saw Kale," I replied, my voice low.

Roman whistled. "How was *that* meeting?"

I blew out a breath. "Surprisingly civil. He is acting like nothing ever happened. He greeted me just like an old friend he hasn't seen in a long time."

"Is that a bad thing?" Roman questioned. "I mean, you don't want it to be awkward while you're there and have your past aired out again, do you?"

Do I? I shook my head. *God, no, I couldn't deal with that. It's just a little – a lot – upsetting that he is acting like there is nothing between us. Not even awkwardness. He is completely at ease in my presence and shooting the shit like before things went to hell with us, which is weird because the last time I saw Kale . . . it was bad. There were declarations of unrequited love, tears and a lot of screaming.*

"Lane?" Roman's voice broke through my thoughts. "Are you still there?"

I cleared my throat. "Yeah, I'm here, and no, I don't want it to be awkward."

Roman was silent for a moment, and then he said, "Does he look the same? Or is he fat and bald now? I'm praying for the latter."

I unexpectedly laughed.

"Unfortunately, it's the former." I lowered my voice to a whisper. "He looks incredible, and he's been going to the gym with my brothers. They were talking about changing up their workouts at the dinner table, and then they told me they took their health and exercise seriously now."

Kale was always a healthy size. He'd never had huge arms or shoulders, but now he had both of those things and more. His arms were chiselled, so was his chest, even his thighs were thicker. I didn't get a visual of his bare torso, but I could imagine the defined abs that hid under his T-shirt and jumper.

"Damn, does that make it harder?" Roman quizzed.

I sighed, my shoulders sagging. "Yes and no. It would be just as hard no matter what he looked like, 'cause it's Kale. But the fact that he is too hot for words is making it . . . difficult."

Roman snorted. "Your poor vagina must be a quivering mess."

I slapped my hand over my mouth when laughter flew free.

Damn it, Roman! my mind cackled.

"I'm going to beat the shit out of you when I'm back!" I stated, but giggled like crazy.

This was exactly why I loved Roman; he could always lift my spirits no matter how many shadows tried to shade me from the light of life. He had managed to resurrect my old sense of humour, which was no small feat.

He gleefully laughed. "When will *that* be exactly?"

"I'm honestly not sure," I admitted. "I'm going to stay awhile to help sort everything out with my uncle's belongings, and to spend time with my family. The tension is thick between us, but I've missed them. I didn't realise how much until I saw them."

"Of course you do, they're your *family*," Roman said, his tone soothing. "Look, I'm going to let you go. I won't bother you while you're with your family, but if you need me for *anything*, just pick up your phone. Okay?"

This was why I loved him. He was one of the most thoughtful and considerate people I had ever met. "Okay," I replied, nodding even though he couldn't see me.

"I'll see you soon, honey," he chirped. "I'll collect you from the airport; just send me the date and flight info when you decide."

I nodded again. "I will."

"Bye, sweetie. You hang in there! I love you."

I smiled and closed my eyes. "I will. I love you too. Bye."

The line went dead, and I took a minute before I opened my eyes. When I did, I walked down the hallway and into the kitchen, where I found my father getting a start on the dirty dishes from dinner. I instantly felt rude for not cleaning up after myself, so I rolled up my sleeves and prepared to help, but when my father saw me, he shook his head.

"You sit down," he said, and nodded to the kitchen table. "We'll take care of this."

Then he called my brothers and Kale in to help with the dishes. They filed into the room without a complaint and got to work. I sat down at the kitchen table and looked at my nanny when she entered the room and sat across from me. She stared at me, so I stared right back at her.

"Do ye have a boyfriend?" she randomly asked me, her eyebrow raised.

I wanted to roll my eyes when my father and brothers grew quiet as they cleaned the dishes in the sink. Lochlan was passing dirty plates to Layton, who washed them, then handed them to my father, who sprayed them down with clean water before handing them to Kale, who was on drying duty. I could see them stilling, not moving a muscle, as they turned their attention to my conversation with my nanny.

"No," I replied. "No boyfriend. I don't have time for one."

That was a lie. I had nothing but time for a boyfriend. I just didn't want one.

Lochlan looked over his shoulder. "Who is Roman then?"

Kale's shoulders tensed, and he began drying off the dinner plates with unnecessary speed and force. I focused on Lochlan and raised a brow. "How do you know about Roman?" I asked.

My brother shrugged. "I heard you mention his name on the phone in the hallway. Heard you also tell him you love him."

What a bloody eavesdropper, I silently grumbled.

I wanted to glare at him, but I didn't, I kept my cool and replied honestly. "Roman is my friend, and before you ask, no, he is nothing more." My lip twitched. "He bats for a different team."

My nanny snorted, and the men relaxed. I shook my head at the four of them; they were acting like I was sixteen again and talking about a boy for the first time.

"Although," I added just to annoy them, "he *did* say he would be my baby daddy if I ever needed sperm. I may take him up on the offer because he is *really* good-looking. His has dark chocolate skin, a killer jawline and eyes that are always bright. I think we'd make a cute baby."

My nanny burst into laughter while Layton shook his head with a grin on his face. Kale glanced at me, and in that moment I wished I knew what he was thinking, because he was staring at me with an intensity that caused my knees to lock together. I broke free from his stare when my father clucked his tongue. He and Lochlan were less than pleased with my humour.

"You aren't funny, Lane," Lochlan grumbled.

I gestured to our laughing grandmother. "She would beg to differ."

My nanny snorted then as she laughed, and it made me smile. Lochlan turned away from me and shook his head, and I couldn't help but shake my own at him. He was a huge pain in my arse, but only because he loved me so much. He felt that I was his responsibility because I was the baby of the family, and it was why he had been more overbearing than Layton. Sometimes even our father wasn't as harsh as he was.

Lochlan was the sole reason I never had a boyfriend growing up. He never admitted to it, but I knew he roughed around Blake Cunning, who asked me out on a date when I was sixteen. The next day Blake had a black eye and told me he didn't think it was a good idea if we dated, and then he walked away from me without looking back.

"Lochlan?"

He looked over his shoulder when I called his name. "What?" he asked.

I held his gaze and said, "I love you."

Lochlan stared at me for a moment before he turned away from me and went back to passing dirty dishes to Layton. Layton stared at our brother, waiting for him to reply to me, and I was surprised when Kale leaned over and said, "Say something back to her. Now." I was even more surprised that Lochlan listened to Kale.

"I love you too," he replied, his voice low.

I looked to my nanny, who was smiling at me, and I couldn't help but smile back. I gestured to her knitting, when she picked it out of a bag next to the table, and pulled a face. "I can't believe you're *still* knitting."

She smirked devilishly. "Do ye want ta help me make some—"

"No!" I cut her off, my voice slightly raised. "No bloody way. I have nightmares about knitting to this day. I *told* you I'd die before I ever picked up needles and wool again."

Snickers filled the kitchen.

I looked around the room and found the only smiling face missing was my mother's, and my uncle's, of course. I sighed and relaxed into the chair. I had to make things good with my family. I had to make things how they used to be before I left and life went to the gutter. They didn't deserve to be blocked out because things didn't end the way I wanted them to with Kale.

They deserved better than the way I had been treating them the last six years, and it rightly fell on my shoulders to make everything better. I just hoped the relationships I walked out on could be mended.

All of them.

CHAPTER FOUR

Ten years old (sixteen years ago)

Kale," I whispered, and then held my breath to keep all noise to a minimum.

I couldn't sleep.

All week, since I'd got home from a shopping holiday with my mother and nanny in New York, I'd found it difficult to go to sleep. I quickly got used to bright lights and noises in a city that never sleeps, and found that the silence in York screamed louder than any noise could. Tonight it wasn't my jet lag or the deafening stillness that was keeping me awake though. It was something very distinctive. It was the reason I was trying to be deathly quiet as I called Kale.

I was so scared the monsters would hear me and come get me before he woke up. I kept staring at my open wardrobe while I blindly reached down and shoved at Kale's shoulder as hard as I could. He was sleeping on his blow-up mattress on my floor, as he always did when he stayed over, and it was pretty much his own piece of furniture inside my room.

It was probably the last time he would be allowed to sleep in my room. My father said now that he was thirteen, he would have to sleep in my brothers' room when he stayed over, which delighted him and my brothers.

I blew out a frustrated breath when he grunted in his sleep, as if he refused to wake up.

"*Kale!*" I pleaded, my emotion shining through my voice.

He groaned and moved around on his mattress, trying to get away from me.

"What is it, Lane?" he grumbled. "I'm sleeping."

The wardrobe door creaked, so I let out a little whimper, and like a shot Kale was up from his mattress and climbing onto my bed.

"What's wrong?" he asked, now wide awake.

I threw my arms around him. "The wardrobe – it's open. They're gonna get me."

Kale released a laboured breath but kept his tight hold on me. He placed his hand on my back and rubbed up and down. The action calmed me down a little, but not enough to let go of him.

"The latch on the door is broken," he murmured, his voice low to soothe me. "That's why it opens when it's been closed – you know this. We talked about it, remember?"

I refused to believe that.

If that was true, then why did the door just magically decide to open in the dead of night? Why not during the day when it was bright out and *not* scary? I'd tell you why: it was because there was no stupid broken latch on the door. It was the hideous monsters that lived inside my wardrobe that opened the door at night. They were planning to take me away.

"It's them," I mumbled into Kale's chest. "I know it is."

He sighed but chuckled a little. "I'm not going to argue with you. Move over and I'll sleep on the outside of your bed, so that way, if they come out, they'll have to fight me to get to you."

I gasped in horror. "No! What if they take *you* away?"

They couldn't take Kale away from me. No one could. I wouldn't allow it.

"I'm not going anywhere – now move over. It's really late, and I've to get up for my football match tomorrow morning."

I did as Kale asked; I moved to the inside of my bed and shivered because that section of the bed was cold. Kale settled next to me, and I thought he was going to turn his back to me so he could watch the wardrobe, but he didn't. He lay on his back and used his left hand to tug me over to him. I was wide-eyed as he settled my head on his shoulder. His arm was hooked around my body and his hand rested on my hip.

My. Hip.

I began to breathe heavily, and I felt myself blush like crazy. I could actually feel the heat crawl up my neck and spread out over my cheeks like wildfire.

What the heck was happening?

"You okay?" Kale mumbled to me, then yawned.

I cleared my throat. "Yep . . . just scared about the monsters."

That was a lie; I wasn't bothered about the monsters anymore. I was freaked out that I was feeling strange lying like this on Kale. He was on my bed, and I was just lying on him. I liked it. A lot. And that was super weird because Kale was like my brother, but I didn't feel all *tingly* in my stomach when I lay with my real brothers, so why was it like this with Kale?

I'm coming down with a severe case of the flu, I thought. *It's the only explanation.*

"Lane, are you sure you're okay?" Kale pressed, worry laced throughout his tone. "You're breathing really fast."

I swallowed and tried to control the rise and fall of my chest.

"Yep, I'm good, like I said . . . just scared of the monsters."

He sighed. "There are no such thing as monsters, Lane. I told you to pay no attention to those stupid lads in your class at school."

I grunted and sat up so I could look down at Kale. My room was dark, but the night-light plugged into my wall helped brighten the place up a little. It was enough for me to see Kale's face anyway.

I looked down at his tired features, my eyes scanning over them. "But what if they're right? What if monsters *do* come through the wardrobe at night and kidnap me? What if they eat me and spit out my bones? That would be horrible, Kale. I'd never survive it."

I frowned when Kale shook with silent laughter.

"I'm *not* playing right now!" I huffed.

He laughed harder and had to put his hand over his mouth to muffle the noises.

I shoved at him. "You're horrible!"

I turned my back to him and lay down on my side of the bed. I tugged my duvet up and covered myself with it completely, but the darkness creeped me out, so I poked my head out of the duvet, leaving everything else covered. Kale was lightly chuckling as he turned to me and grabbed at me with his hands under the covers. I slapped at his hands and kicked at his legs, and he found it bloody hilarious.

I was just about to explode with anger when Kale suddenly grabbed hold of my body and pulled me back into his. He wrapped his arms around me and pinned my arms to my sides, trapping my legs together by throwing his leg over them. I felt his bare chest pressed against my back and felt his breath on my neck.

"Kale," I breathed, "what are you doing?"

I was feeling something, and I wasn't sure what. I was very aware that it was Kale who was holding me, and I was also aware that I really liked it. I liked it in a way that I didn't quite understand.

"Protecting myself," he chuckled. "I knew you were about to snap and hit me."

He was provoking me by laughing on purpose then.

I growled. "You're *such* an idiot."

"Possibly," he said, chuckling, "but I'm an idiot who is going to protect you from all harm. Especially monster harm."

Huh?

"How are you going to do that?" I murmured.

Kale untangled himself from me and slid off my bed. I was shocked at how badly I wanted him to stay, but it felt wrong because Kale was my best friend, like my brother, so I knew I shouldn't want him to hold me . . . not in a way that made my skin tingle and my tummy hurt.

I shook my head clear of my very sudden and weird thoughts and focused on Kale, who was walking over towards my wardrobe. I gasped and gripped onto my duvet cover.

"Be careful!" I squealed.

Kale glanced over his shoulder, smiled at me and I just about died because he looked so . . . cute.

Oh, my God. I thought Kale looked cute. *My* Kale.

K–A–L–E.

"What are you doing?" I asked, my heart slamming against my chest.

He turned and nodded at the wardrobe. "I'm going to stand guard until you fall asleep or until the sun comes up. Whichever one comes first. You don't have to worry. I'll protect you."

I licked my suddenly dry lips. "You – you would really do that? For me?"

Kale reached into the wardrobe and grabbed my baseball bat, then shut the door and leaned against it and winked at me. "Only for you."

Butterflies exploded in my stomach, and I got giddy with excitement.

"I don't know what to – thank you, Kale," I breathed, completely in awe of him.

He smiled at me once more and gripped onto the baseball bat. "Don't thank me. I can't have monsters kidnapping you, right?"

I lay down and pulled my duvet up to my face so he wouldn't be able to see my smile.

"I guess not," I murmured.

"You guessed correctly," he said, winking. "Now go to sleep, Laney Baby. I'll protect you."

"You promise?" I whispered.

"I promise to protect you always, silly."

I stared at him as I remembered when I asked my Uncle Harry how he knew he loved my Aunt Teresa and he told me what he felt like. He said his stomach got butterflies, and his heart pounded really fast when he saw her. He said she made his heart happy, so it beat really fast when she was around, like it was singing for her.

He felt like I did at that moment when I looked at Kale. My heart was singing for him.

It was a daunting thought, but I positively knew in that instant, even though I didn't know exactly what real emotion was, that I'd fallen wholeheartedly in love with Kale Hunt, and it frightened the living daylights out of me.

CHAPTER FIVE

Day one in York

"What are you doing here, Lane?"

I jumped and looked over my shoulder when the voice of my father jolted me from my thoughts and brought me back to my sombre reality. I didn't answer him straight away as I turned and looked back at the freshly dug hole.

"I needed to think, so I decided to go on a walk," I replied.

When it had got late and my parents' house became very quiet, my thoughts suddenly seemed to be too loud, so I'd decided to go on a walk. My feet brought me to my Aunt Teresa's grave, and my Uncle Harry's soon-to-be grave. I stared down at the grave plot that, starting from tomorrow, would house my uncle until the end of time, and it gutted me.

"You scared us," my father said. "Everyone is out looking for you."

I blinked with surprise and looked to my father when he came up beside me. "I'm sorry, I didn't think to tell anyone I was going out. I never have to do it in New York; I guess I forgot."

My father sent out a text on his phone, pocketed it, then sighed and slid his arm around my shoulder. "I'm just glad you're okay."

I felt bad, but since I'd already apologised, I remained quiet.

"Since we're alone, I want to tell you something that I should have told you years ago."

I blinked. "Okay."

"I'm so sorry for what I said to you the day you told us you were leaving. I should have never said it, and I didn't mean it. I've regretted it for years but was too stubborn to admit it."

I wasn't surprised at my father's apology. I knew what he'd said was out of hurt and anger.

"It's okay," I assured him. "I forgave you the moment you said it."

My father's shoulders sagged a little. "I've missed you, my love."

I swallowed the lump that formed in my throat. "I've missed you too, Dad. I know it doesn't seem that way, but I have. I just . . . it's very hard to be here."

"I know, sweetie, I know."

Did he really? my mind whispered.

I glanced at him. "You do?"

"Of course." He nodded. "You think Kale got off easy for driving you out of the country?"

That caused me to stare blankly at him.

"What exactly does *that* mean?" I asked, my eyes wide with curiosity.

My father grinned. "It means I knocked around a man who is like my son."

I gasped in alarm. "You didn't!"

My father shrugged. "Only for a little bit, but I stopped myself before anything serious happened."

I shook my head. "You hitting Kale *is* serious."

"Your moving away because of him was a lot more serious," he countered.

I looked back down at the earth before me. "It's complicated, Dad."

"Love always is," he said.

I forced a smile. "And don't I know it."

My father squeezed my shoulder. "I told him I was sorry – don't worry."

"When?" I asked.

He hummed. "About six weeks ago."

I widened my eyes and pressed my hand over my mouth. "Are you being serious?"

"No," my father chuckled as I dropped my hand to my side. "I apologised about six months later. It was very hard for me to forgive him. You're my daughter, and to know you left home partly because of him really hurt me. I hated him for a while because of it."

My laughter dried up, but my eyes grew damp.

"I didn't want anybody to hate anyone," I whispered, and licked my dry lips.

My father exhaled. "I know that, but sometimes emotions can't be tamed, as you know."

I knew that *very* well, so I nodded.

"He was very forgiving when I did eventually say sorry," my father continued. "He actually judged me for apologising at all. He said he deserved the beating I gave him and more."

That, again, surprised me.

"So why didn't you beat him further that day?" I quizzed.

My father was silent for a moment and then said, "Because he did a good enough job of beating himself up about it. Everything about his life changed after you left."

I squeezed my eyes shut. "Do I want to know?"

"No," my dad replied instantly. "You don't want to know, but you're going to have to know in order to understand how things are with him now."

That scared me.

"I don't understand," I replied.

My father was silent for a long time, but he eventually took me by the arm and led me away from my aunt's grave. "Come with me, my sweetheart," he said softly. "I want to show you someone."

He wants to show me someone in a graveyard?

We walked slowly, passing by grave after grave, me holding my hand in his.

"Where are we going?" I asked as I scanned the dark cemetery, feeling goosebumps rise on my arms.

"You'll see," my father replied solemnly.

I nodded and nervously gnawed on my lower lip.

"Can you talk to me as we walk? I'm suddenly scared to be here," I admitted.

My father tightened his hold on me. "Don't be scared. I have you."

"I know," I said, "but I want to listen to you talk. I've missed your voice."

My father chuckled. "Your mother would laugh hearing you say that. She offered to pay me one hundred quid to shut up last week. She gets sick of listening to me talk."

My lip twitched. "She just pretends she does."

"She's a cracking actress if that's the case," my father stated.

My laughter filled the dark space of the graveyard, and I stopped just as quickly as I started. It felt wrong to laugh so loud in a place where many were resting.

"What is New York like?" my father asked, completely catching me off guard.

I glanced around. "It's not right to say this in a graveyard, but it's alive. Pulsing with life, day and night. It never stops."

My father glanced at me. "It sounds exciting."

It wasn't.

"It can be," I murmured. "I don't get out much, though, if I'm being honest. The constant activity isn't for me. I like the peace I find in my apartment and my books. New York isn't exactly my ideal place to live, never mind grow old."

I knew I shouldn't have revealed that bit of information to my father, but it felt nice to finally say it out loud and know it was honest truth and not a fabricated lie to please others. Roman thought I loved New York, but that was only because when I was with him, I shared in his zest for life. He didn't know that when I was on my own I sometimes wished I wouldn't wake up when I went to sleep.

"Why not move someplace else then?" my father asked, scanning our surroundings as we walked.

I noticed he didn't mention I should move back to York.

I shrugged. "It seems pointless to move somewhere else, I feel the way I feel because I'm sad, Dad. The environment I'm in won't change how I feel."

He nodded in agreement, then said, "No, but *you* can change how you feel."

Here we go, I inwardly sighed.

I smiled a little. "I can't change how I feel until I resolve why I feel the way I feel."

"Ah, I see." My dad smiled too. "If that's the case, then when are you moving back home?"

I pulled on my father's hand and stopped us walking.

"What?" I asked him, and fully turned in his direction.

My father raised his eyebrows at me. "Your problem started at home. You can't fix it anywhere but here because your problem is rooted here . . . He lives here."

I groaned. "Why can't you just tell me to get over it and move on from Kale?"

"Why should I repeat what you've told yourself a million times before? It won't change how you feel."

I glared at my father. "When did you become so philosophical?"

"The day you left me."

I froze. My father's reply was instant, and it gutted me.

"I'm so sorry, Dad," I breathed.

He frowned at me. "I know you are."

I leaned in and placed my head on his chest. "Being here is really difficult."

He put his arms around me and kissed the crown of my head. "I know, honey, but deep down you knew you couldn't stay away forever."

I sighed and mimicked my father, putting my arms around him. "Staying away – that was my plan."

"Until Harry?"

I nodded against my father's chest. "Until Harry."

"He always did say he would get you to come home. Little did he know he was right."

My eyes welled with tears.

"He understood it wasn't just a silly crush I had with Kale. He knew that I was devastated when things ended the way they did between us. Then after Lavender . . . he knew I had to leave after she collided with the bombshell Kale dropped. It's why he helped me. I probably would have started on my downward spiral again without Lavender, as I watched Kale and Drew start a family together while I looked on from the outside."

I pushed away the thought of Lavender and the surfacing memory of Kale revealing to me that he was having a child with another woman, but I knew when I was by myself I would relive that day over again just like I had a million times before.

"That's actually what I wanted to talk to you about," my father murmured.

I pulled back and looked at him. "What do you mean?"

He frowned. "We're nearly there."

He took my hand and starting walking again. "I'm sorry if this upsets you," my father said as he brought us to a stop in front of a grave.

The white marble teddy bear plaque was the first thing I noticed about the grave. My eyes picked up the carved-stone toys and artificial flowers a few seconds later. My heart hurt when I realised what I was looking at.

"You want to show me a baby's grave?" I asked, annoyed. "Why would I want to see this, Dad? Of course it will upset me."

I avoided looking at the picture of the little angel on the headstone because I didn't want to see the face of the beauty that was taken far too soon from the cruel world I still roamed.

"Because I want you to hear it from me before you hear it from anyone else," my father replied.

"What the hell are you talking about?" I asked, my mind a pool of confusion. "You want me to know *what*?"

My father looked away from me. "About a year after you left, something awful happened."

My stomach instantly began to churn.

"Wh-What do you mean?" I asked, my voice tight.

My father rubbed his face with his free hand. "You knew Drew was pregnant when you left, but what you don't know is that she gave birth to a boy four months after you went to New York. The baby was two months premature. At first everything was perfectly perfect. Even though he was small, he was healthy and everyone was happy. Then when he was two months old, he was diagnosed with leukaemia. He fought hard for a few months, but eight months after he was diagnosed, his little body couldn't take any more—"

"Dad. Please," I cut him off, not wanting to hear anything further.

My father ignored me and pressed on, "The doctors tried everything they could, but he—"

"Stop it," I snapped. "Just. Stop."

"He died," my father finished.

I whimpered and flung my hands over my mouth as I took a step away from my father and from the grave. "Dad, no," I whispered. "Please be lying."

My father's features shone with pain. "I wish I was lying, sweetie, but I'm not."

I looked at the grave and at the grass that covered it. "This baby . . . this is . . ."

"Lane," my father sorrowfully said, "this is Kale's son."

My eyes grew blurry, but when I looked at the gravestone once more, I could make out a single sentence that completely destroyed me: "In loving memory of Kaden Hunt."

CHAPTER SIX

Thirteen years old (thirteen years ago)

"Where is Kale?" my Uncle Harry asked as I pulled on my brand-new leather ankle boots that my mum bought me for fifty per cent off in River Island. They were the cutest boots I had *ever* seen and possibly were the most fashionable, trendy item of clothing that I owned.

"Lane," my uncle chuckled, "are you listening to me?"

I looked up when I got both of my boots zipped up, and for a moment I just stared at my uncle. Aside from Kale, he was definitely my favourite person. He was, quite literally, the coolest uncle I could have ever been blessed with. He was like a best friend to me – no, scratch that, he *was* a best friend to me. We hung out all the time and did a bunch of stuff together. He brought me fishing – which I didn't like; the quiet time with him was the only reason I went along – and bowling and a million other places that don't seem fun, but were brilliant because my uncle was the one sharing the experience with me.

My Uncle Harry was my mother's twin; he was older than her by five minutes, a fact that he liked to remind her about often. And the reason I was so close to him was because they were so close. They saw each other every single day, and I mean that literally. My father had even become close to my uncle; it got to the point where they hung out all the time too. He lived only five minutes away from our house, so I was round at his place just as much as he was around at ours.

I made sure I went round to him every day, even if it was just to say hello, because I didn't want him to be alone. He was only forty-one years old, but had to endure one of the hardest things a man would ever have to do. Last year he had to bury his wife, my Aunt Teresa. She had breast cancer and didn't even get a chance to fight it because she found out when it was too late.

I didn't like to think about her, because it made me miss her. We hadn't been very close because she was only in my life for a few short years before she died, and I was too young then to make time for her, but I knew my Uncle Harry loved her very much, and that saddened me because I knew he felt lost without her.

I personally thought my Uncle Harry was the bravest man to ever walk the earth because I loved Kale with all of my heart, and I wasn't even married to him. If he died, I think I would die too because I would be too sad to live without him. That's how I knew I could never be as great as my uncle – because I could never be as strong as he was. It took a lot of strength to live on without someone you loved as much as he loved my Aunt Teresa. It made me idolise him.

"Lane," his voice prompted.

I blinked. "Sorry, what?"

My uncle laughed and shook his head. "Where. Is. Kale?"

I rolled my eyes. "Where do you *think* he is?"

My uncle was silent for only a moment before he said, "With your brothers."

I wish.

I huffed. "He is with Drew. He is always with her, he never spends time with me *or* my brothers anymore."

That was a lie; he still hung out with my brothers. It was me who was getting the elbow recently. I just thought saying that my brothers didn't receive any of his time either made me sound a little less pathetic.

My uncle's low rumbling chuckle irked me. I turned to face him and folded my arms across my chest. "It's *not* funny, Uncle Harry."

He smiled lovingly at me. "I'm not laughing at your distress, sweetheart, I'm laughing at your attitude. You remind me of your mother when we were your age."

I do?

I beamed. "She was also fabulous with brains to burn?"

My uncle laughed loudly, and it brought a smile to my face. I loved his laugh.

"She liked to think so," he said, shaking his head good-naturedly.

I felt my smile fall as I sighed. "I'm sorry for being snarky. I'm just . . . annoyed."

My uncle kept his focus on me. "Why?" he quizzed.

I shrugged. "I don't know."

The corners of my uncle's eyes creased slightly as he said, "Yeah, darling, you do."

I gnawed on my lower lip, looked at my uncle and then to my feet. I felt my stomach churn as the realisation of what I was about to say hit me.

"I'm jealous," I admitted, still looking down. "I like Kale. I like him as *more* than a friend, and I hate it because it means I'm always going to be stuck next to him watching him be with older, prettier girls. It sucks, Uncle Harry. It sucks arse."

I felt heat stain my cheeks when silence fell between us.

"How long have you been feeling like this?" he questioned after a moment.

I blew out a relieved breath that he didn't laugh at me.

I swallowed. "Since I was around ten, but it's getting worse now 'cause I keep getting upset about it, whereas when I was younger, I didn't give it much thought when he was hanging around with other girls."

I looked up when my uncle snorted. "It's your hormones, kid," he said with a matter-of-fact tone. "You've hit puberty. Shit goes downhill from here."

I was a little embarrassed to be talking about hormones and puberty with my uncle, but I laughed when he finished speaking, because his expression was dead serious.

He smiled at me. "Why don't you talk to your mum about this?"

Is he joking? I was horrified at the suggestion.

"I couldn't," I stated. "She loves Kale like he is her own. She'd probably disown me."

My uncle's eyebrows shot up. "That's a *little* far-fetched, don't you think?"

"No," I replied, "I think it's perfectly accurate."

My uncle's eyes twinkled as he smiled. "Your vocabulary is growing."

I pushed strands of hair that fell into my eyes back from my face. "I read a lot of books," I said, shrugging. "Some that aren't for kids either."

My uncle cocked an eyebrow. "Romance novels?"

I nodded. "Young adult stuff – nothing explicit or anything."

Nothing *too* explicit anyway.

"I've no doubt those kind of novels make you more upset about Kale," my uncle said.

I frowned. "Not exactly. Well, they make me want a boyfriend more. I like reading about people's happily-ever-afters. It seems like it would be nice for someone to love me."

"*I* love you," my uncle quickly stated.

I rolled my eyes. "I mean a *boyfriend* type of love. Family love is a different kind."

"Family love is everything," he specified. "Once you have the love of your family, you can do anything."

I snorted. "Okay, Oprah."

"Cheeky mare," he tittered. "All jokes aside, are you okay? We can skip seeing *The X-Men* film if you want to."

"Not a chance. I am *dying* to see that film."

My uncle stared me down. "Are you sure? Because if you aren't up for it, we can do something else?"

I smiled at his concern. "I'll be okay. I just get like this whenever he blows me off. I guess it's just something I'll have to get used to."

My uncle scratched his neck. "Or you could just, I don't know, *tell* Kale you like him and—"

"Are you out of your bloody mind?" I cut my uncle off with a dramatic screech. "Kale can't *ever* know that I like him. It would be the end of my life!"

"Darling," my uncle said, his lip twitching.

"No!" I stated, and wagged my finger at him. "You promise me right now that anything I ever tell you about Kale stays just between us. *Just* between us."

"Lane—"

"Promise, Uncle Harry."

My uncle laughed so hard he had to rub tears from his eyes. "You're *exactly* like your mother," he cackled. "So demanding."

I folded my arms across my chest. "That doesn't sound like a promise to me."

My uncle had a bright smile on his face as he shook his head at me and said, "I promise, I'll keep all things Kale-related *strictly* between the two of us."

I eyed my uncle, then stuck out my right hand, with my pinkie finger erect. "Make the unbreakable vow," I said, my eyes narrowed.

My uncle laughed again. "I *knew* I'd regret buying you all those *Harry Potter* books."

Say what? I inwardly balked. That was possibly the best decision he had ever made; I loved those books.

"Pinkie-swear," I pressed. "It's *my* version of the unbreakable vow."

My uncle gnawed on his lower lip for a moment, then lifted his hand and hooked his pinkie finger around mine. "I, Harry Larson, pinkie-swear to you, Lane Edwards, on my honour, to never share any chats or spats about Kale Hunt to Kale or to any other living, breathing human."

I overlooked his obvious amusement and focused on his words. "Good," I said, nodding. "Now I don't have to kill you."

My uncle's lip quirked. "A girl protecting her heart from possible love – what could *conceivably* go wrong?"

"Nothing," I answered. "Absolutely *nothing* can go wrong; I've got it all figured out."

"Are you sure about that?" my uncle questioned, scepticism laced throughout his tone. "Keeping feelings like the ones you have all bottled up will only hurt in the long run."

I waved my uncle's concerns off; I knew that telling Kale I liked him would be what *would* hurt because I was aware he didn't like me back, not in *that* way. Based on that knowledge, I was certain my choice to keep him in the dark when it came to my feelings for him was the best decision. It was part of my love-Kale-from-a-distance plan.

"Trust me," I said to my uncle. "My plan is foolproof."

"Yeah." He nodded, his lips curling at the corner. "It sounds that way."

I playfully shoved him. "I don't want to talk about Kale anymore. I want to talk about the café Nanny just bought. Do you think she'd give me a summer job there?"

My uncle raised his brows. "You're thirteen."

"So?" I frowned. "I want to get out of the house, and working at Nanny's new café would be perfect for that."

"Why do you want to get out of your house?" my uncle asked.

"Because" – I dramatically sighed – "when Kale isn't with Drew, he is with my brothers, and since he is my only *real* friend, I don't have anything else to do when he isn't around. I'm only allowed one new paperback book a week because Dad says they're expensive, and I read quickly, so that only kills a few hours of my time. Mum and Dad *never* let me out on my own, and if by some miracle they do, Lochlan volunteers himself to keep an eye on me, as if I'm going to do bad stuff. It's *so* annoying."

"Your parents *and* your brothers just worry about you. You know that poor girl from the countryside that was raped and murdered was *your* age. She lived forty minutes away, and they still haven't caught the son of a bitch that did it. You can't blame everyone for being protective of you."

No, I can't, but being suffocated by everyone isn't very protective either.

"Yeah, I know," I grumbled.

"Why don't you invite those girls you study with sometimes – Hannah and Sally is it?"

I snorted. "Anna and Ally?"

"Right." My uncle snapped his fingers. "Those two, they seem nice."

I shrugged. "They can be, but we had a bit of a fight in school the other day, and we haven't made up yet."

I didn't know if we would make up either, because Anna had said some really mean things about my appearance. Ally didn't stop her or defend me, so I took it that she agreed with Anna and what she thought of me. I tried not to let it bother me, but it was hard when Anna kept throwing the same horrible words around.

Fat. Ugly. Nerd.

They were simple words, only a few letters long, but they had an impact on me even if I didn't want them to.

"Friends fight – it happens – but have a little faith; you'll make up."

I nodded for my uncle's sake, adjusted my new glasses, and said, "Okay."

"Atta girl," he said, smiling.

I leaned back in the chair and glanced around my uncle's kitchen, smiling too. "I love this house."

"You do?" my uncle asked, surprise obvious in his tone.

I nodded. "It's my favourite place. Didn't I tell you that before?"

He shook his head. "Why is it your favourite place?"

"Because I have millions of cool memories of being here with you." I smiled as I thought of a few. "Like that time we made a pillow fort out of the sofa cushions in the living room, or that time we flooded this room when we were filling water balloons to get my brothers out back."

My uncle snorted. "Your Aunt Teresa was so mad at me over that last one."

I smiled. "I know, but it was still a really great day."

"It was," he agreed, smiling fondly as he was no doubt thinking of my Aunt Teresa.

"I love my own house, *obviously*, but I don't know, your house just feels right. Like, I feel super safe when I'm here, like nothing can touch me. Is that weird?"

"No, not weird at all. Everyone should have a favourite place, and I'm glad this house is yours, darling."

I smiled. "Are you ready to go see *The X-Men?*"

My uncle stood up and puffed out his chest. "Born ready."

I shook my head, laughing as we left my uncle's house, cracking jokes and teasing one another. I knew I was blessed: I had an incredible family, and even though Kale annoyed me a lot, he was still the best friend I could have ever asked for. I knew I'd never be with him the way I wanted to be, but even if I couldn't have that, I'd want us to be always as close as we were now.

I hope things never change, my mind whispered as I ventured out with my uncle to make more memories.

CHAPTER SEVEN

Day one in York

Kale's baby died.

"No," I whispered, and stumbled back.

"I'm sorry you had to find out this way, sweetheart," my father said, looking at baby Kaden's grave once more. I lifted my hands to my face and covered my mouth as I shook my head in dismay.

This couldn't be real.

"Dad," I whispered, not knowing what else to say.

I moved my hands from my ears to my neck as I had difficulty swallowing the bile that threatened to rise up my throat. I dropped one hand to my abdomen as my stomach churned, and squeezed my eyes shut, trying my hardest not to cry.

"I'm sorry, Lane."

I opened my eyes and looked up into my father's.

"Kale . . . his baby *died*?"

My father's expression was broken as he nodded. I wrapped my arms around myself and slowly rocked from side to side as heartache swirled within me. I couldn't imagine what that must feel like for Kale, and for Drew. My father's arm closed around my body as he drew me against him, hugging me tightly.

I didn't know how long we stayed that way, but when we broke apart, I wanted nothing more than to be in his arms again.

"I ca-can't believe this," I whispered, shaking my head in utter shock and dismay.

My father scrubbed his face with one hand. "I know, sweetheart; it's still hard for everyone to come to terms with."

I blinked dumbly. "How can you come to terms with something like that?"

My father winced. "I worded that badly. I should have said it's still hard for everyone to *live* with."

I didn't think I would be able to live with something like that; I wouldn't be strong enough to survive the loss of a child. I could barely survive the loss of Kale and my uncle, let alone something as soul-crippling as losing a youngster.

"I was so focused on *not* focusing on him that I didn't even notice how truly different he is now," I said, looking off into the distance of the graveyard as I recalled Kale when I was briefly in his presence. "His eyes, they're colder, darker . . . emptier. Now I know why."

Kale wasn't Kale anymore, just like I was no longer the Lane he knew. We were both different people now, and that saddened me.

"He hardly ever smiles or laughs now unless you're mentioned," my father commented.

I looked up at my father with surprise. "Me?"

"Yeah," he said, his lip slightly twitching. "You."

I didn't know how to respond, so I stayed quiet.

"Your Uncle Harry always kept us informed on what you were up to, and when he told us about some of your conversations, it made Kale smile and laugh," my father chuckled, thinking of those times. "The first few months after Kaden died, Kale's mum used to beg me to have Harry over at the house when Kale was there, just so he could talk about you and smile."

Butterflies filled my stomach before they were replaced with dread.

"That was a long time ago," I whispered. "He must hate me now."

"Why would Kale hate you, darling?"

I swallowed. "Because I wasn't here for him when he needed me the most. I wouldn't blame him if he hated me."

My father clucked his tongue. "Lane, you couldn't have predicted what happened any better than the rest of us could."

That didn't excuse my absence.

"I should have been here for him," I said, frowning. "If I wasn't so stubborn and hadn't told Uncle Harry not to tell me about what any of you were up to, maybe he could have—"

"Kale didn't want you to know." My father cut me off mid-sentence.

"Wh-What?" I stuttered.

"When Kaden died, one of the first things Kale did was make Harry swear he wouldn't tell you. He knew things were still very hard for you and didn't want to add to it."

I felt like my throat was going to close up.

"He felt like telling me his son died would add to what I was going through?" I asked, balling my hands into fists. "I would have gotten the first flight home to be here for him in any way he needed, even if it was just to attend the funeral or be in the church. I would have done anything."

"He knew that, Lane, but deep down, I think he couldn't handle it if you were there. Everything was falling apart around him."

My heart hurt.

"But maybe I could have helped him," I whispered.

My father's hands gripped my forearms. "You listen to me," he said firmly. "We were there for Kale constantly, but his mind was absent. It's taken him this long to be able to live with Kaden being gone. You couldn't have helped him; he was so far gone during the time of Kaden's passing, no one could get through to him."

I could have reached him; I knew in my heart I could have.

I blinked numbly. "Couldn't Drew help him?"

My father shook his head.

"A few months before Kaden passed away, they split up and called off their engagement. The strain of Kaden's illness put a wedge between them that they couldn't overcome. They lived together for a few months after Kaden died, to help one another cope, but Kale eventually moved out, and Drew remained in their house. She didn't want to leave because she felt like Kaden was still there with her in spirit. She is with somebody new now, and she seems happy, but Kale never dated anyone else. Losing Kaden almost killed him, and every day is a desperate struggle for him."

I used to dream of a time where Drew and Kale would break up for good, and she would be out of his life, but now that it had happened, I found myself wishing for nothing more than for them to be together again. Maybe she could help him, and he wouldn't be so sad and alone.

"I wish I could have done something," I whispered.

My father kissed my head. "Don't we all, honey?"

I leaned my head back and stared up at the starlit sky, watching my breath turn to fog when I exhaled. It was cold as ice outside, but for the life of me I couldn't feel it. My body was just as numb as my heart.

"You can do something now."

I looked at my father when he spoke and said, "It's been years; what can I possibly do for him?"

"Just being there for him will help him. You have no idea how much he worships you, Lane."

I licked my dry lips. "He idolises a girl from his past, Dad, but I'm not the same Lane he, or any of you, knew. She's gone," I whispered, my voice tight with emotion. "I've changed so much that I don't even recognise myself anymore."

My father hooked his arm around my shoulder and tugged me against him. "You need to be here just as much as we need to have you here, Lane. You can find yourself again and possibly help Kale find peace in the process."

I exhaled a deep breath and looked up at my father's lined face. "That's a lot to achieve in a short amount of time."

He winked. "Your Uncle Harry believed that you would achieve great things. I trust in his judgement, and I trust in you. You can do anything you set your mind to, my love."

A lump formed in my throat.

"You're making wanting to run away again very difficult to do."

"Good," my father swiftly replied. "The time for running away is over. It's time now to face things head on."

Damn him.

I sighed. "I feel like you would be good in any pep talk-related situation."

My father grinned. "It may be my calling, but I'm retired now. I'll have a crack at it in my next lifetime."

I laughed and threw my arms back around my father, hugging him tightly.

"I love you, Dad."

"I love you too, sweetheart," he replied, and kissed the crown of my head.

We were quiet for a few moments, and then we separated.

"Do you want to visit Lavender while we're here?" my father quietly asked me.

You'll never be without me, Lane Edwards; we'll be best friends forever. I shook my head and shook her voice away.

"I'm going to spend time with her on Monday when not many people will be here."

My father nodded and extended his hand to me. "Let's go home, darling."

With a lump in my throat, I placed my hand in my father's and held on for dear life, knowing that eventually I would have to let go, no matter how much I didn't want to. Together, we walked hand in hand back to my parents' house. When we entered through the front door, we were met with silence.

"Stay here tonight."

I hesitated in replying to my father, so he quickly said, "Just for tonight. Spend our last night with Harry here with us."

When he put it like that, there was no question about where I would be sleeping.

"Is there a bed in my room still?" I questioned.

My father lifted a brow. "Your room is still the same way it was when you left."

I blinked. "It is?"

My father tilted his head to the side as he scanned me with his eyes. "Why wouldn't it be?" he asked.

I shrugged. "I thought you might convert it into something else."

He snorted. "Like what?"

I glanced to his gut. "Not a gym, obviously."

He reached out and clipped me around the ear, making me laugh. "Cheeky mare," he chuckled.

I smiled and replied lightly, "I'm only teasing, but I did think you would change it to storage or something like that."

My father shook his head. "We would never do that. Your brothers' room is still the same as it has always been. They both often drop in and sleep here. We left yours the same way for the same reason."

They hoped I would drop in and sleep here. I wondered how long my mother and father had prayed for that. Before I started crying once again, I leaned into my father and gave him one last hug before I went into the parlour, where I found my mother and nanny both asleep on the sofa across from Harry. I stared at the two most important women in my life, and I made a silent vow to always be there for them, no matter the cost.

They had lost a son and a brother; I wouldn't add a daughter and granddaughter to that list.

I took the blanket from the back of the sofa and placed it over the pair of them, kissing their foreheads while doing so. "I love you both so much," I whispered.

I stood up and turned to my Uncle Harry, and without hesitation tears filled and spilled from my eyes. "Tomorrow is going to be the worst day of my life," I murmured to him. "I thought the worst day happened years ago, but you leaving us trumps that."

Like before, I was expecting a reply, and when it didn't come, my heart ached.

"Goodnight, Uncle Harry," I sniffled. "I'll see you tomorrow."

I ignored the voice in my head that cruelly whispered, *For the last time.*

I kissed my uncle's head and then quietly slipped out of the room and went upstairs to my old bedroom. I placed my hands on the newly sanded and varnished banister, feeling its smoothness as my hand glided over the polished wood. I shook my head when I stepped onto the landing and the floorboard just before the bathroom creaked loudly.

That bloody step is a curse, I silently mused. *It ratted me out when I was younger and would sneak downstairs for late-night snacks.*

I passed by the bathroom and my father's office before I came to the familiar door of my old bedroom. I reached out and ran my fingers over the sign I'd proudly hung when I was thirteen.

"DO *NOT* ENTER LANE'S ROOM!
THE CHANCES OF YOUR DEATH ARE *INCREDIBLY*
HIGH IF YOU IGNORE THIS SIGN.
KALE GETS A PASS, AND HIM *ALONE*!"

I'd been such a little hellcat.

I chuckled and reached for the handle of my door, and chuckled even more when I heard it creak loudly as I pushed it open. I shook my head. *Out of everything that has been fixed in this house, they couldn't have fixed my bedroom door after all of these years?*

I reached to the left wall, felt for the light switch and flipped it. I blinked rapidly against the harshness of the light, but my eyes quickly adjusted and began to scan around the room.

It was the same, and only a little different.

There were bed sheets on my bed that I'd never seen before and curtains that were definitely new to the room. Apart from that, things looked untouched. My mother must have put everything back where she'd found it after she did her rounds of cleaning, because it looked like I'd never left, with the exception of it being a lot cleaner than it ever was when I'd lived here.

I looked down to my attire and frowned. My suitcase was back at the hotel, housing my only pair of pyjamas and fresh change of underwear. I looked over to my dresser and curiously walked forward, opening the first drawer. I didn't know why, but I wasn't surprised when I found new packets of underwear lining the wood. I opened the other drawers and found new, plain T-shirts, jeans, leggings, jumpers – you name it; it was stocked in the drawers.

I didn't think my mother would have had the time to do this kind of a shopping haul over the last few days, which could only mean she had been stocking up on new items of clothing for me over the years. She either hoped I would come home, or she knew I would.

It was clear that though the clothes had never been worn, they had been washed a few times and even ironed, which made me feel like an even bigger piece of shit. Washing them, cleaning and preserving my room was her own way of dealing with me being gone.

I opened a packet of underwear and picked out a pair of plain white booty shorts before opening the fourth drawer and taking out a set of adult-sized Pokémon pyjamas that made me laugh. I've always had an embarrassing obsession with Pokémon that only my mother got; her sense of humour on the subject didn't seemed to have faltered.

Laughing, I headed out of my room and into the bathroom, where I showered, washed my hair and scrubbed and shaved every inch of my body before returning to my room, wrapped tightly in a towel. After I dried and changed into my underwear and pyjamas, I got to work on drying my hair. When I got into bed and everything was quiet and dark, my mind screamed my worries at me.

My Uncle Harry's funeral was tomorrow.

Kale's son was dead, and Kale was alone and empty inside.

I forced the thoughts from my mind and stared up, smiling at the glow in the dark stickers of the solar system that lit up the ceiling of my room.

"I can't believe they're still lighting up," I murmured to myself.

I forced my eyes to stay open and prayed that I wouldn't fall asleep, because for once, I didn't want morning to come. Morning meant burying my uncle.

Morning meant a permanent goodbye.

CHAPTER EIGHT

Fifteen years old (eleven years ago)

"Lane, your friend is *sooooo* cute," Anna O'Leary gushed to me as she looked up from her phone. "He just posted a new selfie with your brother Lochlan – who is also *extremely* cute, by the way – on social media and it is *hawt*."

I didn't need to ask for clarification on what cute friend Anna was talking about. I only had one male friend, and he was indeed very cute.

"He's okay, I guess," I mumbled, downplaying the fact that I wholeheartedly agreed Kale was cute, and then some.

Anna giggled again. "Does he have a girlfriend by any chance?"

A girlfriend? I looked up at Anna, giving her my full attention.

"Why?" I quizzed.

She dead-panned, "Because I want to introduce him to a girl I think would be *very* happy to kiss and date him – in other words, me."

I blinked, dumbly.

Anna wants to date Kale and kiss him? I thought. *I don't like that.*

"You're fifteen," I said, stating the obvious.

Anna raised her eyebrows. "I'm sixteen next month. What's your point?"

"What do you mean 'what's my point'? You're *sixteen* next month, and Kale is *nineteen* next month," I said with an arched eyebrow.

Could she not see that the age gap was weird? I knew it was only three years, but we were still little girls . . . I mean, weren't we? We *were* only fifteen.

Ally Day – who was studying with us – giggled, and Anna smirked. "*Exactly.* I always wanted an older boyfriend."

I blinked, unsure of how to feel.

"Kale isn't right for you, Anna. He is pretty much a man."

She sighed dreamingly. "I know. That's why I want him so bad."

Ally was still giggling, so I took it she was on board with Anna. I continued to stare at Anna with a shocked expression on my face.

"You're so stupid," I said, my tone a little shrill.

I resisted the urge to slap my hand over my mouth because I didn't mean to say that out loud.

Anna snapped out of her Kale-transfixed daydream and trained her now-narrowed green eyes on me. "I am *not* stupid. Don't be jealous of me just because *you* got friendzoned by the hottest lad we know."

I felt my cheeks flush with heat when Ally laughed. I didn't know why she was laughing at what Anna said; she was supposed to be my friend.

"I didn't get friendzoned by Kale," I said defensively. "We have just always been friends. It's never been like *that* with us."

I wished it was like that, but it just wasn't.

"Duh," Anna said, and gave me a dirty look. "Like he could ever go for someone who looks like you? *Hello*, ugly alert."

I hate when she does this, a voice in my mind hissed. *She calls me names and upsets me whenever she gets mad at me, and Ally just sits there!*

Anna snorted. "And why do you think that is, Lane? You look eight instead of fifteen. You have no boobs, your teeth still have tracks on them, you wear glasses, you have acne *and* you're fat. You're lucky he even bothers to acknowledge you at all, you ugly cow!"

"Yeah," Ally chimed in, folding her arms across her chest, "I can't believe we even bothered to hang out with you; you're *such* a loser."

My stomach twisted, and my heart pounded against my chest.

"I have to go home now," I whispered, and quickly gathered my textbooks and shoved them into my school bag.

Without a word or look in Anna or Ally's direction, I turned and ran out of Anna's bedroom. I ran down the stairs, flung open Anna's front door and ran out of her garden, down the pathway and all the way home. I didn't stop until I got into my house and up into my bathroom, where I retched and vomited up the entire contents of my stomach.

I only stopped throwing up when I was dry heaving and nothing else came up. I wiped my mouth with some tissue, which I then flushed down the toilet. I moved over to the sink and washed my hands. I cupped my hands together and gathered water, then splashed it on my face. I quickly brushed my teeth and gargled some mouthwash to get the foul taste of vomit out of my mouth.

When I was finished, I dried my hands and face off with a hand towel. I caught my reflection in the mirror and stared at myself. My stomach churned once more as I spotted each and every flaw. Anytime Anna and I had argued over the years, she repeated the same horrible things to me. I couldn't help but see what she had always pointed out. My nerdy glasses, my metal braces, my acne, my slight double chin. I looked down at my flat chest, then to my chubby belly and back up to my face.

Anna and Ally were right: I *was* an ugly cow.

Disgusted with myself, I exited the bathroom and ran for my bedroom, but instead of making a clean escape, I ran head first into my father's chest as he emerged from his office.

"Hello, love," he beamed. "You're home from Anna's house early. How was studying?"

I didn't answer, so my dad looked away from the calculator in his hands and down to my face. When he saw my tear-stained cheeks and red-rimmed eyes, he dropped his calculator to the floor and kneeled before me, placing his hands on my shoulders.

"What's wrong?" he asked, his tone laced with worry.

I looked down to his calculator and blew out a breath of relief once I saw the protective cover on it. My father would have been so mad later if the fall had broken it.

I looked to his perplexed gaze.

"Everything," I answered, my voice broken.

He shook me a little. "Who upset you? Tell me."

I opened my mouth at the same time as my mother shouted, "Dinner's ready."

My stomach churned at the thought of food.

"I don't want dinner. I'm *never* eating anything ever again," I blubbered, then ran around my father and into my bedroom, where I slammed the door shut and turned my lock.

I dove onto my bed and buried my face into my pillow as I sobbed. My chest hurt with the newfound knowledge of my appearance. My cheeks burned with embarrassment, and my heart ached with pain.

How could I not know I'm fat and ugly? I angrily thought. *How could I not see it?*

I had a mirror, a full-length one, but I never saw what Anna and Ally saw, even though Anna had repeatedly pointed it out over the last few years. When we made up, she would tell me she just said the mean things to hurt me, not because she thought they were true, and I stupidly believed her. I thought I looked like a normal teenage girl. I never thought I fell into the fat or ugly category. My father always told me I was beautiful. Kale did too.

They lied. *Kale* lied.

"Lane! Open this door right now!" my father ordered, and banged on my door with his fist.

I could hear my mother shout as she ran up the stairs, then my brothers' voices as they ran in from the back garden upon hearing the shouting.

"No. You lied to me!" I screamed.

My father was silent for a moment before asking, "What did I lie to you about?"

Like he didn't know!

"You told me I was beautiful," I bellowed. "You told me I was perfect. You *lied* to me, Dad. I'm fat and I'm ugly, and everybody knows it! *Everybody!*"

I was sobbing so hard I almost made myself sick again.

"Lane!" Lochlan's voice shouted. "Open the door, or I'm breaking it open!"

"Lochlan, stop it!" my mother snapped, her voice distraught.

"No, we don't know what she's doing in there," he argued. "What if she's hurting herself?"

At that my mother screamed for me to open the door, but I refused to do as she ordered. I didn't even respond to her. I was too busy replaying what Anna and Ally had said to me in my head.

Hello, ugly alert.

"Lane?" Layton's voice suddenly bellowed.

I closed my eyes and hugged my pillow to my body.

They'd all lied to me, every single one of them.

I screamed when a sudden bang erupted, followed by a crunching sound. I shot upright on my bed and stared wide-eyed at my door – which was now wide open.

"You – you kicked my door in!" I stuttered to my father, who stalked into my room and straight over to my bed to me.

I scurried back away from him until my back was against my wall.

"Don't touch me!" I cried, wrapping my arms around myself.

My brothers flanked my father while my mother crawled onto my bed to get closer to me. She stared at me.

"What happened?" she asked, her voice shaking.

I looked at her for a moment before I cracked.

Breaking down, I threw myself into her opened arms and sobbed into her chest. She wrapped her arms around me and cried with me, even though she had no idea what was wrong. She just saw her baby hurting, and it hurt her.

"Anna . . . and Al-Ally," I sobbed. "We were in Anna's house, th-they called me fat and ugly, and they're ri-right. I am disgusting."

My mother whimpered. "You are not. You're beau—"

"Don't," I wailed. "Don't lie to me. I ha-have braces, I have gl-glasses, I have acne, and I'm fat. I'm ev-everything they said I was. I'm an ugly cow. I want to die!"

"Lochlan!" my father's voice shouted as my brother ran out of my room. "Where are you going?"

"To get those little bitches here to fix this!" Lochlan replied, his voice a bellow.

"Oh, shit. He's going to the O'Leary house," Layton hissed, then ran out of my bedroom after our brother.

"Goddammit. Take care of her – I'll be back soon." My father ran out of the room after my brothers.

When they were gone, I fully turned into my mother's embrace and buried myself against her. I held onto her as my body trembled. I felt so bad about myself, and I didn't know how to deal with it. I had never given my appearance much thought, but Anna was right: if I ever wanted a boyfriend, I would have to "look the part". The only problem was, I had no idea what that meant.

"Why did Anna and Ally say those mean and *untrue* things to you?" my mother asked as she continued to rock us from side to side.

I sniffled. "Anna, she told me Kale was cu-cute, and she wanted him to be her b-b-boyfriend. I told her it wasn't a good i-idea because he was older. I told her he was almost a man, and we w-were still girls. She didn't care though, so I-I called her stupid," I said, quickly adding, "I'm sorry. I didn't mean to call her that. It just sl-slipped out."

"It's okay, she *is* stupid for saying those things to you," my mother assured me. "It's all going to be okay."

She continued to hold me, and before I knew it, I'd closed my eyes and slipped into an unsettled slumber. I awoke sometime later with my blanket pulled up over my body and my glasses removed. I reached out to my bedside table, picked up my glasses and slid them on. I was tired and wondered why I'd woken up, but when I heard voices downstairs, I realised I must have heard *his* voice in my sleep, and my body reacted by waking up.

I sat up and switched my lamp on. It was dark outside. One look at the clock on my wall and I groaned. It was after 8 p.m. I'd slept for hours, which meant I was going to be awake all night and be miserable in the morning when I got up for school.

The thought of school, and Anna and Ally in my class, made me feel ill. I decided then that I wasn't going; I would persuade my parents to let me stay off since it was a Friday. I needed the entire weekend to figure out what I was going to do about my appearance.

I needed to think.

I looked at my door when I heard footsteps come up the stairs. I tilted my head to the side and focused on my door. It was closed and looked fine, but the panel that surrounded the lock was gone.

My father had kicked it off.

"Lane?" my mother's voice called out softly as she knocked on my door. "Honey, Kale is here. He would like to see you."

"Why?" I shouted at the closed door. "Why would he want to look at me?"

Seconds went by until his voice spoke. "Can I come in, Lane?"

Never.

"No, I don't *ever* want to talk to you or see you again, Kale Hunt! You're a *liar*!" I screamed, and lay back down on my bed, turning over to face my wall.

I was hurt, embarrassed and mad.

I was mad that Kale had never told me I was fat and ugly. He was supposed to be my best friend. We told each other everything. So why hadn't he ever told me something so important?

Why did he lie to me? I thought hopelessly.

I sat on my bed and remained quiet until I heard their footsteps walk away from my bedroom and descend the stairs. I waited a further five minutes before I stood up from my bed.

I didn't want to leave my room, but I needed to go to the toilet.

I walked over to my door slowly and carefully pulled the damaged wood open, wincing when the damaged hinges creaked. I hesitated, but then quickly pulled it open very fast, hoping the noise would be kept to a minimum. I was right: the door didn't make much noise, but it didn't matter if it did or not; he still would have heard. Sitting next to my room with his back against the hallway wall didn't leave much room for him to miss anything.

"Go away, Kale," I said, and stepped over his legs and walked down the hallway and into the bathroom.

He didn't reply to me, didn't make a single noise, and that irked me.

I relieved myself in the bathroom, and when I was cleaning myself up at the sink, I made a point not to look up into the mirror. I didn't want to see what everyone else was forced to look at.

I exited the bathroom and headed back down the hallway towards my room. I glared at Kale, who still had his arse parked on the floor right next to my doorway. I shook my head as I stepped over his legs and entered my room, closing the door behind me.

Again, he said nothing to me; he didn't make a single sound.

Damn stubborn lad.

I busied myself for the next hour with homework and some reading. I couldn't get into either one, though. Anna's cruel words and Ally's shrill laughter replayed over and over in my mind on an endless loop. I glanced at my bedroom door, and after a moment I stood up and walked over to it. I reached out for the handle, and after a few seconds of hesitation, I gripped the handle and pulled the door open.

He was still there.

Still sitting outside my room, waiting for me to let him in. I stepped back and opened the door as wide as it would go. I said nothing, but Kale knew what I was offering. He pushed himself to his feet and entered my room.

I closed the door and turned around to face him. He was standing in the middle of my room, with his hands shoved into the front pockets of his jeans as he stared at me. He gazed at me with sad hazel eyes. I was more than ready to tell him off and be mad at him, but when he silently lifted his arms and opened them to me, I broke down.

I felt a lump form in my throat as I walked into his embrace. I wrapped my arms around his waist and pressed my head against his chest. His arms tightly closed around me; he even rubbed his right hand up and down my back to soothe me like he usually did when I was sad.

Damn him.

Why does he make it so hard to stay mad at him? I angrily thought.

I didn't know how long we stood there holding onto one another, but when I calmed down enough to speak, I pulled back and looked up at him. He smiled down at me, his beautiful barely there dimples creasing his cheeks.

"Hey, Laney Baby," he whispered.

I burst into tears and rewrapped my arms around his body. He lightly vibrated as he chuckled and put his arms back around me.

I pulled back once more. "I'm sad, Kale."

He looked at me, his eyes heavy with anguish. "If I have to convince you that Anna O'Leary and Ally Day are just jealous of you, then you aren't the smart girl I know you are."

I grunted and moved away from him, and walked over to my mirror, where I glared at my appearance.

"They were right, though," I said as I gazed at the hideous flaws Anna had evilly pointed out. "Look at me. I'm disgusting."

Kale came up behind me and looked me in the eye; he was over a head taller than me, so he did this easily.

"Tell me what you see when you look into the mirror and see your reflection," he urged.

I felt heat stain my cheeks. "A fat, ugly cow."

He shook his head. "Do you want to know what I see?"

"No, not really," I replied.

He ignored me and said, "I see a beautiful girl whose smile brightens up a room. I see a beautiful girl whose eyes are so warm and welcoming, they make people feel at ease with one glance. I see a beautiful girl who cares for others and loves so hard it's impossible not to love her back just as hard. I see a beautiful girl who is so stunningly gorgeous, she will break her father's and brothers' hearts when she realises just how incredible she is and decides to give her heart to another. I see a beautiful girl who just doesn't see how beautiful she really is."

That was it; I was once again a blubbering mess.

"Damn you, Kale Hunt," I cried, and turned to him once more, wrapping myself around him.

He held me to him and kissed the crown of my head. "There isn't a hair on your head that isn't beautiful, Laney Baby. Everything about you is beautiful; I've known that since the first day I saw you."

I surprisingly laughed through my blubbering. "You first met me when I was two hours old. I probably looked like a shrivelled-up prune."

"You did," Kale agreed, "but a beautiful shrivelled-up prune."

I shoved him, and he laughed, so I laughed with him. I pulled back from him and walked over to my bed.

"How can you remember back so far? You were only three when I was born." I climbed onto my bed and turned to face Kale, who took a seat on the chair in front of my desk.

"I remember everything about the day I first saw you, Lane. It was the first time I ever saw an angel in the flesh."

I covered my face as it burned up.

"Shut up. You're *so* full of it!" I screeched.

He laughed. "Give over – you know you're my angel."

On the inside I purred with delight; on the outside I played it off with a roll of my eyes.

"Yeah, well, this angel is getting a makeover," I said and pushed my long, dull brown hair over my shoulder.

Kale raised his eyebrows. "A makeover? What does that mean exactly?"

I shrugged. "I'm going to get a haircut and buy make-up and clothes that don't come from the kids' sections in shops."

He blinked. "Lane, you don't need to change your appearance to seek approval from people who don't matter."

I shook my head. "I'm not doing this for Anna and Ally; I'm doing it for me. I want to be the one that boys notice. I'm *so* done with being everyone's 'friend'."

The latter was directed at Kale, but he didn't need to know that.

He stared at me for a long moment, and then he licked his lips and dug his phone out of his pocket when it rang. He answered it and had a brief conversation, then shook his head and looked up to me.

"What's wrong?" I asked.

He shrugged. "Just Drew being Drew. Nothing to worry about."

Drew Summers was his current girlfriend.

I didn't like her. I never had.

I didn't like any of Kale's girlfriends, but Drew was different because she kept reappearing. She and Kale would be together, then break up for a while and then get back together. They were on and off like a light switch. It bugged the hell out of me that she wouldn't just go away and stay away.

"Are you sure?" I asked, hoping to be a shoulder to cry on if he needed one.

He nodded. "Yep, she'll get over whatever is up her arse eventually."

I chuckled. "Always the charmer."

Kale gestured to himself. "But of course."

I smiled and looked down to my fingers, picking out the dirt from under my nails.

"Can I stay tonight?" he asked.

I looked up and raised an eyebrow. "It's a Thursday, though. When you stay over, it's usually on the weekends."

"I know, but your mum said it was okay for me to crash since you weren't feeling so hot – uh, I mean good. Shit. I didn't mean that as in appearances—"

I cut Kale's brain fart off with my laughter. "I get what you mean, loser."

He relaxed. "Good."

I glanced at my bedroom door and then back to him. "Are the lads okay with you staying?"

He snorted. "Please. Your brothers love me."

Everyone in my house loved Kale; he was part of our family.

Kale never looked at me like anything other than a sister, and while I hated it, I respected his respect for me. He was completely fine with sleeping in my brothers' room, and so were my brothers. I seemed to be the only person who wanted him to sleep in my room with me; I kept that to myself, though. I kept everything about how I really felt about Kale to myself – unless my Uncle Harry was around for me to vent to.

"So it's cool to stay?" he asked.

I crossed my eyes at him, making him burst into laughter.

My lip twitched. "Like you even have to ask."

He thought about this for a second, then said, "True."

He ignored his phone when it rang again, and switched it off instead. "I'll have your mum call my mum and let her know I won't be home. Then I'll be back, and we can totally talk lads and do each other's nails."

I fell sideways on my bed, laughing.

"You're *such* a freak."

Kale beamed at me. "If it'll make you smile, I'll be the biggest freak this world has ever seen."

I continued to laugh. "That wouldn't take much."

He gripped his chest. "Your words, they wound me deeply."

"Go call your mum already!" I howled in laughter.

Kale chuckled to himself as he left my room, and I beamed after him, not surprised that I felt so happy being in his presence after being so sad without him.

~

The next day Kale helped me convince my parents to let me have the day off school. He had the week off college and promised my parents he would take me out and help cheer me up. My father wanted to know what that entailed, and Kale had to explain my makeover plan to them.

My father didn't like it, but my mother was completely on board. She gave Kale a bunch of money from her savings jar and told him to help me make good decisions.

"Come with us, Mrs Edwards – you know more about fashion and hairstyles than I ever will," Kale said to my mother.

She patted his shoulder and said, "I think a boy's opinion is what is needed here, not a mother's, because I think Lane looks beautiful as she is."

"Then it's pointless for me to go too, because I wholeheartedly agree with you."

"My God," I grumbled as embarrassment heated my cheeks.

We eventually left my house, *without* my mother, and made our way into town, laughing and joking the entire bus ride in. When we got off the bus, we were in shopping heaven. There were clothing shops, nail bars and hair salons in every direction. I'd never come into this part of town before, and the overload of people made me nervous.

"I've got you." Kale threaded his fingers through mine. "Don't let go; you're tiny and would get lost in the crowd."

Oh, my God. I could have died. I could have died right there in the middle of the shopping district.

Kale was holding my hand and leaning protectively into me like a boyfriend would to his girlfriend. I knew we were just friends, and he was making sure I didn't venture off, but I let myself pretend that it was real and he was really just hanging out with me as his girl.

"Okay, what do you want to get done first? Hair, nails or do you want to hit the clothes shops first?" Kale asked as he leaned his mouth down to my ear so I could hear him over all the voices around us.

I trembled as shivers ran up and down my spine.

"Hair," I squeaked, and then I cleared my throat. "Hair first."

"Hair first it is," he said, weaving us through the crowd until we entered a Toni and Guy hair salon.

I stood staring at all the different hairstyle pictures in black and white on the walls for a long moment, and when Kale pulled on my hand, I almost jumped out of my skin. He laughed at me, and so did the woman behind the counter.

"Follow me," the woman chirped after she smudged a little white gel behind my ear, a skin test for future appointments that involved hair dye. I didn't want my hair dyed this time around; I just wanted a different style, but I did the test anyway.

I swallowed and looked to Kale and found him sitting behind me in the mini waiting section next to the doorway. "I'll be here and I'll be able to see you. Go on – you'll be fine," he said, and then hesitated. "Just don't cut too much off, 'kay?"

I smiled and nodded my head, then walked over to a chair to be introduced to Kevin, a stylist. Kevin was in his early twenties, with spiky hair the colour of the rainbow. He also had so many piercings on his face and in his ears that I lost count at fifteen. He was lovely, though, and very excited that he was giving me my first haircut in, well, forever.

"What are we thinking of doing today?" he asked me, his voice bubbly.

I blew out a breath. "Okay, so I don't like my hair being so dull. I like the colour, because it's dark brown but it has a natural red-wine tint when the sun hits it. I'm thinking of five inches off the length and a full fringe like that picture over there. With some layers thrown in too."

Kevin snapped his fingers at me in a "Z" formation. "Honey, your lad over there won't be able to take his eyes off you when I get done with you."

I knew Kevin was talking about Kale, but I didn't correct him because I liked the fact that someone didn't think it was as crazy an idea as I thought it was. A half hour went by, and after getting my hair washed, cut, blow-dried and cut again, I was ready. Kevin spun me around and told me to open my eyes. I gasped when I saw myself in the mirror. I looked . . . pretty!

Not beautiful or anything, but pretty, and I was so happy with that.

"Oh, my God," I squealed. "I love it. I love it *so* much."

I hadn't been trying to look older, but I could easily pass for sixteen now, and I thought that was beyond brilliant.

"Told you," Kevin said, beaming, and ruffled the hair on the sides of my head.

He brushed stray hairs off my clothes and brought me back over to the desk, where I checked in so I could pay. Kale still sat in the waiting area. He was slouched down on a seat, his long legs bent as he paged through a magazine. There were two girls sitting across from him, watching him with keen interest. I wanted to roll my eyes. He got attention like this everywhere he went, and he didn't even notice.

"Kale," I said when I walked over to him.

He looked up at me when I reached him, and his eyes widened. His immediate expression made me very nervous.

"What do you think?" I asked, my voice a whisper.

He put down the magazine and stood up to his full height, which caused me to take a step back so I could look up at him. He was so much taller than me now. Over the last two years, he'd taken a big stretch and got lanky on me.

"I think" – he reached out and brushed the back of his fingers against my fringe – "you look just as beautiful as I knew you would."

"Oh, my God," one of the girls said out loud while her friend stared at him in complete awe.

I felt heat crawl up my neck and spread out over my face.

"Kale!" I hissed with embarrassment, and turned to Kevin, who was smiling brightly at me.

"I told you he wouldn't be able to keep his eyes off you, didn't I?" he beamed. "I can spot a good boyfriend from a mile away."

Oh. My. God.

Kill me. Please, just kill me now.

I looked down and tensed when Kale stepped up beside me and paid for my haircut out of the money my mother had given him. I thanked Kevin as we left the salon, and swallowed when Kale placed his hand on my lower back.

"He thinks I'm your boyfriend?" he murmured in my ear.

Shit.

"Yeah, sorry about that," I said, laughing nervously. "He just assumed."

Kale grabbed a hold of my arm and turned me to him. "Why are you sorry?" he asked curiously.

I shrugged. "Because I don't want you to be embarrassed if people think we're together."

He frowned. "Why would that embarrass me?"

I blinked. "Because I'm not Drew. I don't look like her, or any of her friends. I'm not stupid, Kale; I know I'm homely compared to her. That isn't news to me."

He stared down at me, a frown on his face, but he said nothing.

I looked over my shoulder and spotted a River Island shop. "Let's go in there."

Kale took my hand in his – I got excited shivers again – and led me to River Island without muttering a single word. He was acting very strange. He followed me around the shop as I picked up different items of clothing. I came to a black pair of skinny jeans I really liked, but I wasn't sure if I could pull off such a look or not.

"Do you think I could wear them?" I asked Kale, and picked up a pair, showing them to him.

He looked at the jeans and nodded. "Sure, why not?"

"Because they are *skinny jeans*," I said in a *duh* tone.

Kale blinked. "I don't know what that means."

Lads.

I rolled my eyes, making him snort.

He followed me to the changing rooms and waited outside as I began the process of trying all my outfits on. I tried on a few different dresses and T-shirts, then decided to get the jeans out of the way. They were a size twelve and slid on me fine; they even buttoned up great.

They looked good; at least I thought they did.

I turned around and looked at myself from every angle to see if my bum looked okay. I turned to the front and grunted at my tummy; it was chubby, but not exactly flabby. I wished it were flat and toned.

"What are you trying on?" Kale asked me from outside the changing room.

"The jeans," I replied.

"Can I see them on?" he asked. "Or do you not want my opinion?"

I did want his opinion; I just didn't want him to see *me* in the jeans, if that made any sense. I was going to throw on a T-shirt to cover up my stomach, but I thought the hell with that because I would need him to help me get a certain dress on in a few minutes, which meant he would see my stomach anyway. Besides Kale wouldn't care if he saw my bra or chubby belly. He probably wouldn't even notice. He never noticed anything about me.

I opened the door of the changing room and gestured to the jeans. "What do you think?"

Kale widened his eyes and quickly entered the changing room, closing the door behind him.

"Kale!" I snapped as I stumbled backwards. "What was *that* for?"

He turned to me and growled. "You're in your *bra*!"

His eyes lingered on my chest before he snapped them away like his eyes burned.

I looked down at myself and then back up at him. "So? You're the only one who can see me."

"No," – he glared, fixing his eyes on mine – "two lads are just down there with their birds, I'm not having them see you naked."

Naked?

"Oh, give me a break." I rolled my eyes and, turning around, asked, "Does my arse look flat in these?"

I watched in the mirror as Kale's eyes dropped to my behind. "What kind of question is that?" he asked, staring at my arse without blinking as he spoke.

"A good one," I argued. "I don't want to have a pancake arse. I've been doing squats with my mum. I think they're working."

I turned around and looked at my behind again over my shoulder, and to be honest I was pretty happy with how it looked. I was fifteen – I wasn't expecting to have a Beyoncé bum, but I was pleased with what I was rocking. Well, as pleased as I could be with my newfound knowledge about my looks anyway.

"I don't think . . ." he began slowly, "I don't think your dad, or brothers for that matter, would let you wear *that* out in public."

He spoke as if I would be walking around bare.

I snorted as I grabbed a tank top and pulled it over my head. "I'll be wearing a T-shirt with it, not just my bra. *Duh.*"

"Yeah, I get that . . . but the jeans – they're skintight."

"What did you think *skinny jeans* meant?" I questioned.

Kale grunted. "I didn't think you meant the skintight ones."

"Well, I do. Do they look okay on me?" I asked, and then frowned. "Be honest."

He looked down at the jeans, then back up to my eyes. "Yes, but you're far too young for them."

I felt my jaw drop open. "Kale, come on."

He shook his head. "I'm serious. You're only fifteen—"

"Sixteen in two months," I growled, cutting him off.

"And I'm nineteen next month. If *I* notice you in them, so will other lads my age. I don't like that. I don't want you getting attention from lads in that sort of way. It's not right."

I frowned. "Why not?"

Kale opened his mouth, then closed it after a moment. "I don't . . . I don't know why exactly. I guess I feel protective of you. I just know I'd lose my head if I caught some lad staring at you for too long, Lane. I know what goes through a lad's mind, and I don't want you to be the centre of it. You're *fifteen*."

I knew how old I was, and it bugged the hell out of me.

"You're going to have to accept that I'm getting older, and I'll start dating soon."

Although I had no idea if I'd ever start dating because I needed boys to be interested in me for that to happen.

"I'll accept it when you're fifty." Kale grinned.

I laughed and shook my head. "You're worse than Lochlan."

He snorted and turned around while I took my jeans off and placed them in the "yes" pile. I tried on a few pairs of different-coloured leggings with long T-shirts then, and I didn't need Kale's opinion on them. They were cute, casual and something everyone could pull off, no matter their size.

I stepped into a sky-blue sundress that buttoned up in the back. I shimmied it up to my chest and slid my arms into the armholes, holding it against my chest so it wouldn't fall down.

"Can you turn and button this up?" I asked Kale.

I watched as he turned around and glanced at my back like it was a foreign object. He stepped forward and began to button up the dress. He paused a few times when his fingertips brushed against my skin, but eventually he buttoned it up the entire way. Though it looked like he broke a sweat doing it.

I did a little twirl in the dress and beamed. "I love it."

And that was the truth. Without looking for the faults that I was sure I would find, I took the dress at face value, and I thought I looked a little pretty in it.

"Me too," Kale murmured.

I squealed with happiness at his agreement.

"Really? You aren't just saying that because you're my friend?"

"No," Kale stated. "I'm *definitely* not saying it just because I'm your friend. Trust me."

I lifted my hand for a high five, which Kale delivered half-heartedly.

I frowned. "Is everything okay?"

He nodded. "Everything is great. Why do you ask?"

"Because you're being weird?"

"Weird?" he questioned, and folded his arms across his chest. "I'm not being weird – you are. How am *I* being weird?"

Yep, he is definitely being weird.

I shook my head and laughed. "What is going on with you today?"

"I have no bloody idea," he grumbled, and scrubbed his face with his hands. "My stomach is hurting. Might be hunger pangs."

I instantly felt bad for keeping him out so long without feeding him.

"I'll finish here and we'll go get food, okay?"

He nodded. "Okay."

Ten minutes later we were in the queue to pay for my clothes, and just as we got to the till, I realised my jeans weren't in Kale's hands. "My jeans," I murmured, and ruffled through the pile of clothes in Kale's arms.

I looked at Kale but found he wouldn't directly look at me.

I set my jaw. "Where did you put them?"

He groaned. "I don't want you to buy them."

I could have whacked him around the head.

I glared at him. "You're unbelievable, Kale Hunt."

I didn't bother to look for them because I knew he would have hidden them. Instead, I walked to the rack I'd found the jeans on, got another size twelve and walked back to where Kale was waiting at the till.

"I didn't anticipate this part," he grumbled when he saw the new pair of jeans in my hands.

The man behind the till laughed at our exchange. "Don't underestimate women, mate. They'll surprise you at every turn," – he glanced at me – "no matter *what* their age."

I looked back to Kale and found he kept his eyes on me as he said, "I'm beginning to believe that."

I felt smug as I put my jeans on the counter and watched the man scan the price tag. I cleared my throat and glanced at the clothes in Kale's arms, causing him to sigh and drop them onto the counter. He stood back and folded his arms across his chest as he watched the man behind the till scan and bag each item of clothing.

When we were finished in River Island, we went to McDonald's, and Kale didn't speak to me until we were sitting down and he was halfway through eating his food. I was starving, but I didn't want to eat fast food. I wanted to eat healthy food to help me not gain any more weight.

I made a mental note to talk to my mother about it when I was home.

"Who do you like?" he randomly asked me.

I nearly choked as I swallowed some water Kale had got me.

"What?" I rasped, wiping my mouth with the back of my hand.

"Who do you fancy?" he clarified.

I stared at him for a moment and then said, "No one – why?"

He raised his eyebrows. "There isn't a single lad in school you fancy?"

Well, my heart sang, *there is you.*

I scratched my neck and said, "Nope."

"I don't believe you," he dead-panned.

I frowned and played with my fingers. "Why not?"

"Because you won't look at me when you answer the question, and you're playing with your fingers. You do both when you're lying."

I clasped my hands together.

"Can we not talk about this?" I asked.

"Fine," Kale quipped.

Great: he was mad.

I tilted my head as I looked at him. "Why do you care if I fancy a lad?"

"I don't," he retorted.

Bullshit.

"Then why ask?" I pressed.

He shrugged. "Just starting a conversation to kill the silence."

He was lying.

"Since when have you ever started a conversation like this one?" I questioned.

Kale dipped his burger in sauce. "Never, which is why I brought it up. I mean you do like *boys*, don't you?"

"What do you mean? Omigod!" I gasped when I got his meaning. "I'm *not* gay."

He bit into his burger and said with a mouth full of food, "It'd be cool if you were – I mean, there's nothing wrong with it."

My stomach churned.

"I know there isn't, but I'm not gay. To be honest, I'm fairly bloody pissed off you assume I'm gay just because I say I don't fancy a lad in school."

I stood up from my chair, grabbed my many shopping bags and stormed out of McDonald's.

"Lane!" Kale shouted. "Shit. Wait. I'm sorry."

He thought I was *gay*? God, this was mortifying. The person who I was in love with thought I batted for the other team. It was so embarrassing and completely hurtful. Not to mention utterly devastating for my already shot self-esteem.

Kale caught me outside of McDonald's and jumped in front of me, his hands raised. It was then that I noticed he had his half-eaten burger in one hand and his tub of chips in the other. He'd brought his food with him?

"You're such a pig," I commented.

"Your mum paid for this – I'm not letting it go to waste," he frowned.

He said this with such a serious face that it made me laugh.

"There is something wrong with you," I said with a shake of my head.

He locked his eyes with mine. "Yeah – you."

I grinned. "You love me."

He waggled his eyebrows. "It's the only reason I put up with you."

I sighed. "You're such a pain in my arse."

"Your squatted arse?" he asked, grinning.

I didn't reply to him, so he said, "You forgive me, right?"

I sighed. "Have you ever known me to stay mad at you for long?"

"No," he proudly announced. "It's my superpower – that and being incredibly good-looking."

I flushed and playfully swatted at his arm, making him grin. I had a small smile on my face as we turned and got lost in the crowd heading back towards the clothing shops, because I had more money to spend. I hated that deep down I knew no amount of money could change how I now felt about my body and overall appearance.

Anna and Ally's words were drilled into my brain, and they couldn't be forgotten. Kale could only distract me from reality for so long, but I'd make damn sure the time with him wouldn't be wasted.

CHAPTER NINE

Day two in York

It was time.

I pressed my forehead against the oak door of my old bedroom, praying time would somehow reverse and give me a few more days with my uncle. I wasn't ready to lower him six feet below the earth and cover him up with dirt. I knew on some level I would never be ready to permanently say goodbye to someone I loved, but I felt like I physically couldn't do it for my uncle.

I wasn't ready to say goodbye to him. I just couldn't do it.

"Lane?" I heard a soft voice call out from the other side of my bedroom door, gaining my attention.

I blinked and realised it was my grandmother.

"I can't do it, Nanny."

I stepped back when the handle of the door wiggled until it pressed down fully, and my door opened. My grandmother stood in my doorway, wearing a stylish black trouser suit. She had crumpled up a tissue in her hands, and her eyes were red-raw and bloodshot from crying.

"Baby," she sniffled, "ye can do this."

My eyes welled with tears. "I'm not ready."

She smiled at me, tears falling onto her lined cheeks. "We'll never be ready, sweetie, but death waits for no one."

I nodded and sniffled as tears fell from my eyes and splashed on my cheeks and dress. I looked down at my black dress, momentarily admiring the black lace sleeves. My mother had gone out and got me the dress, tights and shoes I wore because I had nothing in my suitcase that was appropriate attire for a funeral.

When I'd read Lochlan's note, I'd just thrown in my suitcase the first items of clothing I thought of from my apartment back in New York. Something to wear for the funeral never entered my mind. At the time it didn't feel real. I was trying to wrap my head around the fact; I was trying to come to terms with it. It *still* didn't feel real, and I didn't think it ever would.

I would always be expecting the usual phone call, Skype call and daily email from him, and I was sure my heart would break each time I realised they would never come.

"You're the last person ta say goodbye to 'im, baby," my nanny whispered, pulling me from my thoughts and back to my haunting reality. "The hearse will be here soon ta close the coffin and take 'im ta the church for the funeral mass. I want ye ta have some time with 'im first."

I nodded once more, my heart thumping inside my chest as my stomach churned.

My nanny led me out of my room and down the stairs. I heard numerous voices as I descended the stairs. Then I saw a crowd of people inside the house and another crowd outside in the garden through the open front door. Everyone quietened down when I reached the bottom stair, but I avoided looking at anyone's face. I didn't want to speak to anybody. I just wanted to be with my uncle, and my nanny sensed that. She ushered me into the parlour;

gave me a long, warm hug; glanced at the coffin one final time; and then turned and left the room.

When the door to the parlour closed behind me, and I was left alone with my uncle, the silence in the room was deafening. On trembling legs, I walked up to the side of my uncle's coffin, and I lifted my gaze. Through blurred eyes, I scanned over every inch of his handsome face, making sure I would never forget it. I placed my shaky hands on top of my uncle's cold ones.

"This really is the worst day of my life," I said to him, remembering what I'd said to him last night. "I thought the day I left here was soul-crushing, but putting you to rest is killing me."

I didn't know why, but like before I was expecting my uncle to reply to me and assure me that everything would be okay, but when silence answered me, it made his death feel more real. How stupid was that? I was standing right next to his deceased body, and only when he didn't answer me back did it make him being dead feel real.

"I'm not . . . I'm not ready to let you go," I whispered.

I broke down into audible sobs when I heard a car pull up outside our house. I glanced at the window, and through the netted curtain I saw the hearse. It would take my uncle from my parents' house and bring him to the church for the funeral mass, then on to his final resting place in the cemetery.

I began to panic. I was out of time.

"I love you with all of my heart. You have b-been the best uncle and fr-friend any girl could have ever asked for. I want you to kn-know that I've always adored you, and I'm so sorry f-for leaving you. I'm sorry, Uncle Harry. Please forgive me."

I leaned over the coffin and placed my head on his hard, cold chest as sobs racked through my body. I hated that my cries rose to a point where it caused my mother, grandmother and family friends to break down outside of the parlour. I didn't mean to upset them any more than they already were, but I couldn't control the emotion that surged through me. I didn't know how long I cried on my uncle's chest, but when I felt hands on my hips, I lost it altogether.

"No!" I cried, and I stood upright over my uncle. "I n-need a few more m-minutes."

I felt a forehead press against the back of my head, and the hands on my arms gripped me tightly.

"Come on, Laney Baby."

Kale.

"I can't, Kale," I whimpered. "I can't leave him. I c-can't do it."

I couldn't even let my mind settle on the fact that Kale was touching me; I was too distraught over saying my final goodbye to my dear uncle. I looked to the parlour door when it opened, and men dressed in black suits entered.

The footmen.

"Kale, please," I wailed, and turned in his arms. "Don't let them t-take him, *please*."

I looked up at Kale, and through blurred eyes I saw his bloodshot whisky-coloured eyes staring down at me. "I'm sorry," he whispered.

"Please," I wailed. "I can't be w-without him. Pl-please."

Kale squeezed his eyes shut, the anguish he felt written all over his face.

"Who will be present for the final closing?" a male voice murmured.

"I will," my father's voice replied.

I turned and gazed upon my uncle once more and whispered, "Goodbye, Uncle Harry."

I knew I was supposed to leave then, but I couldn't work my legs, which were frozen in place. I didn't care because I didn't want to leave anyway, but this wasn't about what I wanted. This was about my uncle and him receiving the best send-off possible. Yet, even though I knew all of that, I still couldn't bring myself to leave the room.

Kale knew this too, because without warning, my feet were lifted off the ground, and for a moment I fought against him as he lifted me from the room, but once we were outside in the hallway, I latched onto him and cried until there wasn't a single tear left in my body. He mutely held me the entire time, kissed my head and swayed us from side to side until my sobs became mere sniffles.

"I'm sorry," I whispered, feeling awful for using him as my shoulder to lean on when I had no right to ask that of him. I had no right to ask anything of him.

He squeezed me. "I'm here for you, Lane. Always."

More tears came then, and regret wrapped around my sadness and thrust me further into misery. I wished more than anything that I could have been here for him when he needed me like he was here for me now, but that was the difference between myself and Kale.

He was selfless, and I was selfish.

"It's time, sweetheart," he murmured.

I mutely turned and headed out front, where I found the garden, as well as the road and pathways, was full of people. That made me cry harder. My brothers found Kale and me, and both of them hugged me when they saw what a state I was in. We moved over to my grandmother, mother and father, who was no longer with my uncle, and that meant his coffin had been closed for the very last time.

I held Kale's hand and squeezed it as my uncle's coffin was removed from my parents' house and loaded into the back of the hearse. My family and Kale all got into the black family car that drove behind the hearse. I sat next to Kale, which wasn't surprising considering I hadn't let go of his hand since he'd offered it to me.

I leaned my head on his shoulder as we rode to the church for the funeral mass. The journey to the church was quicker than I would have liked. When we got out of the car, Kale let go of me so he, my brothers and father could join the footmen to carry my uncle's coffin into the church.

I took hold of my grandmother's and mother's hands, and we cried together as we slowly walked behind the coffin into the church. I watched as the coffin was lowered from the men's shoulders onto a stand that sat at the front of the altar, along with multiple bunches of flowers, flower nameplates and a beautiful picture of my uncle smiling happily.

I took my seat on the bench at the front of the church and nestled next to my father, then scooted down when Kale sat next to me, put his arm around my shoulder and tucked my body against his. I heard loud murmurs and movement as the priest prepared for the service. Glancing over Kale's shoulder, I saw a sea of people. I wasn't surprised to find the church so full. My Uncle Harry had been one of a kind, and the hundreds of people who came to see him off were just a testament of how truly incredible he was.

I was so thankful for Kale. He didn't have to give me the time of day, yet he sat beside me and held my hand through the entire mass. He hugged me to him when both of my brothers read out their prayers, and rocked me as I cried during my father's eulogy. It made people laugh to hear of the crazy side to my uncle, but it mostly made people cry, knowing they had lost such a character from the town.

While the priest was reading one of the final prayers, my mind drifted to my last Skype conversation with my uncle, and it brought me both comfort and heartache.

"You would not believe the day I've had," I said to my uncle when his face filled my laptop screen.

My uncle snorted. "Hello to you too, darling."

I grinned and adjusted my headphones so I could hear him clearly. "Sorry – hi, how are you?"

"Great now that we're chatting." He winked, then waved his hand. "Go on: tell me about the day you've had that I won't believe."

"Smartarse," I chided, making him laugh. "Okay," I began, "so you know how I've been editing a horror series for K.T. Boone?"

"The one where the little girl is really the killer?" my uncle asked warily.

Reading that series scared him.

"Yes," I said, nodding.

"What about it?" he asked.

I had to contain my squeal because even though I was tucked away in the back of my local Starbucks, I would still draw attention to myself.

"The latest book in the series hit the New York Times *list at number one!" I gushed. "Uncle Harry, something I edited, and helped shape, is a best bloody seller!"*

My uncle cheered and clapped his hands together. "I knew it! I knew you'd do brilliantly. I'm so proud of you."

For once, I felt something that resembled happiness.

"Thank you," I said. "I can't believe it. My name is associated with it, and because of that I've gotten three emails from different publishers – big publishers might I add – looking to hire me to work with some of their clients. Can you believe that?"

"Darling," my uncle said with a beaming smile, "I'm not one bit surprised."

I chuckled. "You knew this would happen, then?"

"I knew you'd be very successful at what you do, so yes, I did know. You're rocking that city."

I laughed. "I'm over the moon. Finally, something good has happened to me."

"Will you still freelance?" my uncle questioned.

"Of course," I said, nodding enthusiastically. "Indie authors are superstars, and it's because of one of them that I'm getting job offers like this in the first place."

"Good on you, darling. I'm so proud of you, and your parents will be delighted with the news."

I slumped a little. "Do you think so?"

"Lane, of course. They're so proud of all the books and articles you've edited. I told you that your father and I read everything you work on."

That touched my heart in a way that I couldn't describe.

"I can imagine you both huddled around the kitchen table discussing the books," I said, laughing.

"We have to sit in the sitting room; your nanny and her friends knit at the table now."

That caused me to laugh harder.

"You should call your brothers and give them the great news."

"I don't think so," I grumbled. "I called on their birthday, and when I told Lochlan to stop asking me to come home, he told me never to call him again. I'm just abiding by his wishes."

My uncle shook his head. "You're every bit of your brothers: stubborn beyond compare."

I grinned. "Like you aren't stubborn?"

"I am," he agreed. "I'm just not as bad as you and your brothers."

I groaned. "I don't want to argue with you."

"I'm not arguing. I'm just mentioning something that you don't like hearing."

I rolled my eyes. "What did you do today?"

He thought on it, then said, "I went up to your aunt's grave and put down fresh flowers. I put some on your friend's grave too."

My voice was tight with emotion.

"Thanks, Uncle Harry," I said. "You're the best."

"That'd be you, darling."

~

I blinked a couple of times when Kale moved next to me. Looking around, I realised the mass was over. The priest came down to my family and shook each of our hands as he offered his condolences. I couldn't reply to him, so Kale did it for me.

"Thank you, Father," he said.

I retook my mother's and grandmother's hands as Kale, my brothers, my father and two footmen lifted my uncle's coffin back onto their shoulders and walked him out of the church, with everyone in attendance following slowly behind. Once my uncle was safely placed inside the hearse, we got back into the black car and journeyed to my uncle's house for one final drive-by.

It hurt like hell.

It tore me up as we passed by the house and headed to his final resting place at York Cemetery. Everything seemed to fly by at that point. Within a blink of the eye, we were at the gravesite, standing next to the grave plot as my uncle's coffin was lowered down into the ground and the priest spoke his prayers.

A friend of my mother's passed a single red rose to each of my family members and Kale, for us to throw down on top of my uncle's coffin. I was the last person to throw my rose, but before I let it fall, I kissed the petals and whispered, "I'll miss you forever."

The rose seemed to fall in slow motion and landed on the nameplate of the coffin, where my uncle's name was engraved as clear as day. The priest spoke some more about what a well-loved man my uncle had been and how many lives he had touched.

Not long later, "Time to Say Goodbye" by Andrea Bocelli and Sarah Brightman began to play once the priest had said his final prayers. I managed to hold it together for the first minute of the song, but as soon as the chorus began to play, and the words "time to say goodbye" were sung, I broke down.

Arms came around me from behind, and a face rested against the side of mine.

"He'll always be with you," Kale's gruff voice whispered.

I sobbed and turned into his body, holding onto him as I cried through the heartbreak that was surging through me. I didn't know how long I cried, but I was soon in my parents' arms as we wept for my uncle. People began to leave then, once the song drew to a close, signalling the end of the funeral.

I looked through the crowd of people that was dispersing, and my eyes landed on Kale. He was standing in front of Kaden's grave, which was only thirty or so plots down from my aunt and uncle's grave. He was staring at the headstone with his hands thrust deep in the pockets of his slacks. I was about to walk over to him, simply to be there for him, like he had been for me, but I froze to the spot when, out of nowhere, I saw Drew making her way over to Kale.

I took the time to take her in, noticing that while she still very much looked the same, her face showed signs of her loss. It wasn't as vibrant as I remembered. I didn't know if she spoke to Kale when she reached his side, but he glanced down to her and, taking his left hand from his pocket, put his arm around her shoulder, hugging her to him before they both turned their focus to the headstone of their son.

Jealousy swirled around in my stomach, and I wanted to beat myself into a pulp because of it. Why did I still have to feel envious at the sight of them together when it was so obvious that the only connection between them now was the memory of their lost son?

I looked away from them so they could share their moment with their son in private instead of having my roaming eyes lingering on them. My focus quickly landed on my grandmother, who was hugging Kale's parents. I hadn't seen them in years, but they were just how I remembered them; they just had a few extra lines around their eyes and less of a spring to their step.

Losing their grandson, and watching their son go through his struggle, was the cause of that, no doubt.

When I approached them, Mrs Hunt spotted me first.

"Lane," she gushed. "Oh, my girl, it's *so* good to see you."

I smiled wide when she rushed at me and wrapped her arms around me, hugging me so tightly I was afraid she would break me.

"Let the poor lass go, Helen – you'll crush her," said Mr Hunt, his Geordie accent as thick as ever.

I was always surprised that Kale had never picked up even a hint of his father's accent. The Newcastle accent was strong, but it just went to show that he was a Yorkshire lad through and through.

I chuckled when Mrs Hunt let me go only to hug me again. When she finally separated from me, Mr Hunt cut in fast before she got another chance to enfold me in her arms.

"It's brilliant to see you, love," he said, smiling down at me, and then kissed my forehead like he had done so many times before, when I was younger.

"And you, sir, you're looking well."

He was; he had lost a lot of weight and looked great.

He winked. "Kale and your brothers have taken over my diet and have me eatin' healthy. Trust me, I'd rather be with your da down the pub and chippy a few nights a week than countin' how many calories I'm eatin'."

I joyfully laughed. “It seems my dad has been eating and drinking enough for *both* of you.”

Mr Hunt laughed, and it brought a genuine smile to my face.

“So,” he said after he settled down, “how is living in the Big Apple?”

I lost my smile.

“It’s . . . okay.”

Mr Hunt’s lip twitched, but he said nothing further.

I looked in the direction of a couple that called out my name. They were my parents’ friends, so I excused myself from Mr and Mrs Hunt and greeted the couple, as well as many other people who stopped me and gave me their condolences. I didn’t know how I managed to keep it together, but I did, and I was mildly happy about it. I knew tears would lead to sympathy, and sympathy would lead to more tears. And by God, I didn’t want to cry any more.

When I finished greeting and thanking people, I made my way over to the car that had brought me to the graveyard, and I bumped into my mother along the way.

“Are you coming to the pub?” she asked.

I shook my head. “I just want to go back to your house and go to sleep. I will only cry around everyone in the pub, Mum.”

My mother nodded in understanding. “I know, baby. I can’t see myself staying very long either. I just want to go and thank everyone for coming.”

“Give those I know my best, will you?” I asked. “Oh, and say bye to Kale too. I didn’t get a chance to.”

My mother nodded once more and kissed my cheek. “I will. Now go on home and get some sleep. I’ll check in on you when I get in. Ask the driver of the black car to bring you back. Ally and Samantha drove here. They’re bringing us back to the church.”

I hadn’t seen either of them since I arrived at my parents’ last night, but that wasn’t surprising given the number of people who had turned out for the mass and funeral itself.

I hugged my mother tightly before heading over to the black car. The driver was having a cigarette, but he quickly dropped it and covered it with his foot when I neared him.

"Hello, miss," he said, dipping his head in greeting.

I nodded. "Hello. Could you bring me home, please?"

"You don't want to go to the afters venue?"

I shook my head. "I'm not feeling up to it today, I'm afraid."

He frowned. "I'm very sorry for your loss."

With his line of work, it saddened me to think of how often he had to say those words to people.

"Thank you, sir."

He opened the door behind the driver's seat for me and gestured me into the car.

"I'll have you home in just a few short minutes," he promised with a wink.

One minute I was in the black car driving through town, then the next I was climbing the stairs of my parents' house. I wanted to go straight to bed and just curl up into a ball, but I needed to shower and try to wash this day off my body.

After my shower, I grabbed a large towel from the rack, wrapped it around my body and walked out of the bathroom and into my bedroom, where a cold chill wrapped around me, causing me to shiver. I found myself smiling and shaking my head when I found another set of Pokémon pyjamas, and it only caused my love for my mother to grow.

She was so thoughtful.

After I was changed, I put on some fluffy socks and slipped on a pair of new slippers before I blow-dried my hair. I didn't bother with keeping it straight, but just blasted it dry, and when I was finished, I tied my hair on the top of my head in a messy bun.

I felt relaxed then.

Just as I was about to crawl into my bed and resign myself to the quiet and darkness, the doorbell chimed. I closed my eyes on a sigh and momentarily contemplated ignoring it, but I decided against that when I thought of all the people who had been by since I'd arrived, to pay their respects and offer their condolences for my uncle's passing. I left my room and headed downstairs to greet whoever was at the door. My uncle deserved everyone's respect and condolences, and I would happily accept them even if it killed me.

I opened the door, and through my sore eyes, I saw a very familiar face instead of a strange one. "Kale," I said in surprise. "What are you doing here?"

His lip twitched as his eyes flicked down to my pyjamas before they resettled on my own. "Your mum said you came home because you couldn't deal with everyone in the pub, so I came here to keep you company. I don't want you to be alone right now."

I whispered, "But I don't deserve your comfort, I don't deserve anything from you."

Kale's brow furrowed. "Why not?"

I shrugged. "Because I made everything horribly complicated for you, then just left and never spoke to you for six years."

Kale's lips thinned to a line. "Let's get you into the sitting room, and we can watch a film or something. I'm not talking about this today, tomorrow or the next day. When things aren't so fresh about your uncle's passing, we *will* talk, but for now let's just hang out."

I widened my eyes for a moment but quickly nodded, turned and went into the sitting room while Kale shut the front door. I was glad for the few seconds alone because I felt like I was about to freak out. While I knew Kale and I would have to talk – and talk about *everything* – hearing him say it out loud sent me into a bit of a tailspin.

I dreaded to think how that conversation was going to go.

"Are you okay?" asked Kale, his voice startling me.

I numbly nodded. "I'm great."

He raised an eyebrow. "You can't lie to me, Lane."

Isn't that the bloody truth?

"Okay, I'm not great, but I'm not in bits either – not right now anyway."

He gestured to the sofa. "Sit down and turn on something for us to watch. I'll be back in a minute."

I blinked. "Where are you going?"

"To make us tea, obviously."

I was surprised when I snorted, and even more surprised when it brought a bright smile to Kale's face. "A cup of tea would be *perfect*."

He chuckled and turned on his heel. "Three sugars and loads of milk. On it."

I felt my jaw drop open. "You remember how I take my tea?" I asked, my shock laced throughout my tone.

He stopped by the sitting room door and, without turning around, he said, "You think I'd forget it?"

I said nothing, so Kale proceeded to walk out of the room and down the hall to the kitchen. I gazed at the space he vacated for a few moments, before sitting down on the sofa and staring ahead at the blank television screen.

He remembered how I took my tea. I didn't know if it was just an afterthought, because he'd made me so many cups of tea during my lifetime, or if it was a bit of knowledge he held onto after I left, and it killed me because I couldn't ask. It would have been awkward. I couldn't ask him any kind of question that related to feelings between us. I knew how that conversation went, and it wasn't pretty.

Besides, a conversation about our past would be on Kale's terms; I owed him that much.

I turned the television on and scanned through the channels until I landed on *The Big Bang Theory*. That was safe. It was a comedy show, and there was a low probability of me bursting into tears as we watched it. A few minutes passed by before Kale re-entered the room with two cups of tea in his hands. He placed both cups on coasters on the coffee table in front of the sofa.

He settled next to me, sitting just a few inches away, with his arm thrown over the back of the sofa and his long legs parted as he watched the show. I couldn't concentrate on anything other than how close Kale was to me. He was so close I could smell his delicious scent, and it was torturing me as it begged me to bury my face in his neck and inhale.

Rein it in, my mind warned.

I bit the insides of my cheeks, then leaned forward and picked up the cup in front of me, blew lightly and took a sip of the heated liquid. I audibly groaned as the sugary goodness slid down my throat to my empty stomach.

"Oh. My. God," I breathed. "You still make the best cup of tea I have *ever* tasted."

Kale didn't reply, so when I looked at him, I found his eyes were focused on my mouth, and it caused my pulse to spike. After a moment or two, he lifted his gaze to mine and grinned. "I'm glad I still hold onto my title of World's Best Cup of Tea Maker."

I snorted, thinking back to the time when I'd given him that title. I was fourteen and had my period, and I was cramping and miserable. Kale made me my first cup of tea, and it changed everything. Every. Thing. From that moment on, whenever I was in his company, he would be on duty to make me a cup of tea.

I was glad to see it was one tradition that didn't fade to nothing.

We sat in a comfortable silence for a few minutes before I felt on edge. I wanted to offer my condolences for Kaden, to acknowledge his existence, but I didn't know how to say it. I was so scared

I would mess it up and not come across as completely sincere. I was also afraid it would upset Kale, and that was the last thing I wanted.

I decided it was best for me to leave before I said something that would upset one of us, most likely me.

"I think I'm going to go up to bed before I fall asleep down here."

That was a cold-hearted lie. I was so wired being in his company, and it was freaking me out.

"Go ahead. I'll stay down here until your parents and brothers get in."

What did I do to deserve his generosity? I thought, then frowned when my mind sneered, *Nothing.*

I got to my feet and shifted from foot to foot.

"Thank you, Kale."

He gazed up at me. "You don't have to thank me, Laney Baby – I've got you."

My heart thudded against my chest, surprisingly still working.

"Laney Baby," I mused. "That won't ever change, will it?"

Kale smiled, shook his head and said, "Things haven't changed around here, kid."

I glanced around and frowned. "Are you sure? Because from where I'm standing, everything is different."

"I'm the same," he replied, and licked his lips. "Mostly, anyway."

I looked at him, *really* looked at him, and found him staring right back at me, his hazel eyes focused on mine.

"Everyone changes, Kale. Nothing stays the same forever," I murmured.

He frowned. "Have you changed?"

He looked, and sounded, like it pained him to ask that question.

I reluctantly nodded. "I'm not the same Lane you once knew, pup."

Surprisingly, my answer brought a glorious smile to his face. It was the kind of smile that caused butterflies to flutter in my stomach, my heart to beat fast and my breath to catch.

It was a true thing of beauty.

"My Lane is still in there somewhere," he said, his tone matter-of-fact. "Only she would call me 'pup'."

I always called him that because he had the biggest puppy-dog eyes I had ever seen, and that was one thing about him that would never change. The glint in them had, but not the size.

I didn't know what to say to that, so I gave him a small smile and bid him goodnight. When I got into my bedroom, I closed the door behind me, pressed my back against the wood, then sank down to the ground and stared into the darkness.

He called me his. Kale said I was *his* Lane.

I shook my head at that because I wasn't his. You could never belong to someone without owning a piece of him or her in return, and I'd learned the hard way that I didn't own any part of Kale. I had a memory of what owning him was like, but that was it. And that memory was fading. Fast.

CHAPTER TEN

Seventeen years old (nine years ago)

My brothers were going to bloody *kill* me.

Layton might be reasoned with, but not Lochlan, who would run through me like a murderous bull. Even Kale would tear me a new one when he understood how I'd lied to my parents and snuck out to a party instead of staying over at my friend's house like I'd told them I was going to.

The plan was unassailable – that was until my brothers, Kale *and* their friends walked into said party.

"I'm so dead," I whispered to myself as I sat on the lid of the toilet of the upstairs bathroom.

I was in this massive house on the edge of town, where a huge party happened a few times a year. I had heard about them over the last two years from older girls at school, and they were always ragers. The man and woman who owned the house were always away on business, so their son had parties to keep from being bored.

I regretted ever agreeing to come, even though I *was* having fun before my brothers and Kale showed up. No amount of fun was worth dealing with the three of them when they were mad at me, though.

"Lane?" a familiar voice whispered through the bathroom door; then three hard knocks rapped against the wood.

It was Lavender.

Lavender Grey – that was her real name – was my friend. She'd moved down the road from me nearly two years ago, and we instantly became friends. She showed up in my life shortly after everything went to hell with Anna and Ally. I was so happy when she didn't take to either of them or any of the other mean girls in our year at school; she saw them and their true colours without me having to tell her they could be nasty.

We hung out every single day and became best friends rapidly. She was unlike any other person I had ever met. She was straight-up honest and took no bullshit. The first day I'd met her, I was annoyed with Kale for ditching plans we had made at the last minute, and I literally bumped into her in the supermarket where Kale and I were supposed to meet. I mumbled an apology, and she said if I was going to say sorry, then I had to mean it. At first I thought she was a bit of a bitch, but I quickly found that she was up front and said what she thought, and I liked that. I liked how different she was from me. She didn't keep things bottled up like I did; she was an open book.

She didn't just distract me from Kale's absence in my life, but helped me become more independent with her I-don't-need-a-man-to-be-happy attitude. It rubbed off on me a little – not a lot because I was still obsessed with Kale, but enough to keep me from thinking about him every second of every day.

At that point in my life, Kale and my brothers only came home on weekends from their university in London, and sometimes they missed a weekend here and there. I was still close to them, but it wasn't the same with Kale. After our shopping day out, things changed between us. I felt like I was losing him. He was currently broken up with Drew and was off doing God knows what with God knows *who* in London, while I was stuck in York with my parents, uncle and nanny for company. If it wasn't for Lavender coming into my life, I may have just up and died of loneliness and boredom.

"Lane," Lavender's voice hissed. "Let me in."

I got to my feet and unlocked the door, stepping to the side so she could enter. I quickly relocked it, much to the displeasure of houseguests on the other side who needed to use the facilities.

"Hurry bloody up!" a voice shouted, and there was banging on the door.

"One more minute!" I called out.

I looked from the door to Lavender, and when I saw her hands were empty, my face fell.

"I'm sorry." Lavender winced when she saw my expression. "I tried to find you something to wear, but it's only a boy that lives here, and the girl clothes I found in his room – that I assume belong to a girlfriend – are in a size bloody *four*."

"Shit," I groaned, and placed my face in my hands before dropping them and looking down to my attire.

I was wearing a washed-out denim miniskirt and a black crop top that had "TEASE" printed across the front in white block letters. It was a stupid decision to wear such revealing clothing. I didn't like the stares or advances from random guys at the party, and I had only myself to blame.

They wouldn't have looked twice at me if I'd worn my regular clothes, and my thick-framed glasses. At the thought of my glasses, I lifted my hands to my eyes and gently rubbed them, wincing at the sting. I was wearing a pair of contact lenses my parents had recently got me, but I hated them. They made my eyes feel very uncomfortable.

"I shouldn't have worn these clothes," I mumbled as I sat back down on the lid of the toilet.

Lavender was sporting a similar outfit to mine, only instead of a miniskirt she wore short shorts. Now she hunkered down as best she could next to me and placed her hands on my bare thighs.

"You look seriously hot, and you wanted to try something different – there's *no* harm in that. You don't ever have to wear clothes like this again, or ever come to a party again, but at least you can rest assured that you did *something* teenagery in your bookish life."

I raised a brow. "'Teenagery' isn't a word, Lav."

"I know it's not," she huffed. "You're missing the point here, Bookworm."

Bookworm: that's what she called me.

I chuckled. "I'm not. I hear you loud and clear, and I agree with you, but my brothers and Kale won't."

She grunted. "Your brothers I can understand, but Kale *cannot* rag on you for this."

"You don't know Kale," I mumbled.

She stood up and stuck out her hand to me just as someone rapped on the bathroom door and shouted, "Hurry up in there!"

I placed my hands in Lavender's and sighed as she pulled me to my feet.

"Don't frown – we might be able to sneak out of here without being spotted," she said with a wink.

I nodded and tried to remain optimistic.

"Just stay close to me and *don't* look up."

I used my free hand to salute Lavender, then followed her out of the bathroom once she opened the door. I grunted as two lads both rushed by two girls waiting in the queue for the toilet and knocked into me.

"Arseholes!" Lavender snapped at them and tugged me closer to her.

We wound around body after body of the people who littered the hallway, until we came to the top of the staircase. I blew out a nervous breath, and Lavender gave my hand a reassuring squeeze before she took the lead and began to descend the steps.

When we reached the bottom of the stairs, Lavender suddenly came to a halt, which caused me to walk straight into her back. My face hit the back of her head, and I yelped in pain. I instinctively let go of Lavender's hand and lifted both of mine to my throbbing nose.

"What are *you* doing here?" Lavender snapped at someone.

I heard a male chuckle. "I'm here to have a good time. No doubt you are too, dressed in *that* outfit, babygirl."

"*Don't* call me that!" Lavender growled.

I looked around my friend and to the person she was ready to tear apart and sighed. Daven Eanes. Lavender's on-again – and currently off-again – boyfriend.

"Don't be like that, Lav. I'm only teasing."

Lavender grunted. "Sure you are."

She usually loved the nickname, but because they were broken up, it hurt for her to hear him call her it. She'd told me so.

"Look," Daven said and moved closer to my friend, "can we talk somewhere private? I miss you, babygirl. We need to hash this out; we're meant to be together. I love you."

Don't fall for it, Lavender, I willed.

"I have to leave with Lane," Lavender replied to Daven, instead of telling him to piss off like she should have.

Daven blinked his bright grey eyes, then flicked them past Lavender, and after a moment they landed on me. He raised his eyebrows when Lavender stepped to the side, exposing me completely. I felt like I needed to take a shower when Daven lazily rolled his eyes over my body from head to toe and back up again. It made me feel dirty, and *not* in a good way.

"Lane?" Daven said, the shock in his tone obvious. "Damn, you look *hot*."

I did? I mean, Lavender told me I did, but I didn't really believe her.

"Are you fucking kidding me?" Lavender snapped at him, asserting her body back in front of mine.

Thank God.

"I didn't mean it like *that*," Daven quickly pleaded to Lavender. "I just meant she looks different from what she usually looks like, that's all . . . You're so gorgeous tonight, babygirl."

Oh, please.

"You can't really be falling for this crap, Lav," I grumbled to Lavender, who stiffened.

Daven heard me and narrowed his eyes at me while he reached out and took Lavender's hands in his. He refocused on her and smiled his breathtaking smile, which always captivated my poor lovesick friend. I couldn't argue that it wasn't distracting because it was. He had a smile that made you stop and stare, and he knew it.

Daven Eanes was a bastard who used his incredibly good looks to fuck over my friend time and time again. We were constantly arguing over his lack of respect for her, and it drove Lavender insane to listen to the pair of us.

"Just give me five minutes, babygirl," he pleaded. "I *need* to speak to you."

I shook my head when I heard Lavender sigh, indicating she was already giving in to him before verbally saying so. She turned to face me, her eyes begging for me not to cause a scene. I ignored Daven staring at her arse, and focused on my best friend.

I rolled my eyes. "You're going to be crying over him tomorrow, but if you want to talk to him, go ahead. I'll wait for you."

Relief flooded Lavender, and a bright smile took charge of her face. "I owe you one, Bookworm."

"If my brothers catch me, you owe me *more* than one," I grumbled as Daven took hold of Lavender's hand and led her away from me.

One second Lavender was right in front of me, and the next she was replaced by some tall, drunk lad who was blatantly staring at my breasts while swaying on his unsteady feet.

"Can I help you?" I asked angrily.

The lad's hooded, bloodshot eyes flicked to mine, and he nodded as a sick-looking grin curved his mouth.

I backed up away from him and said, "Not in this lifetime, buddy."

I intended to give him the finger, but my back hit something hard, and hands grabbed hold of my waist, bringing me to a halt.

"Easy, darling," *his* gruff voice said.

Life could not be this cruel to me.

"Sorry," I said in a voice that was not my own, hoping Kale wouldn't notice that it was me who'd just backed my arse into his body.

"Don't worry about it – hey, are you okay?"

Why the hell did he have to care about *everyone*? Why couldn't he be like a regular lad and just mind his own business? I knew the answer to my questions before I thought of them. Because Kale was caring and an all-round perfect human being – *that* was why.

In a last feeble attempt to hide my identity, I covered my face with my hands when Kale rounded on me. "Are you sure you're – wait a second. Drop your hands."

He knew. I heard his voice change when something familiar about me registered in his mind. "Why?" I grumbled into my hands.

"I *better* be seeing things," he growled. "You better not be who I think you are."

I groaned and dropped my hands from my face down to my sides.

"Lane?"

Oh, bugger.

I should have kept my face covered; it would have saved me the torture of looking at him while he looked like a bloody Greek god. He had on dark jeans and a buttoned-up, collared blue shirt with the sleeves rolled up to his elbows. I never thought rolled-up sleeves could be so attractive on a man, but damn it, they were. He had on a beanie hat matching the dark colour of his jeans too. I swear to God that the sight of him did unholy things to my lady parts.

He. Looked. Fucking. Hot.

I stared up at him with wide eyes and found I couldn't respond to him because my throat was clogged up with naughty proposals. I quickly cleared the sin from my throat, and lifting my hand to my neck, awkwardly scratched it.

"Hey, Kale."

He drilled his bloodshot eyes into mine.

"Hey, Lane," he growled.

I innocently smiled. "Fancy seeing you here."

"Yeah," he replied, his voice dangerously low. "Fancy that."

I lowered my hand to my side and frowned. "You won't tell my brothers that I'm here, right?"

He didn't respond, and it made me nervous as I glanced around, making sure they weren't in close proximity. "Kale, you're my *best friend*; you can't throw me under the bus here," I pleaded. "You know Lochlan will go crazy and embarrass me."

Layton would just be disappointed and give me a lecture about the dangers of partying, alcohol and boys. Lochlan, on the other hand, would go insane, and if I didn't have Layton on my side to defuse the situation, I would be toast.

Kale grunted to himself, then said, "You shouldn't be here." He lowered his eyes to my body and swallowed. "*Especially* dressed like that."

I felt a little giddy when his eyes lingered on my midriff and legs a little longer than necessary. "Please, it's just a skirt and crop top," I said, waving his worries off.

He licked his lips. "Have your legs always been this long?"

I looked down at my legs, then back up to Kale, my eyebrow raised. "I've been five foot nothing since I was twelve. They're still short and stumpy."

His eyes didn't waver from said legs. "They don't look stumpy. They look longer."

I snorted and shook my head. "You're losing your mind."

"I think I am, because your legs are seriously looking good to me right now – and so is the rest of you. Since *when* do you dress like this?" he asked, and swayed a little.

"Are you drunk?" I quickly grabbed his arms. "How much have you had to drink?"

"I'm good, just a little tipsy." He shrugged. "Just a couple cans of Bud, but we did some Jack Daniel's shots when we got here. Three of them, I think. Or maybe it was four?"

Whisky? I thought on a groan. *Brilliant.*

My Uncle Harry loved Jack Daniel's, but he always said it was a grown man's drink for a reason, and seeing Kale struggle to keep his balance proved that theory correct. He wasn't slurring and still had his wits about him, but he was slowly starting to fade.

I opened my mouth to ask if he wanted me to get him a glass of water, but out of nowhere two girls appeared at his side and shamelessly pressed their bodies up against him, giggling. "Hey, Kale," the red-headed girl on his left purred. "Do you remember me?"

"And me?" her blonde friend murmured.

I glared at the both of them, anger and jealousy swirling inside of me. "If you have to ask, maybe neither of you was very impressive."

I clamped my mouth shut when I realised I'd just spoken out loud, while Kale, on the other hand, laughed. Both girls ignored him and narrowed their eyes at me, moving to step towards me, but Kale prevented them from getting near me – thank God. He stepped forward and blocked my body with his.

"I don't think so, ladies."

I heard annoying complaints, and threats, but instead of Kale getting mad at the obvious ex-mattress-dancing partners he was turning down, he politely sent them on their way with the wish of them having a great and safe night.

Even tipsy he was almost too perfect, and it irritated the hell out of me. He turned to face me, grinning down at me. "Are your claws stowed, kitty?" he asked.

I pretended not to know what he was talking about. "Can I get you some water?" I asked.

He chuckled and took hold of my hand, sending jolts of electricity up and down my spine. "Come with me. I want to talk to you somewhere I can hear you clearly."

I followed him then and was surprised to find he was leading me back up the stairs Lavender and I had just descended. At the thought of my friend, I cringed. "Shit, Lavender," I grumbled, and looked over my shoulder but saw no sign of her.

She was probably still with Daven, the prick.

"Where are you bringing me?" I shouted over the blaring music to Kale.

"Somewhere quiet," he replied, and led me down a long hallway and took a right, then opened the first door on the left. We entered a white bedroom that was dimly lit by a lamp in the corner of the room.

"Whose bedroom is this, pup?" I asked Kale.

I heard the door close.

"It's a guest room."

I blinked and turned to face him, only to find him leaning against the now closed bedroom door. "How do you know it's a guest room?" I quizzed.

He grinned. "I've been here to party a few times."

I rolled my eyes, not wanting to know how many girls he'd shagged in this house, or in this room. "I don't want to be in here if you bring girls here for sex."

He raised his eyebrows. "I've never had sex with anyone in here. I just know it's a guest room."

I eyed him, and when I saw the truth in his hooded eyes, I nodded.

"Come here," he said.

I blinked. "Why?"

He shrugged. "'Cause I want you to."

"Okay," I said with a quizzical look, and I walked over to him, stopping a few inches away.

"You never answered my question downstairs," he mumbled and reached out, placing his hands on my bare hips, causing my eyes to widen.

I blinked at the sound of my thudding heartbeat.

"What was your question?" I asked, not recalling anything I had said, because he put his hands on me.

He smirked. "I said, since *when* do *you* dress like this?"

I nervously swallowed. "Since tonight. They're Lavender's clothes; I'm just borrowing them."

He sucked his bottom lip into his mouth and let his eyes roam over me once more. He looked at me like he appreciated what he saw. He looked at me like I wasn't a kid, or his best friend. He looked like he . . . *desired* me.

"Since when do *you* look at *me* like that?" I asked, my breathing becoming a little rapid.

Kale's eyes flashed with fire as he grinned at me. "Since you wore those skinny jeans and I saw you in your bra two months before you turned sixteen. You started looking more like a woman than a little girl."

I almost fell over. He'd noticed me back *then*?

I rolled my eyes as if what he said didn't affect me. "It's my boobs, isn't it?" I asked, teasing.

I was trying my hardest to play it cool.

Kale's eyes zeroed in on my chest. "It's always the boobs, Lane."

I couldn't help but laugh. "You perv."

"Hey," he smiled, flicking his whisky-coloured eyes up to mine. "You asked."

I playfully shoved him. "If you're done teasing me, we can go back downstairs."

He didn't move an inch.

"Who says I'm teasing you?" he murmured.

I cleared my throat. "I say."

"Why?" he asked.

Did he want the list?

"Because I'm your best friend, like your sister and I'm under eighteen," I rattled off. "Three things you always remind me of when we talk about *anything* related to sex."

Kale's tongue swiped across his bottom lip and got my full attention. "I say those things for *your* benefit, not mine."

"What the hell does *that* mean?" I asked, furrowing my brows.

He blinked and looked away from me. "Shit. Nothing. Forget I said—"

"Oh, no you don't," I stated and grabbed hold of his T-shirt when he tried to turn away from me.

Kale grunted but didn't resist against my hold on him.

"Explain that," I demanded. "Now."

He looked up at the ceiling, then back down to me and said, "What do you want me to say, Lane?"

"I want you to tell me what you meant."

His jaw set. "You sure you want to hear this?" he asked.

"I asked, didn't I?"

He licked his lips and said, "I know . . . I know that you . . . like me."

I felt my pounding heart drop to my stomach.

Be cool.

"Wh-Wh-What?" I stuttered.

Be bloody cooler!

I cleared my throat. "Run that by me again?"

He gazed down at me. "I've known for a few years that you like me in *that* way."

I didn't understand what was happening.

"Why do you think that?" I asked, trying not to appear as dumbfounded as I felt.

"Come on, Lane," he said, his lip slightly quirked. "I've seen the way you look at me, how you get when I talk about Drew and other girls – *and* I've seen your scribbles on the back pages of your school journals."

He. Did. Not.

I gasped in horror. *"What?"*

"'Lane *loves* Kale'" – he fully grinned – "and my personal favourite, 'Mrs Lane Hunt'."

This wasn't happening.

"Omigod," I breathed, and tried to push away from him.

He laughed and swayed again as he grabbed hold of me. "Don't be embarrassed."

Embarrassed? my mind screamed. *I am fucking mortified.*

"Let me go," I begged. "Omigod, I can't *ever* look you in the eye again."

Kale continued to laugh as I struggled against his hold, and it got under my skin.

"Stop laughing at me!" I shouted.

He pressed his face against my hair, and it halted my movements. "I'm not laughing at you, just at your reaction to me knowing you fancy me."

The surface of my face felt like a supernova.

"Shut up, Kale!"

"Oh, give over," he said, laughing again. "If it will make you feel better, I fancy you too."

Everything stopped.

My heartbeat.

My breathing.

Time.

"You're playing," I whispered after a stretch of silence.

He nudged the side of my head with his face. "Look at me."

I did.

I lifted my head until I was staring up at his transfixing face. "I'm not playing; I do fancy you." He said this while looking into my eyes, and his eyes spoke to me too.

He was telling the *truth*. I felt my mouth drop open.

"Since *when*?" I asked, astonished.

He sheepishly smiled. "I told you. I noticed everything about you two months before you turned sixteen. You were upset over Anna O'Leary and Ally Day, and you got it into your head that you wanted a makeover. I noticed before that day that you were, um, *filling* out, but when you got your haircut and a new wardrobe, it highlighted everything that I found attractive about you. It was like a jolt of pure lust shot straight to my dick. I spent most of that day, and many more following it, trying to hide my hard-on from you."

I could do nothing but stare at him with wide eyes as I thought, *Is he saying all this because he's had a bit to drink?*

"I know," he breathed, taking in my reaction. "This admission is very sudden and out of the blue, but fuck, you look *insanely* hot tonight, and when you looked at me downstairs with the want in your eyes and got catty with those girls over me, it took everything in me not to kiss and touch you."

I lifted my left hand to my right arm and pinched the skin. I winced as pain filled me, and Kale frowned. "Why did you do that?"

"Just making sure I'm not dreaming," I replied.

He stared at me for a moment, and then a breathtaking smile curved his luscious lips. I smiled back at him but grabbed hold of his arms once more when he swayed on his feet.

"Shit," he grumbled and lightly shook his head clear. "The whisky is hitting me at the *worst* time."

I giggled. "I feel like I should make a joke about you not being able to handle your liquor."

Kale's lip twitched. "You try drinking Bud and downing some Jack Daniels, and we'll see how long you're on your feet for."

I smirked. "Ten quid says I'd be up longer than you."

Kale licked his lips and dropped his eyes to my mouth. "I'd take that bet."

I grinned. "Stop looking at me like you want to eat me."

"I *do* want to eat you."

My playfulness disappeared. "And how would that go exactly?"

Kale growled. "Aren't we bold tonight?"

I smiled teasingly. "I've dreamt of conversations like this with you. Let's just say I'm ready to play them out in real life."

He bit down on his lower lip, looked down at my body and took a small step backwards. "Let me see you."

I cocked an eyebrow. "You can see me."

He smirked as he lifted his hand, stuck up his index finger and rotated it in a circular motion. He wanted me to twirl. I playfully shook my head, smiling as I slowly twirled in a circle, swaying my hips from side to side as I moved.

"Damn, Laney Baby," Kale whispered in a low, husky voice.

I blinked with surprise as I watched his eyes slowly scale their way down from my face to my chest, which had finally decided to develop over the last year and a half. He licked his lips as he read the word across the front of my crop top and snorted to himself before lowering his gaze further.

"You got your belly button pierced," he murmured, more to himself than to me, then flicked his eyes up to me and asked, "What else do you have pierced?"

I licked my lips, and heat flooded my core. "No more piercings, but . . ."

"But?" Kale prompted.

"I have a tattoo on my inner thigh," I said in a rushed breath. "I got it a couple of months ago with Lavender, like a pre-birthday present to myself for my eighteenth next month."

Only Lavender, and now Kale, knew about my tattoo. If it got back to my parents or brothers, they'd kick my arse, never mind what they would do if they knew what kind of tattoo I got.

Kale's features hardened. "What did you get?"

He looked in pain.

"Just two words," I whispered.

He moved close. "What words?"

"Taste me."

Kale's sharp intake of breath caused my legs to shake. "You. Are. Perfect."

My heart thudded against my chest so hard it almost hurt. "Such a sweet talker," I murmured.

Kale lifted his hand to my face and cupped my cheek, rubbing his thumb under my left eye. "Where's my girl gone?" he mumbled.

I frowned. "I'm right here."

He lightly shook his head. "No, my girl wears glasses and is terrified of other people seeing her with hardly any clothes on."

Was terrified.

Lavender helped build my self-esteem up when she realised how shot it was. She had observed me a lot during our first few weeks of friendship, and she held off in calling me out on what she termed "hiding behind my books". At first she thought I was just quiet, but when I let about to how Anna and Ally had made me feel about myself, she hit the roof. She blew a fuse and vowed then to always be completely honest with me, and she told me I was beautiful and that I shouldn't hide behind the books I love so dearly because the real world was much better than fiction.

She started off by giving me small compliments every day. She repeatedly told me I had lovely penmanship and that she wished her ears and lips were like mine. Silly things that most people would overlook. Her compliments were only the beginning; she brought me on new adventures too. She was a daredevil and believed most things should be tried once, and she took me along for the wild ride. She broadened my perception of the world and myself, and eventually I became content with who I was. I wasn't freaky or a nerd because I loved reading, and I wasn't fat or ugly because I didn't measure up to society's version of beauty. Lavender made me appreciate my own beauty.

I didn't understand what Lavender saw in me because I felt I didn't offer anything great to our friendship, but she told me the way I cared for her was enough. She said that she noticed when I cared about someone; I treated them like one of my favourite books. I treasured and loved them. She said that was what was special about me.

I narrowed my eyes. "I'm growing up."

"*This* is you growing up?" Kale asked as he continued to stroke his thumb under my eye, his eyes getting more bloodshot by the minute.

I nodded. "This is me having some *fun*, Kale. I wanted to come to a party and see what the fuss was all about; I'm tired of just reading about them in my books. I wanted to experience what one was really like."

He growled, and the sound caused me to jump and lick my own lips as a thunderbolt of excitement shot up my spine.

"Dressed like *that* you wanted to experience a party?" he asked, maddened.

I stood my ground. "I'm eighteen next month, I can dress like this – and be with lads if I want to be."

Kale's breath hitched and he dropped his hand from my face. "You haven't been with someone . . . have you?"

I felt heat spread across my cheeks. "Why do you care?"

I gasped when my back was suddenly pressed against the wall behind me, and Kale was up against me, moulding his hard body to the front of mine.

My centre began to throb.

"Have. You. Had. Sex?" Kale asked me, his eyes narrowed and non-blinking.

I was so twisted for finding him incredibly sexy when he was angry.

"What will you do if I have?" I questioned.

He placed his hands on either side of my head and said, "Rip the bastard's dick off."

My eyelids fluttered, and I couldn't help but laugh. "And if I haven't, what will you do?"

He dropped his roaring red eyes to my lips, and my heart almost came to a complete stop.

"Answer my question and I'll show you."

Show me. Not tell me.

"No," I squeaked. "I haven't had sex with anyone."

Kale lowered his face to mine until our lips were centimetres apart.

"I've had a fair bit to drink," he hiccupped. "So kick me in the balls if kissing you isn't okay."

I bit down on my lower lip, and the action caused him to groan as I felt him harden against me. Fuck. Shit. It was happening.

Finally.

"I'll kick you in the balls if you *don't* kiss me."

Kale pressed his forehead against mine and said, "I don't want to do something that will ruin things."

"It's too late for that," I replied, terrified he would change his mind. "You want to kiss me, and I *really* want to kiss you."

"We can't be friends after this," he whispered, swaying into me. "We can't ever be just friends anymore."

I lifted my hands and gripped onto his T-shirt. "I don't want to just be your friend."

He blinked. "You really want me?"

"Hell. Yes."

His eyes lit with fire then, and he applied more pressure against my body.

"Think carefully about this," he said firmly, groaning when I moved, causing my hip to brush over his hardened length.

Yeah, he's hard, I thought. *For me.*

I swallowed. "I've thought about this non-stop the last couple of years."

Kale growled. "You're making this *very* hard."

I couldn't help but grin. "I think that's the point."

He looked at me, his hooded eyes filled with lust. "Last chance for you to run away from me."

Like hell.

"I'd never run away from you."

Kale lowered his face dangerously close to mine. "Promise?"

"I promise," I breathed, and fisting his shirt in my hands, I pulled him towards me.

He didn't protest; in fact, he almost glided across the room with me, but he halted and said, "The door."

I let go of him as he scurried over to the door, turning the lock. When he turned back to face me, I started to lose my cool and become nervous. Extremely nervous. I continued to back up until the back of my legs came into contact with the bed.

"You're sure about this?" Kale asked as he stumbled towards me.

I caught him just as he was about to trip over his own two feet.

"I'm sure, but are *you*?" I asked. "You've had a bit to drink, and I don't want to take advantage—"

"Let me stop you right there," he said, laughing. "You aren't taking advantage of me, Laney Baby – trust me."

I did, but he wasn't exactly in his right mind, and I didn't want this to be something that was really good tonight but turned out really bad in the morning.

"Okay," I whispered.

Kale looked down at me and licked his lips.

"Lie back for me, sweetheart."

Shit.

Okay, this was *really* fucking happening.

I sat down on the bed and lay back like he asked. I looked up at him as he knocked his knees against mine and took off his beanie hat, tossing it on the floor behind him. His hair was sticking up all over the place, which only added to the Greek god look he was rocking. He kept his inflamed eyes on me as he kicked his shoes off and began to unbutton his shirt.

Ohhhhhh, my God.

I licked my lips when the shirt left his body and floated onto the floor. I watched it fall until it was out of sight, so my eyes automatically went back to the show Kale was giving me. His hands were on his belt, and he was unbuckling it. My hands itched to do it, so I boldly sat up and covered his hands with mine in silent question as I gazed up at him.

He let go of his buckle and placed his hands on either side of my face, grinning down at me. With a surge of bravery, I opened Kale's belt and unbuttoned his jeans. I lowered his zip and then tugged on his jeans until they fell to the floor. I gasped when I found he was going commando, and saw the really impressive body part that had had me wondering for years.

It measured up to my expectations.

Trust me.

"Fuck," I whispered.

Kale huskily chuckled as he moved his hand to my hair and scraped his nails against my scalp. The sensation prompted me to angle my mouth towards him, but he quickly stopped me by pulling his hips back.

"What's wrong?" I asked, frowning up at him.

Kale stepped closer to me. "I want your mouth on me more than *anything*, but just not now. I don't have enough control."

I realised what he meant, and my cheeks flooded with heat.

"So beautiful," he murmured, rubbing his thumb over my cheek.

Confidence filled me, but nervousness took over once more when Kale leaned me back onto the bed and said, "I want to make this good for you."

I hesitated, confused. "I don't understand."

He lifted my legs and rid me of my heels.

"Kale," I pressed. "*What* do you mean, you want to make it good for me?"

He moved from my legs to my skirt, and I watched with wide eyes as he unbuttoned it and hooked his fingers through the belt holes. He pulled, and without thinking I arched my back and lifted my behind from the mattress so the fabric could freely slide down my legs.

Suddenly, Kale was on his knees, his hands on my spread thighs. It took me a second, but when I knew what he wanted to do, shock filled me.

I gasped. "You can't!"

He devilishly smirked. "I plan to."

The pulse that was slow and steady between my thighs came to life with a vengeance at the thought of what Kale planned to do to me . . . *there*.

"Kale," I whispered.

"Hmmm?"

"Can you kiss me first?" I swallowed. "Before, you know, you do *that*."

I hesitantly looked at him to gauge his reaction, and when I saw the swirl of lust and desire in his hazel eyes, I gasped. His touch was like fire as he moved up my body and brought his face to mine.

"I've wanted to hear you ask me that for *months*," he murmured.

I blinked. "You have?"

He nodded. "Say it again, but this time *tell* me to."

My heart hammered against my chest.

"Kiss me, Kale," I breathed. *"Now."*

"Yes, ma'am."

His lips touched mine, and magic happened.

After all the years I'd spent admiring Kale, I thought I knew all there was to know about his lips, but nothing I imagined about kissing them came close to the real thing. Goosebumps broke out over my skin as a shiver raced up and down my spine, before it was quickly replaced with warmth that spread throughout my body.

He tasted of whisky, and I knew I would never be able to separate him from that taste and scent. It was purely him.

I parted my lips when Kale's tongue flicked against them, asking for entry. The wicked pulse between my thighs throbbed with every thrust of his tongue against my own. I mimicked his actions, and we quickly fell into a rhythm of kissing one another with a hunger that meant more than our next breath.

His mouth was warm, and the caress of his lips was softer than I could have ever imagined. I opened my mouth with a low moan as Kale imprinted himself on my lips.

The kisses obliterated every thought.

I greedily sucked air into my lungs when his lips left mine minutes later. He pressed his forehead to mine, and with his own chest rapidly rising and falling, he inhaled and hummed low in his throat.

"I knew it'd be like this," he breathed. "I knew we'd be like fire together."

The need I felt for him consumed me.

"Kale, please," I pleaded. "Touch me."

He made a sound close to a growl when he lowered his face and nuzzled my neck. I swallowed as he kissed his way down my body, stopping at my lower abdomen when I gasped.

He lazily grinned up at me. "You'll love it, darling, I promise."

I didn't doubt that, but what if *he* didn't love it.

"What if you don't like . . . because you'll taste . . . oh, God."

I flung my hands over my face when Kale started to laugh.

"Laney Baby, your innocence is killing me."

Yeah, well, mortification was killing *me*.

"Just let me die here and – *Kale*!"

I dropped my hands from my face to the sides of my body and fisted the bed sheets around me as pure pleasurable sensation attacked my core in the form of a wicked tongue. I wasn't new to the sensation I was experiencing – I had pleasured myself on many occasions – but my fingers were no match for Kale's tongue.

"Oh, God!" I groaned, and bit down on my lower lip.

I lifted my head and looked down at Kale, who was kissing and licking me through the thin material of my lace underwear. The sight was just as good as the sensation, if not better.

I couldn't take my eyes off him, but the moment he pushed the material of my underwear to the side and put his mouth on me bare, I was forced to. My eyes rolled back as my head fell against the mattress underneath me. I heard the cries, pleas, and moans echo throughout the room, but I was so twisted up in what Kale's mouth was doing to me that it took me a few minutes to realise the sounds were coming from me.

"Lane," Kale growled against me, "you taste like heaven."

He sucked my clit into his mouth and rubbed his lips back and forth over the bundle of nerves until I was putty in his very capable hands.

"Oh, God," I cried out. "Kale, please."

He moved his arms under my thighs and slid them around to my hips where they met above my lower abdomen. He locked his hands together and held me in place and full-on assaulted me with his tongue. I screamed as the feeling suddenly became too much.

I found that my hips were involuntarily bucking into Kale's face while the rest of my body was trying to scramble away from him.

"Too mu-much!" I pleaded.

Kale didn't let up, and if possible he sucked harder, causing my back to arch off the bed as white spots dotted my vision. I momentarily stopped breathing as a wave of pure ecstasy slammed into my body in the form of delicious pulses that throbbed between my thighs.

This only lasted ten or so seconds, but for that short amount of time I was in complete bliss.

I blinked my eyes open when I felt the mattress dip, and watched as Kale climbed onto the bed and hovered over me. He grinned down at me and lowered his head to mine.

"I want you for breakfast every day."

I felt my face flush with heat, and it seemed a little juvenile to be embarrassed considering the orgasm he'd just given me, but I couldn't help the colour that stained my cheeks.

"Are you sure?" I asked, my body trembling. "Having the same thing to eat every day can get boring."

"Not *this* chosen meal," Kale growled, and covered my mouth with his.

I was very aware of where his mouth had just been, and tasting myself on his lips and tongue was so erotic that the aching pulse between my thighs that Kale had soothed came back with a bang.

"Kale," I groaned into his mouth.

He hummed back in response before detaching his lips from mine and nudging me into an upright position. I was momentarily confused about what he was doing until he lifted my arms and the fabric of my crop top slid over my head, causing me to gasp with surprise.

Kale chuckled as he reached around and unclipped my bra. The straps fell down my arms, and my breasts were exposed when he tugged the material away from me completely. I was bare in both flesh and heart.

Breathe, just breathe, my mind soothed. *You want this. No, you need this.*

I repeated the thought over and over as Kale laid me back on the bed and moved his body over mine.

"Lane," he murmured.

I swallowed and looked up at him.

"I can't tell what is real and what's not right now," he breathed. "So tell me now *loud and clear* if you don't want this."

My heart almost burst with love for him; his consideration for me meant everything.

"I want this," I assured him. "Trust me."

"My Lane," he whispered as he rubbed his nose against mine.

I could smell the whisky on his breath, and the urge for me to taste his lips again consumed me. I reached up and gripped onto his biceps. "Please, don't stop."

Kale looked down at me, his eyes clouded with lust. "Is this real?" he whispered, and lifted his hand. He touched my cheek with his index finger to make sure I was really there with him. I nodded as my eyes welled up with tears. "Yeah, pup. It's real."

He began to tremble. "Is . . . is this okay with you?" he asked, and shakily pressed himself between my legs.

I began to tremble too, but with anticipation.

"Yes," I whispered and opened my legs wider. "This . . . this is what I want. *You* are what I want, what I've always wanted."

I couldn't believe I'd admitted that out loud.

"Lane," he whispered again, and leaned his face down to mine. "Can I have you?"

My heart warmed, and my stomach exploded into a mess of fluttering butterflies. "All of me," I murmured. "You have all of me."

You always have, a voice in my head whispered.

With a groan, Kale ran his fingers down my slit until he felt how ready I was for him, and then he lined himself up with my entrance, and just before he thrust forward, he whispered, "I'm sorry."

I didn't know what he was apologising for until I felt a sharp pain tear through me as he embedded himself within my body. I gasped, squeezed my eyes shut and clenched my hands into fists. I tried to breathe through the sudden hurt, but I wasn't expecting it to sting as much as it did.

"Jesus Christ," Kale breathed and leaned his face down to mine. He let his lips hover above my mouth for a few seconds before I gently pressed against them. I parted my lips and nervously slid my tongue into Kale's mouth, tangling it with his. This was the first time I had initiated a kiss with him, and I was so worried I would mess it up, but thankfully he took control of it, and I quite happily followed his lead.

I was thankful for the kiss because it distracted me from the pain between my legs, which stung with Kale's every thrust. I was about to throw in the towel, when I suddenly groaned into his mouth and the sting began to lessen, and the aching pulse from before began to take over my senses.

Yes, I thought as the pain I felt faded away and pleasure mounted.

I moved my mouth in sync with Kale's and ground my pelvis upward when the kiss, and friction of Kale's thrust, caused the growing throb between my legs to intensify.

I locked my ankles around the back of his knees, and gripped onto his shoulders as he put some of his weight down on me. He removed his mouth from mine and brought his lips to my jaw, where he trailed kisses down my jawline and onto my neck.

"You feel . . . *Fuck.*"

He sounded like he was in bliss.

I wanted to reply, but I was ticklish and he was breathing on and kissing my neck, so I was squeamishly trying to pull away from his lips as they pressed against my skin. I was about to tell him to stop, but what left my mouth was a loud groan. He sucked on my neck harder, and the sensation caused my back to arch and goose-bumps to break out over my body.

"Oh, God," I panted, and rolled my eyes shut as an orgasm consumed me and slammed into my body like a train. I felt my eyes roll back as wave after wave of ecstasy rolled over me until I was nothing but sensation.

Kale growled against my neck when I came down from my high, and then pulled up off me. "Lane . . . I can't wait."

I opened my eyes and I *saw* him. All of him. And I loved what and who I saw.

"So don't," I urged him.

His gaze locked on me, and there was something different about it. I felt *incredibly* beautiful in that moment and knew I would remember for the rest of my life the look of need in Kale's eyes for me.

Not want. *Need.*

"I don't have a condom, but I'll pull out. I promise."

A condom. I didn't even *think* about a condom. My mother's "talk" last year reflected in my mind. She made me swear never to have intercourse without protection, but Kale's promise was protection enough for me. I trusted him in every way possible.

"I trust you."

Kale shuddered. "I – God, I've wanted this for so long with you."

He had? My eyes bugged out of my head, but I managed to keep my cool.

"Me too," I replied, my heart going into overdrive against my chest. "I've always wanted you."

Kale closed his eyes and hummed in response. I gasped as he pulled out of me and used the head of his length to rub over my pulsing bundle of nerves. I was about to ask him to do it again, but he seemed to know what I wanted, because he did it without direction.

I groaned.

Kale watched me for a moment, then dipped back inside me. He leaned his head down to mine and covered my mouth with his. He kissed me long and deep, and just as I fell into his kiss, he pulled out of me and thrust back just as fast.

"Oh!" I moaned.

Kale growled and thrust into me harder, heightening the pleasure and the volume of my moaning. The soothing pleasure turned to heated magic. My entire body was alive and singing with delight.

"Lane," Kale almost roared. "I'm sorry. I can't hold back – you feel too good."

I wrapped my arms around him. "It's okay."

A few rapid thrusts later and Kale pulled out of my body, groaning out loud as spurts of hot liquid jetted onto the sheet next to me. When he finished his release, he stared down at himself for a few moments before he collapsed on top of me. His weight wasn't crushing; I could still breathe, but it wasn't exactly comfortable. I didn't care, though. This was my version of heaven, and I didn't want anything about it to ever change.

I remained under Kale for a few minutes until his weight started to hurt.

"Kale," I murmured.

Silence.

I frowned. "Kale?"

Again, silence.

I grunted. *"Kale?"*

I gasped when a snore responded to my calls.

He couldn't be. There was no way he was asleep, he was still on top of me, for God's sake! "Kale Hunt," I rumbled, my patience wearing thin, "you better answer me."

He groaned against my chest, then rolled off me. I looked to my left and found him on his back, out cold. I gawked at him, not understanding how he could fall asleep so quickly.

He was still naked as the day he was born! I was too, *and* I was sporting the evidence of Kale's release on my body. I looked over at him and found that he was too. When he fell forward onto me, his leg hung off me for a moment and pressed against the sheet he'd ruined, rubbing the aftermath of our lovemaking onto his skin before he transferred it to mine.

Even though it was only a little bit on us both, I grimaced.

I wasn't a prude. The idea of a man's come didn't bother me, so Kale's come *definitely* wouldn't, but never mind that he was the love of my life, I was not leaving it on my skin, or his, any longer than need be. I stood up from the bed and scurried over to the open door that led to a nicely decorated en suite. I gathered some tissues, soaked them with water and washed down my thigh as well as gently cleansing between my legs.

I was a little startled to see blood on the tissue as I was cleaning myself up, but I reminded myself that bleeding was normal after having sex for the first time. It wasn't much anyway, so I wasn't concerned in the slightest. After I finished cleaning myself up, I gathered some wet and dry tissues and, back in the bedroom, did the same for Kale, who didn't move a muscle.

He was snoring his head off, and I didn't know why, but I was a little bit angry with him. I hadn't known what to expect from Kale when I bumped into him earlier, but ending up in a bedroom, admitting we liked one another and having sex with him definitely was *not* it. However, I had hoped we would stay awake and talk and cuddle afterwards. Him falling straight to sleep was not on the agenda, not for me anyway.

When I got him all cleaned up, I quickly got under the covers of the bed and pulled them over him to keep him warm. When I was settled next to him, I lay on my side, still and quiet for what must have been an hour or even two, just simply staring at him in awe.

I couldn't believe I finally had what I'd wanted my whole life.

My Kale.

I had him, and for the life of me, I never wanted to let him go. I scooted closer to him, careful not to wake him up. I hesitated for a moment but decided to put my nerves aside and lie on his chest.

With an enormous smile on my face, I closed my eyes, blocked out the sound of the party downstairs and focused on Kale's breathing. Oddly, his snores helped lull me into a relaxed state, and not long after, I fell into darkness, with a full and happy heart.

I never wanted this moment to end.

~

I blinked my eyes open when I heard a door slam, and then flinched when shouting voices followed loud laughter. It was dark, and for a fleeting moment I had no idea where I was, until I looked down to my left.

Kale.

Visions of kissing him, touching him and making love to him came tumbling back to me and put an instant smile on my face. I relaxed next to him and found he was on his side facing me. I simply gazed at the perfection that was before me. It wasn't a dream. I'd really had sex and slept in a bed with Kale.

Oh, my God.

My heart was so happy I could have burst into song. My stomach was aflutter, and my body was shaking. Adrenaline was surging through my veins, and all because I woke up next to Kale. He gave me a high like none other, and I loved it. I loved *him*.

I looked past Kale's body to the clock on the dressing table next to the bed and saw it was after five in the morning. I listened out for music but couldn't hear it any more. I could hear distant laughter and voices, though, which told me the party was still going strong.

I didn't like how dark the room was now that I was awake, so I turned on the lamp on the bedside table next to me and relaxed back into the pillow I was lying on. I closed my eyes on a sigh but snapped them back open when I heard groaning next to me.

"My head is killing me," Kale grumbled, and lifted his hands to his face, covering it completely.

I snorted. "That's what you get for downing Jack."

Kale's entire body tensed when I spoke, and he slowly lowered his hands from his face and turned to look at me.

"Good morning," I said, beaming.

"Lane?" Kale whispered, then rubbed his eyes and repeatedly blinked them.

He choked on air when he glanced down to my naked breasts, then widened his eyes. Lifting up the bed sheets that covered him, he looked down at his naked body.

"Oh, Jesus," he panicked. "Oh, Christ."

I frowned at him. "What's wrong?"

Kale snapped his gaze to me. "What's *wrong*? Are you fucking serious?"

I was taken aback by his sudden anger. "I don't understand why you're so mad," I replied, my temper rising to match his. "You were fine a few hours ago!"

He shook his head in dismay. "I was drunk a few hours ago, Lane."

Sickness attacked my stomach, and hurt gripped my heart.

"Wh-What are you saying?" I whispered, not wanting to hear the answer to my question.

Kale looked at me once more and frowned deeply. "I'm *so* sorry. Please, forgive me."

Forgive him?

"For what?" I asked, my eyes welling up with tears.

He grunted. "You know what for . . . We had sex, Lane."

I was instantly gutted when I saw the regret on his face. "You . . . you're sorry we had sex?" I asked, trying my hardest not to allow my voice to crack.

He placed his head in his hands. "Of *course* I am. You're my best friend, you're only seventeen and I don't even remember sleeping with you. Oh, fuck, what have I done? Did I hurt you? Did I use a condom?"

I couldn't speak.

I couldn't move.

I couldn't think.

"Lane," Kale breathed, and turned to me, the bed sheets still covering his lower body. "Please, forgive me. I'm begging you. I'm so sorry if I hurt you."

"You didn't have a condom, but you promised you would pull out, and you did." I looked at him and blinked. "You didn't hurt me either."

He just fucking destroyed me.

Kale closed his eyes. "I'm such a fucking prick."

Yes. Yes, he was.

"Do you remember anything?" I asked after a lengthy silence.

He was looking at me, but turned away from me when I asked my question, and said, "No."

How on earth was that possible?

"Kale, you weren't *that* drunk," I stated. "You were tipsy at most."

He moved away when I reached for him, and it really hurt my feelings. "I don't know what to tell you, Lane. I was drunk. I'm just not a messy drunk, I guess, but that doesn't mean I remember shit."

Did he have to word it like that?

I swallowed. "You weren't even slurring, though—"

"I don't remember it, okay?" he bellowed.

I wasn't expecting him to shout at me, and it caused me to almost jump out of my skin.

"I'm sorry," he said when he saw that he'd scared me. "I'm so sorry about all of this. It's all my fault."

I was so confused.

"You told me you liked me," I whispered.

"If I said that, then I wasn't lying. I do like you – I swear I do. You're fucking gorgeous, but it's been embedded in me to look out for you because you are like a sister to me, and for a long time you have been, Lane."

He *truly* saw me as his sister?

Oh, my God.

I felt sick.

"It's okay," I breathed, forcing back the bile that wanted to rise up my throat. "We'll just forget about it. It's not a big deal."

It was a big deal; it was a huge fucking deal.

"Lane."

I refused to look at him; the tears that were in my eyes would fall, otherwise.

"No, Kale, I swear it's fine," I said, and fumbled with the sheets to cover my body. "You're right – this was a mistake."

It almost killed me to say the biggest lie of my life.

"I'm so sorry if I've hurt you," he said, clearly in distress. "I hate myself for upsetting you."

Stop. Talking.

"It's fine, honestly," I assured him.

It wasn't fine, not at all.

"I wasn't . . . I wasn't your first, was I?"

I looked up at him and saw the horror in his expression. He truly didn't remember any of what we did, not even the conversation we'd had before.

That cut me deep.

"No," I lied through my teeth. "No, I've had sex before."

His jaw set before he slowly nodded.

"Can you – can you turn around so I can get dressed?" I asked, an embarrassed flush covering the surface of my face and neck.

I wasn't being shy; I was simply mortified at having to do a degrading redress from the night before, then do the walk of shame from someone who I should never have been walking away from.

I quickly got up from the bed and scrabbled around the room, picking up my underwear and Lavender's borrowed clothes and pulling them on in record time. When I got my heels on and checked that my phone and house key were still in the back pocket of the skirt I was wearing, I moved towards the door, with my head downcast.

"Lane?" his voice murmured.

I froze at the door of the bedroom.

"What is it, Kale?" I asked, tears splashing onto my cheeks.

"You mean the world to me, and you know I'd never be horrible to you or say something hurtful *unless* it was for your own good, don't you?"

My head was pounding, and I had no idea what the hell he was talking about.

I couldn't make sense of it.

"I have to go, Kale."

He was silent for a moment, and then he said, "Just . . . don't hate me. Please."

That was the damn problem. I *wanted* to hate him, but I couldn't, I loved him too much to ever experience another emotion when it came to him, and I hated *that*.

"I don't hate you," I whispered.

I heard Kale exhale a relieved breath.

"Will you be okay getting home?" he asked, concerned.

I nodded. "I'll be fine."

"Look, I'll see you over Christmas break, and I'm telling you, we'll laugh our heads off about this by then."

That was highly doubtful.

"Yeah," I lied. "It'll be hilarious."

"Take my jumper; I left it up here when I got to the party a few hours ago. Please . . . take it. You'll freeze outside wearing just that."

I hesitated in turning.

"Lane, please," he pleaded. "I don't want you to get sick."

I swallowed my hurt and pride, and turned to face him. I made sure not to look at him directly, though, as I walked over to the bed and grabbed his jumper from the floor. I quickly put it on, then moved back over to the door.

Kale was silent for a moment before he said, "See you, Laney Baby."

I squeezed my eyes shut but reopened them as I reached for the handle of the bedroom door. I turned the lock and pulled the door open. I stepped out into the hallway, and without looking back, I said, "Bye, Kale", and closed the door behind me.

I stood there for a moment before I willed my legs to move. I began to walk down the hallway, and just before I took the left turn and headed for the stairs I heard Kale's voice roar, "Fuck! Fuck! *FUCK!*" from back inside the bedroom where I'd given myself body and soul to him.

I broke down then. He really regretted sleeping with me. He really regretted *me*, and he was clearly furious with himself over it. I couldn't take the hurt that welled up inside of me. I ran down the hallway, jumping over a sleeping body here and there, until I got to the stairs and descended them two at a time. When I reached the bottom of the stairs, I glanced around and winced at the state of the beautiful house I'd entered last night.

It looked like a bomb had gone off, and I pitied the poor souls who had to clean it all up. I glanced at the large clock next to the stairs and saw it was close to half past five in the morning. There was no way I could go back to Lavender's house, because she'd told her parents that she was sleeping in my house, but since she wasn't with me, I had a pretty good idea of who she was with.

I reached into the back pocket of my skirt, pulled out my phone and dialled her number.

"Pick up, pick up, pick up," I repeated over and over.

"Hello?" Lavender's husky voice answered.

"It's me. Where are you?" I asked, breathing a sigh of relief that she was okay.

She mumbled something to someone, then to me she said, "I'm in Daven's house. His mum had a late shift at the hospital, so he brought me back here when I couldn't find you."

I was a shitty friend; she'd probably been worried sick about me.

I winced. "Sorry about that, I went AWOL."

"It's okay. Daven's friend said he saw Kale bring you upstairs, so I left with Daven because I knew you would be safe with him."

Safe. Yeah.

"Yeah," I murmured. "I was with Kale."

"Wait," she said, her voice suddenly more alert. "You were with Kale? Like *with* him?"

"Yeah," I said, and burst into tears.

"Oh, babe, no," Lavender whispered.

"It was perfect," I cried, "but he just woke up and freaked out on me. He said he didn't remember us having sex and that he saw me as a sister. He regrets having sex with me, Lav. He regrets me."

"Where are you? I'm getting dressed and coming right over."

I wiped my face and took a few deep breaths to calm myself down.

"No, it's too early." I sniffled. "Stay with Daven, I'm going to go ho-home. My dad will be gone to work, and my mum will be asleep. I'll sneak in and get into bed, and when she wakes up, I'll just say I came home early from your house."

"Are you sure?" Lavender asked. "I don't care about the time. I'll come to you right now if you need me to."

I heard a voice grumble, "Is she okay? Does she need me to pick her up?"

I was surprised that Daven was even the slightest bit concerned; he never usually showed any emotion of any kind towards me. We would either fight over his fights with Lavender or ignore one another. There was no in-between with us.

"She's fine – go back to sleep."

I jerked my head when I heard movement upstairs in the house, and I was terrified it was Kale coming down the stairs so he could go to his parents' house. I did *not* want to see him, so I focused on my phone.

"I have to go, Lav."

"I'll swing by yours on my way home in a few hours, okay?"

I nodded. "'Kay."

"Love you, babe. Hang in there," Lavender said.

I sniffled. "I will. Love you too."

I hung up and pocketed my phone. I hated wearing Kale's fleece jumper, but I folded my arms together and snuggled into the heat that it offered me as I opened the hall door of the house and stepped outside into the freezing morning air.

My attire was a really bad fucking idea.

I felt my teeth chatter as I walked down the never-ending driveway of the party house and headed in the direction of the village. My house was only fifteen minutes away, and because I briskly walked the entire way, I got there pretty fast.

I took off Lavender's wedged heels and held them in my hand as I walked up the driveway. I got my key out of my back pocket and held my breath as I approached the hall door. I put the key into the lock, turned it and gently nudged open the door. I silently stepped inside my house and carefully closed the door behind me, relocking it and then hanging the key on the rack.

I quickly entered the alarm code when the warning sound began to beep. Once that was done, I crept up the stairs and cursed God himself when that stupid loose floorboard next to my bedroom creaked as I stood on it.

I froze to the spot for a solid minute, and when I heard no movement coming from my parents' room, I stepped off the stupid noisy floorboard and escaped into the safety of my bedroom, where I gently closed the door behind me. I tiptoed over to my dresser, opened the first drawer and shoved Lavender's heels inside. I rid myself of her clothes and Kale's jumper and shoved them into the drawer too.

I washed my face clean of make-up, and brushed my hair out before plaiting it back out of my face. I climbed into my bed, where I lay for ages, staring at the glow-up stickers on my ceiling, wondering if my entire night was a dream – or a nightmare.

~

"Lane, darling?" I heard my mother's voice shout later that morning as I got out of the shower. I had scrubbed myself raw, trying to take away some of the pain I felt by replacing it with a physical one.

My mother had come into my room at ten in the morning to collect my dirty washing from my hamper, and got the fright of her life when she found me asleep in bed. Her scream woke me up and nearly gave me a heart attack. I told her I'd come home at 9 a.m., but because she'd still been in bed, I'd gone back to bed too. She didn't suspect a thing about what I had really been up to; she was more concerned about how she didn't hear me come in.

I opened my door and replied to her with a loud "Yeah?"

"Can you come down here?"

I pressed my forehead against my bedroom door and sighed. "Sure. Give me a second to get dressed."

I entered my room, got dried and changed into clothes before heading downstairs.

"What's up?" I asked.

"Nothing," my mother replied. "Just wanted to see what you wanted for dinner this evening."

"I'm cool with whatever you want to make," I said.

"Pizza and chips it is," my mother chirped.

I stared at her back, then sat on a chair next to the kitchen table. I was silent for a moment, and then suddenly I felt like talking to her because I felt really low.

"Mum," I mumbled, pushing my wet hair out of my face.

She glanced at me over her shoulder for a moment, then went back to the dishes as she said, "Yes?"

Talk, I willed myself.

"I like Kale," I blurted out.

I held my breath as soon as the words were out of my mouth. My mother halted her movements and looked at me, her lips parted. "I know."

She knows? my mind screeched.

I exhaled. "You do?"

She nodded. "I always knew you had a little crush on him."

If my being in love with him was described as a "little crush" then yeah, I crushed on Kale hard. "How come you never said anything to me about it?" I questioned, feeling at a disadvantage. First, Kale had known I liked him, and now my mother did? Who else was aware of my clearly obvious feelings for him?

She shrugged and turned to face me fully, a tea towel in her hands, drying them. "I didn't want to embarrass you."

I frowned. "But you talked to me when I liked Blake, before Lochlan scared him off that is."

"That was different," she lightly chuckled. "I didn't know this Blake lad. He isn't a son to me the way Kale is."

I felt my heart sink. "You really think of Kale as a son?"

My mother nodded. "Your father does too. Even your Uncle Harry and Nanny consider him our family."

She wasn't making me feel better. If anything, her words were making me feel worse.

I scratched my neck. "It'd be weird for us to . . . you know, ever wind up together then?" I asked, chuckling to help clear out the awkwardness I felt.

My mother laughed. "Yeah, it'd be strange since everyone considers you his little sister."

I looked away from my mother so she wouldn't see the hurt in my eyes. "Yeah, you're right," I said, and cleared my throat. "I guess I just liked him because he was always around me."

I was surprised at how easily I lied about something, *someone* that was so close to my heart.

"That and Lochlan never let you close to a boy no matter how many times I warned him not to interfere." My mother clucked her tongue, then turned her back to me as she carried on with hand-washing the dishes.

"You know Lochlan." I swallowed. "He just wants to protect me."

"Layton and Kale too," she chuckled. "That's what brothers do."

I'd never thought of Kale as a brother or relative of any kind, not since I was little. "Yeah," I said, and stood up from the table. "Lavender will be over soon."

I heard the smile in my mother's voice as she said, "I'm so glad you have a girlfriend to spend time with. You need to experience life outside of your circle with just Kale."

I hated to admit it, but I needed to experience life entirely outside of Kale, now more than ever. I really needed to speak to my Uncle Harry, because he got me – he always understood me so easily. He didn't need to know about Kale and me having sex, but he could know something serious happened and that the outcome broke my heart in two.

I heard my mother talking, but for the life of me I couldn't hear what she was saying over my own thoughts. I nodded to her, even though she couldn't see the gesture as I left the kitchen and headed up the stairs to my room. When I entered my room, I sat down on my bed and clutched at my chest as pain spread across it.

I wiped under my nose with the back of my hand and looked over to my bedside table, where the vibrations of my phone rumbled against the wood. I dried my eyes with the corners of my towel, picked up my phone and saw Kale's text message. My heart stopped.

I hope u r ok. I'm so sry, I rly hope u dont h8 me. I luv u nd Im sry if Ive ruined evrythin.

I gritted my teeth at Kale's text talk; I hated when he didn't use grammar correctly, but I shoved that annoyance aside as I thumbed out a reply.

Stop it. It's fine. I'm fine. It was a mistake. I know that, and you know that. You're still my best friend. Nothing will ever change that. You haven't ruined anything. You're still my buddy. Things haven't changed. I promise :)

Lie. Lie. Lie.

I didn't voice it, but I suspected things would never be the same between us ever again, and I think Kale knew it too.

CHAPTER ELEVEN

Day three in York

"Lane?"

I blinked away the memory that had taken hold of me and turned my head to the voice that called my name, and when I found the source was Ally Day, my gaze hardened.

It was Sunday, the day after my uncle's funeral, and my family, family friends and a bunch of other people had dropped by my parents' home, some to talk about their good times with my uncle, while others were drinking.

I made sure that I steered clear of alcohol. I hadn't touched a drop of it in seven years, and even though I felt like I was at my lowest point, I kept my private vow never to use alcohol to mask my pain again. I had done that enough in my late teenage years, and I *never* wanted to fall back into that state of mind.

"What do you want, Ally?" I quipped, pushing loose strands of hair from my face. "I'm not in the mood to be put down. I've had a shitty weekend, in case you haven't noticed."

Ally winced. "I deserve that."

"You think?" I sarcastically asked.

She played with the hem of her cardigan as she said, "Lane, I'm sorry."

I turned my body to face her fully. "For what?"

She swallowed and said, "For how horrible I was to you when we were younger. I have no excuse for it. I was mean, horrible and a straight-up bitch to you for no reason. I wish I could take it all back."

I tilted my head as I stared at her.

"I wished for that countless times too," I stated. "I wished every night after that day in Anna's house that I could rewind and not go there. Do you understand how much your words, and Anna's, had an impact on me? I wanted to *die* because I felt so bad about myself. You played a part in making me feel like that."

Tears welled in Ally's eyes.

"I'm terribly sorry. I had no idea of the hurt we caused you."

I didn't bat an eyelid.

"Of course you didn't. You were too wrapped up in Anna to see anything else, never mind seeing the impact your words and actions had on others."

Her tears fell from her eyes and splashed onto her now red-blotched cheeks.

"I hate myself for how I behaved in school. I never wanted to be that person, Lane. I just acted mean to seek approval from Anna. I don't know why I needed to be friends with her, because she was horrible to me, even worse than what she was with you."

I scowled. "Am I supposed to feel sorry for you, Ally?"

"No," she answered, "I'm not trying to make this about me. I just wanted you to know why I was the way I was. I did some horrible things to fit into a nasty friendship with someone who wasn't worth it, and I hurt you and many others in the process. I'll forever be sorry for the things I said to you."

I didn't know whether to accept her apology or not, even though it was obvious she was very sorry for what she had done.

The heartbroken teenager within me wanted to watch her cry and have her feel horrible for what she had done to me, but I shook that version of myself away. If I did that, I would be no better than Ally or Anna back in the day.

"I can see that you're sorry," I commented.

"I am," she sniffled. "I swear it."

I sighed deeply. "I don't know what you want me to say, Ally. I can't just switch off the dislike I have for you. You were a part of making growing up as a teenager more difficult than it needed to be."

"I'd take it all back if I could," she vowed.

I raised an eyebrow. "Why now?"

"Huh?" she hiccupped.

"Why are you saying all this to me now?" I clarified.

Ally shrugged her shoulders. "I've wanted to apologise to you for years, but you've been in the States, and I didn't want to find you on Facebook and send you everything I had to say in a text message," she explained. "Anything short of the apology I'm giving you now wouldn't have cut it, not to me."

That surprised me.

"You've changed since I last saw you," I commented after a moment of silence.

I didn't mean her appearance, and Ally knew that.

"I have," she said, nodding. "I've grown up, and I'll have to live with the things I have done and said, but all I can do now is offer my apology and prove that I'm a better person."

My gut told me that she was being sincere.

"I . . . I can't believe I'm saying this, and *meaning* it, but I forgive you, Ally," I said after a pregnant pause. "We won't be friends anytime soon, but I do believe that you're sorry for what you did, and I accept your apology. We don't have to talk about it again; it's in the past where it belongs."

Ally's crying amplified until she was sobbing so much she couldn't speak. I didn't know what to do for her, so I stood motionless before her and stared. I cringed as I put myself in her shoes.

Is that what I looked like when I cried? I wondered. *Did others feel as helpless as I did?*

"What's going on in here?" Lochlan's voice suddenly boomed from my right.

I looked at him at the same time he locked his eyes on a still blubbering Ally, and I resisted rolling my eyes when Lochlan's hardened gaze switched to mine. If looks could kill, I would have been dead and buried with the glare my brother shot my way.

"What. Did. You. Do?" he growled.

Here we go.

"What are you talking about?" I quizzed. "*I* didn't do anything."

He lifted his hand and gestured towards Ally. "Explain her state then!"

I looked to Ally, who was trying to speak but was now hiccupping and couldn't get any words out.

"I didn't make her cry – she did that herself."

Lochlan growled. "I've never seen her cry like that, and all of a sudden she is alone with you for a few minutes and she's a mess of tears."

Why does he care so much?

"You better close your mouth, turn around and walk off before you say something you regret," I warned him. "I am not at fault here. She is apologising for the shit she did to me when we were teenagers. She is crying because she feels bad about what she did. We're talking it out. That's it."

Some of the tension from Lochlan's body disappeared.

He looked to Ally and asked, "Is that true?"

It pissed me off that he didn't take what I said as truth.

Ally sniffled and nodded her head to Lochlan.

"Oh," he said, then cleared his throat. "I didn't know."

"How could you know?" I questioned. "You never gave me a chance to explain. You came in here pointing your stupid fat finger and jumped to your own conclusion. Typical Lochlan."

The tension that had left Lochlan's body came back tenfold.

"I know you, Lane, and you have a way of starting trouble out of nothing," he sneered.

He might as well have kicked me in the face. It would have hurt less.

"You're wrong, dear brother," I mocked. "You don't know me; you haven't known me for a long time."

"And whose fucking fault is that?" he suddenly bellowed.

Ally jumped, but I didn't. Lochlan didn't scare me. I was used to his outbursts.

"I'm sorry, Ally," Lochlan murmured, his voice incredibly soft towards her. "Can you give me a minute with my *sister*?"

He said the word "sister" like one would say "cancer".

Ally nodded to both of us, tenderly touched Lochlan's arm, then scurried out of the room, closing the door behind her. I blinked at the closed door, then looked to Lochlan, and my face lit up when I put two and two together.

"I'm so stupid," I said, laughing. "No wonder you defended her yesterday in the sitting room and just now: you're shagging her."

Lochlan scowled at me. "Don't talk about what you don't know."

I laughed harder. "I'm right, aren't I?"

He glared at me, his silence screaming a resounding yes.

I shook my head. "For *years* you never let older boys near me, and now you're shacked up with someone the *same age* as me? The exact age as your *little* sister, Lochlan. This is just bloody brilliant."

"You don't know what you're talking about," he growled.

I ignored him. "Maybe I should take a leaf out of your book and scare her away from you. It seemed to work out well when you did it to me all those years ago."

Lochlan's gaze hardened. "That's different. We aren't kids anymore."

"Since when has maturity mattered between siblings?" I asked.

My brother narrowed his eyes to slits. "Leave. Ally. Alone."

I held up my hands in front of my chest. "No problem, big bro. I won't be here long enough to screw you out of getting laid. Trust me, the first chance I get, I'm out of here."

Lochlan's whole demeanour went rigid. "*Stop* threatening us with that."

I looked away from him. "You know I'm leaving when everything is squared away with Uncle Harry's things. It's not a threat if it's true."

He stepped towards me. "You can stay here if you want to; you know you can."

"Uncle Harry is gone," I replied, gazing out the kitchen window. "What's left for me here?"

"Me!" Lochlan roared.

I almost jumped out of my skin when he shouted. I quickly looked in his direction and backed up against the kitchen counter when I saw how tense his features were. I had never seen him look so infuriated before.

"I'm here," he bit out. "Layton is here. Mum, Dad and Nanny are here for you. Kale is here for you too, not that you've ever given a damn about him."

It was my turn to shout then.

"What the hell are you talking about?" I bellowed, rage flowing through my veins. "I left *for* Kale! I left so he could be with Drew and have their baby. I didn't want to remind him of the bullshit

I put him through every time he saw me, and I didn't want to put a strain on their relationship, because I knew Drew didn't like me around him. I left so he could finally be happy, so don't you fucking *dare* tell me I never cared for him. I loved him with everything in me, you arsehole. I left my entire life for him!"

What I didn't say was that I also left because I couldn't watch Kale's life with another play out before my eyes, but Lochlan didn't need to know that.

He stared back at me with wide eyes.

I shook my head. "I love you, Lochlan, but you make me hate you sometimes."

He swallowed as tension left his features. "I don't mean to be so hard on you, but you didn't just leave Kale or Uncle Harry when you went away. You left me too."

My heart hurt for him.

"And I'm sorry for hurting you, but I didn't know what else to do at the time. I couldn't be here. It was too hard."

Lochlan blinked. "And now?"

I frowned. "And now I don't know how I feel. I'm a bundle of emotions with everything going on. I just need to get a handle on myself and think for a while."

"I've been in a relationship with Ally for the last four years."

Out of all the things I expected my brother to say, that was *not* it.

"What?" I gaped. "Four years?"

He nodded. "We're engaged."

Thank God I had the counter to lean against because I was sure I would have fallen over without it.

"It's not just *shagging*, as you so nicely put it. I love her, and she loves me."

I blinked dumbly.

"We're getting married next June," Lochlan continued, "and I – *we* – want you at the wedding."

I looked away from my brother then, but he shot forward and got in my face.

"Don't do that! Don't turn away from me. If you're not going to come to my wedding, then say it to my face."

I was shocked to the core when I saw unshed tears, *real* tears, sitting in my brother's eyes.

"I just forgave her for everything she did to me when we were younger, but I don't exactly like her, Lochlan. How can I stand in a church and pretend like I do?" I asked, my eyes searching his.

Lochlan's gaze lost some of its intensity, and his lip quirked. "You can sit down the back if it helps?"

I was surprised when a laugh burst out of me. Lochlan laughed too. Then, without warning, he put his arms around me and pulled me into a tight hug.

"You're still the biggest pain in my arse, little sister, but you've always been my number-one girl; you know that, right? I love you to death, and I've missed you with all of my heart."

Tears fell from my eyes as I hugged him back.

"I'm sorry," I whispered. "I'm so sorry for leaving you."

Lochlan squeezed me tightly.

"Congratulations," I said then as I pulled back from our hug. "I mean it. I'm happy for you."

Lochlan winked at me. "Thanks, kid."

I teasingly grinned. "I'll have to share Lochlan's number-one-girl title it seems."

He smiled wide. "Yeah, it appears to be that way."

I got serious then and said, "If she ever hurts you, you tell me, and I'll hunt her down and kick her arse."

Lochlan almost doubled over from laughing, and it caused my lip to twitch.

"I'm glad you find it amusing, but I'm dead serious."

He laughed harder.

I nudged him. "I'm going to kick *your* arse if you don't bring it down a notch."

Lochlan tried to compose himself.

"I'm sorry, Rambo," he snickered. "I'll keep your offer in mind. I'll just have to pray Ally never hurts me."

I rolled my eyes at him, smiling, before going in for another hug.

"So you'll be here for my wedding?" he asked.

I nodded against his chest. "Do you think Mum or Nanny would let me miss it?"

He pulled back from me, thought on it, then smirked.

"They'd personally go over to New York and put you on a plane home."

They would – that was God's honest truth.

I cringed. "I can only imagine."

Lochlan smiled at me, then leaned in and kissed my forehead. I closed my eyes, then reopened them and looked up at him. "Are we cool?"

He gazed at me for a moment and said, "Yeah, Lane, we're cool. I'm tired of being angry with you. I know it's because I just miss you and worry for you, but if you want to live abroad, then I'm going to deal with that. Things will change between us, I promise."

He hugged me again, and just like that, the tension between Lochlan and myself disappeared. It felt damn good too. I pulled back from my brother when I heard the sound of a throat clearing, and froze when I saw Kale standing in the open kitchen doorway, his hands in his trouser pockets. His lifeless eyes were trained on me.

"Lane?" Kale's voice murmured quietly.

Oh, God.

"How . . . how long have you been standing there?" I asked, my voice barely a whisper.

He licked his lower lip. "Long enough."

Did he hear everything I said about him? I panicked. *Fuck.*

I squeezed my eyes shut. "I have to go."

I needed to get away from everyone and be on my own. I pushed myself away from Lochlan and practically ran by Kale, only to be brought to a halt next to the sitting room when a body stepped out in front of me.

"You aren't going anywhere!" This voice belonged to my father.

I refused to look at anyone.

"I meant I'm going to my *hotel* room. I promised Mum and Nanny I'd stick around to help with Uncle Harry's house and his belongings. I'm not skipping town – I just want to be on my own for a while."

My father didn't budge. "You can be alone up in your room, you don't have to—"

"Sweetie, let her go," my mother said softly.

I wasn't so surprised to hear her say that. I looked up and found her in the doorway of the parlour, watching me through exhausted eyes.

"We'll see you tomorrow?" she asked me.

I nodded my head.

"Then go on to the inn and get some sleep, sweetheart."

I walked over to my mother, gave her a big hug and kissed her cheek.

"I love you – you know that, right?" I whispered in her ear.

She nodded and squeezed me tightly. "I love you too, darling."

I turned then and headed towards the front door of my parents' house but froze when *his* voice spoke.

"I'll walk you."

I squeezed my eyes shut. "I'll be fine."

I felt him behind me.

"I wasn't asking for permission, Lane."

Oh, damn.

I licked my lips. "I can't be alone with you right now."

Kale rounded on me and got in my space, not caring that everyone in my family was behind us, watching with intent.

"Deal. With. It."

How? I wanted to scream. *How the hell can I deal with anything when it comes to you?*

I exhaled. "Kale—"

"Lane."

I set my jaw and looked up at him. "Why do you have to be so difficult?"

He shrugged. "It gets results when it comes to you."

What the hell does that mean? I frowned.

I shook my head. "You're being a complete arsehole right now for no reason. You realise that, don't you?"

His lip quirked. "I'm aware of it, yes."

I ignored the snickers from behind us.

Kale's eyes showed that he wasn't backing down on his offer to walk me to the inn, so I shook my head, pushed past him and opened the front door.

"Come on if you're bloody coming then," I grumbled.

I heard the smile in his voice when he said, "Yes, ma'am."

I could hear him chuckle under his breath as I exited my parents' house and walked briskly down the pathway and out of the garden. He was hot on my heels and jogged to my side, where he easily matched my strides because his legs were a lot longer than mine.

"You're going to give yourself a stitch if you don't slow down," he commented.

I grunted. "It's either walk fast or thump you for—"

"For what?" he said, cutting me off. "Making sure you get to the inn safely? You think I'm taking chances when it comes to your safety?"

I sighed and slowed my pace down.

"You're taking the decision away from me about whether you accompany me to the inn."

Kale laughed. "It's been years since I took anything from you. Let's call this a catch-up on due goods."

I rolled my eyes. "You're something else."

"Yeah," – he chuckled – "I know."

My lip twitched.

We walked in an oddly comfortable silence for a few minutes, and when we neared the inn, something clicked within me. Back at my parents' house, my instinct had been to run away because that's what I was good at, but now I got it – that nothing had ever been resolved by leaving them, by leaving Kale, by leaving York. For six years I'd felt exactly the same as the day I left York, if not worse. I'd allowed my fears to blind me. I'd let the "what ifs" win.

What if I couldn't handle seeing Kale happy with a family?

What if I came back home and fell into a deeper state of depression?

What if? What if? What if?

"What's wrong?" Kale asked, clearly wondering why I came to a sudden halt.

I looked at him and blinked. "I've just realised something."

He licked his lips. "What's that?"

"I don't want to stay at the inn; I don't want to be away from my family," I said, and shook my head clear as a cloud of confusion lifted from me. "I've been on my own for so long that I felt like I needed to get out of the house and away from them, but that's not what I need at all. I need their love and support, and I think they need mine too."

A smile broke out over Kale's face. "Then let's get your things from the inn, check you out and go back to your parents' house."

Could things really be that simple? I wondered.

I nodded. "Yeah . . . yeah, let's do that."

We walked to the Holiday Inn, and before we headed up to my room, I informed the lady behind the desk that I would be checking out. It was past checkout time, and I didn't know if she would charge me a fee, but she told me it was perfectly fine, so Kale and I headed up to my room.

He hovered near the door while I walked into the room and lifted my suitcase onto the bed.

"*That* is your case?" he asked.

I nodded. "I left the city in such a rush, I just grabbed what I could think of and practically ran to the airport."

Kale was silent for a moment and then he said, "I'm sorry you're going through this, Lane."

He was still the sweetest, most caring person, even with the hollowness within him now.

When I didn't reply, Kale told me to get any belongings of mine from the bathroom, and he would wrap up my hair appliances, laptop and chargers. I planned on doing exactly what he asked, but the silence between us screamed at me. I didn't understand why he was being so nice to me. I understood his being kind during my uncle's funeral, but why hadn't he so much as hinted at being mad? I'd left on such bad terms and hadn't been there for him when Kaden died.

I swallowed and said, "Why don't you hate me?"

He stopped rolling the wire around my hairdryer, and placed it on the desk.

"I'm not doing this in a hotel room, Lane."

I sucked up my fear.

"And you aren't leaving here until you answer my question," I countered. "I don't want to have our talk right now, I just want to know why you don't hate me when I have given you every reason to."

The muscles in Kale's back tightened before he turned to face me, his hazel eyes locked on mine. "I've never hated you, and I never will," he simply said with a shrug of his shoulders. "You mean more to me than any other living person on this planet, and if you think after not having you in my life for six years that I'm just going to ignore you and play some stupid game, then you've got another think coming, kid."

I felt my eye twitch. "I'm *not* a kid anymore, Kale."

The eyes I loved so much dropped to my chest, then lowered until he was leisurely drinking me in. It made me feel weak; one look from his whisky-coloured eyes and I was done in.

"I can see that," he mused.

I swallowed and felt in my heart it was the right moment for me to say what I had been carrying around since last night.

"Kale, I'm so sorry about Kaden."

He went silent for a long time.

"Who told you about him?" he asked after a deafening silence.

I looked down to my feet.

"My dad. I was at my Aunt Teresa's and Uncle Harry's grave the night before the funeral, and he showed me . . . showed me where Kaden was buried. I saw you and Drew at the plot yesterday after my uncle's funeral, and I wanted to go over to you, but I didn't want to interrupt you."

"Look at me," he said after a moment.

I exhaled before looking up at him, hating that his expression had changed to one of sadness.

"Thank you for your condolences about my son."

I squeezed my eyes shut. I didn't want to be formal . . . not about this.

"I saw his picture on his headstone . . . He was adorable," I whispered, my eyes still closed. "He had your nose and lips; he even had your tiny birthmark on his neck."

Kale's breathing picked up, and I hated myself.

I opened my eyes but kept them downcast. "I'm sorry, Kale. I'm making everything worse. I'll go and finish packing—"

I turned to walk into the bathroom, but Kale shot across the room and grabbed hold of my arm. "No."

I turned my head and looked at him. "No, what?"

He stared at me with his puppy-dog hazel eyes. "Don't leave. I'm not mad at you; I was just remembering my son. You would have loved him. He was the most perfect being I've ever laid my eyes upon, Lane. He was . . . everything."

A sad smile curved my lips. "I've no doubt. He was your son, Kale. He wouldn't be anything less than perfect."

"You think he looked like me?" he asked, surprised. "I think he looked more like his mum."

I smiled brightly. "Men always see the beauty of the mother in their children's faces. He was the perfect mix of you both. You and Drew created someone astonishing."

Kale's eyes bored into mine. "Thank you."

I nodded. "My pleasure."

"Do you want to see a video of him?" he suddenly asked, his eyes alive with pride. "I have loads of videos, and pictures of him too."

"Like you even have to ask," I beamed. "Gimme."

Kale smiled at me and quickly dug out his phone from his pocket. "I only have a few videos and pictures on my phone, but I've loads more backed up onto flash drives and storage sites that I can show you if you want."

A daddy protecting the physical memories of his pride and joy. It hurt me that memories were all he had.

"I've got time to see every second of him, Kale," I assured him.

He did something that shocked me then: he reached out and put his arms around me, and pulled my body into his. It wasn't a hug of sorrow and sadness like the ones he'd given me over the past couple of days; it was a hug of promise. A promise of what I didn't know, but whatever it was, I felt it in my bones.

"I've missed you so much," he said into my hair.

It took me a second, but I lifted my arms and put them around his body and squeezed him. "I've missed you too, Kale, more than you know."

We stayed like that, hugging one another until Kale stepped back and stared down at me. "I know this might sound stupid, but I can't believe you're really here," he said with a shake of his head. "When I first saw you on Friday in the parlour, I wanted to be the one to touch you instead of your dad, just so I could see if you were real. I've dreamt so many times about you being back here, I wasn't sure if I was just seeing things."

His admission stunned me.

"Kale," I whispered.

"It's dumb," he blurted out, flushing slightly. "I know—"

"It's not dumb," I interrupted. "When I'm in my apartment in New York and I'm falling asleep at night, I hear your voice in my head. Sometimes it keeps me awake because I miss you so much."

I wasn't embarrassed to admit something so private; it felt right to tell him.

Kale swallowed. "You're still my best friend."

"I know, pup, and you're mine."

He looked away from me. "I can't believe how our lives have turned out. Everything is so different from when we were kids."

I sighed. "Tell me about it. I've wished for a time machine many a time to go back and change some things."

Kale looked back at me then. "What do you want to change about your past?"

It was my turn to look away then. "You said you didn't want to have *that* conversation here."

He cleared his throat. "I don't . . . sorry, I guess I'm just using every second I can to talk to you, and I'm saying the first thing that pops into my head."

I looked back to him, reached out and pressed my hand against his arm. "I know this will be hard to believe considering I've bolted before, but I'm not running away. I'm going to stay right here in York and make things right with my family, and with you, before I even think about anything else. Harry would've wanted that."

He would have. He had told me enough times over the years.

"What about you?" Kale promptly asked. "What do *you* want?"

"A lot of things," I replied, my heart heavy.

He tapped away on the screen, then lifted his arm and turned it to face me. "This is Kaden."

I gasped and immediately snatched Kale's phone from his hand, which he found amusing. "Oh, my God," I gushed as I stared at the newborn baby in the picture. "He is beautiful, Kale. Just . . . oh, my God. He was perfect. I knew your baby would be perfect, but he really was."

Kale nodded. "He was everything."

"Little angel," I whispered and stroked my pinkie over the picture of Kaden's beautiful little face.

Kale watched me meeting his son, with joy.

"I'm sorry I wasn't here," I said softly as I scrolled through the pictures and watched videos of Kaden at various stages through his short life.

Kale was silent for a long time, but he eventually said, "You were with me; just not in person."

I looked up from his phone and found him watching me. He backed against the wall and had his hands jammed into the front pockets of his jeans. He seemed to be positioned that way a lot whenever he was in my presence. "Why didn't you want me here?" I asked, curious. "You told Harry not to tell me about Kaden's death. Why? I would have come home. I swear I would have."

He walked back over to me and kneeled before me, placing his hands on my thighs, sending my stomach into cartwheels. "I know you would have come home," he said firmly. "Trust me, Lane, God himself wouldn't have kept you away – and sweetheart, I *know* that."

I blinked. "Then why didn't you want me here?"

"Because," he began, "you would have dropped everything for me. I didn't want to hurt you again because I knew deep down I would have been using you to mask the pain over losing Kaden, and you didn't deserve that. I didn't want to take advantage of your feelings for me, and I probably would have to make myself feel better at the time."

I solemnly nodded. "I understand."

"Do you?" Kale prompted. "Do you understand how much it hurt that I needed you, but I couldn't have you?"

"Yeah, Kale, I understand exactly how much that hurts."

He stared at me, his eyes swimming with different emotions. "I'm so sorry for hurting you," he whispered.

I smiled and said lightly, "I hurt myself, Kale – you did nothing wrong."

"But I did," he pressed. "I could have gone after you and brought you home."

"That wouldn't have changed a thing, and you know it."

He frowned and stood up, moving back across the room, where he began to pack my suitcase again. He was silent for a minute or two, and then he said, "I know, but sometimes I wish it could have been that simple."

"Me too, pup." I swallowed. "Me too."

CHAPTER TWELVE

Seven years ago (nineteen years old)

Lane?" Lavender's voice called through my bedroom door. "Are you alive in there?"

I groaned into my pillow as her voice wreaked havoc on my throbbing head.

"Stop screaming at me," I rasped.

I heard Lavender's chuckle as the door creaked open. It had been fixed years ago, but the squeaking noise never left after my father kicked the door in.

"I suppose asking how you're feeling would be a stupid question?"

I grunted, my eyes still closed. "It'd be a *really* stupid question."

I heard Lavender giggle as she crossed my room, her feet pattering across the floorboards. I momentarily wondered what she was doing, so I lazily lifted my eyelids, but I quickly squeezed both eyes shut when blinding light wreaked turmoil on my retinas.

"Bloody hell, Lav," I whimpered, and pulling my pillow from behind my head, I plunged it over my face, coaxing my senses back into darkness.

"If it makes you feel any better," she snickered, "you pulled one of the hottest lads I have *ever* seen last night, even if he is a bit weird."

Though I didn't forgive her morning wake-up call, I had to agree with her conclusion about last night's escapades.

I smirked into my pillow. "He was a bit of all right, I guess."

I chose to overlook the part about him being weird, because I couldn't remember *that* much of what had happened to comment on it.

"You're so full of it." Lavender laughed as she climbed onto the end of my bed.

I smiled and slowly lifted my pillow from my face, wincing at the sunlight that filled my room. After a few moments of adjusting, my vision cleared and I stretched out my limbs.

"Did you wear protection?" Lavender asked, her tone very motherly.

I lifted my head and looked at her with raised eyebrows. "Don't I always?"

She dead-panned, "Your reply makes you sound like a slut."

I devilishly grinned. "I've slept with ten different lads over the last year and a half. I think that *does* make me a slut."

"Hardly," Lavender scoffed. "We both know you only get drunk and lost in the closest body because you feel rejected and hurt over Kale . . . *still*."

My chest ached and my stomach lurched at the mention of his name.

"Not now, Lav," I groaned, lying back down. "I'm too hung over for this conversation."

"Tough," my so-called friend chirped as she whacked both of my feet with her hands. "I'm getting fed up saying this to you, but here I go again. No matter how many people you have sex with, it will *never* erase your night with Kale. You can't replace the person you want for life with the person you want for a night."

I growled at Lavender.

"I'm nineteen and in university," I argued. "Wasn't it *you* who told me to play the field?"

"Play the field? Yes," Lavender agreed, then narrowed her eyes. "Fuck every man in sight? No."

I couldn't help but laugh.

"Give over. It's not funny and you know it's not," she grumbled. "You don't want to be *that* girl, do you? The woman who degrades herself with meaningless hook-ups and loses herself because she is sad?"

I hated when she got deep like this, especially when I felt like shit.

I blinked. "I'm not sad."

"Babe," – she frowned – "yeah, you are."

I looked up at my ceiling and grunted, "I knew I shouldn't have come home this weekend."

Lavender snorted. "We go to the same university and share an apartment. You can't escape me."

That was the sickening truth.

We both attended the University of York and lived in a student apartment close to campus. I studied English, and Lavender studied English in Education. After I got my Bachelor of Arts degree, I wanted to be a literary editor, and Lavender wanted to teach children. Her term was like mine, three years long, and she needed a Bachelor of Education degree to take the first step towards her dream job, and I was happy to take my steps right alongside her. We were in our first year of college life and loving every second of it.

I rolled my eyes at her. "Tell me something I *don't* know."

Lavender grinned. "Okay, Kale and your brothers are downstairs."

I shot upright and quickly reached for my head when the room spun slightly. I closed my eyes, counted to ten and when I was sure I wasn't going to vomit or pass out, I opened my eyes and narrowed them to slits.

"You lie!" I rumbled.

Lavender held up both of her hands in front of her chest. "I'm not – they're downstairs eating. They didn't know you would be home this weekend either."

This couldn't be happening.

"I can't deal with my brothers when I'm hung over, and I can't see Kale, knowing what I did last night with some stranger."

Lavender raised a brow. "Why? I thought you didn't care about him like that anymore."

I gritted my teeth. "I don't."

"Come downstairs and prove it then," she challenged.

I hated her.

"Fine," I bit out, and shoved my duvet covers from my body.

Lavender made a show of covering her eyes. "I'm your best friend and room-mate, but I don't need to see that bloody much of you."

I looked down and saw that my bedtime crop top revealed one of my boobs, and my underwear had given me a wedgie. I adjusted my top and underwear, then laughed as I got to my feet. I got clean underwear from my chest of drawers, a pair of comfortable trousers and a plain bra and black tank top. I went into the bathroom and had a quick cloth wash before putting the fresh clothes on.

I washed my face clear of last night's make-up, tied my hair up in a loose bun on top of my head and put my glasses on. I walked downstairs, letting Lavender lead the way.

"Did you wake her, Lavender?" Layton's voice called out as she walked into the kitchen.

"Barely," Lavender snorted. "I think she's still drunk."

"Great," Lochlan grumbled, making me grin.

I walked into the kitchen and cleared my throat.

"There she is," Kale announced, beaming as he stood up from his chair.

I groaned and placed a hand on my head.

"Not so loud," I moaned.

He grinned as he approached me.

"Sorry," he whispered before folding his arms around me, pulling me tightly against his warm body.

I missed hugging him, and I hated that.

"'S'okay," I murmured.

Kale released me and returned to his seat while my mother gave me her usual morning hug and kiss on the cheek. She did this often when I was younger, but now that I was away at college, she made sure to do it every time I was home and came down for breakfast.

"I heard you getting sick this morning," she said, frowning. "How much did you drink last night?"

Uh.

"Yeah, little sister," Lochlan asked, "how much *did* you drink last night?"

I looked over at his grinning face and glared before I turned back to our mother.

"Not much. I just did too much dancing, I guess, and it made me sick."

Lavender snorted, and my palm itched to smack her.

"What time did you get in?" my mother asked as I moved to the kitchen table and sat on the only seat available, between Lavender and Kale. "I didn't look at the clock when I heard you in the bathroom."

I blinked when I drew a blank at her question, then looked to Lavender, who laughed.

"I dropped her out of the taxi at half seven," she said, shaking her head.

That late? I cringed.

No wonder I had such a headache. I was nursing a hangover as well as running on next-to-zero sleep.

"Your brothers never came in that late," my mother commented.

I rolled my eyes. "My brothers were never as cool as me."

Said brothers snorted.

I grimaced as my mother set a plate of food in front of me. I touched my stomach and decided to wait a few minutes before I tried to eat anything; I didn't trust that I wouldn't get sick again.

"What did you do last night?" Kale asked, happily eating the breakfast that my mother made.

"*Who* did she do last night is more like it," Lavender mumbled as she reached for her orange juice.

It was loud enough for Kale and my bloody brothers to hear. Naturally, all three of their heads snapped in my direction, a scowl perfectly in place on all of their faces, which caused me to laugh.

"She's joking," I said, and kicked Lavender under the table.

Three pairs of eyes landed on Lavender, who winced in pain from my kick but forced an innocent, and convincing, smile. "Of *course* I'm joking."

My brothers stared at her for a few more seconds before they were appeased enough to go back to eating their breakfast. I blew out a relieved breath, then looked to Lavender and glared at her.

"Sorry," she mouthed, but she had a grin on her face.

The evil twit.

I looked away from her and flinched when I looked at Kale and found his eyes on me. He'd watched my interaction with Lavender, and I could see that he thought her smile and defence were pure bullshit. He looked a little mad, but he had no right to be. He wasn't my boyfriend, and over the past two years, he'd barely been my friend, so he shouldn't care who I had sex with.

I hardly ever saw him anymore, and we only texted and spoke over the phone every so often. I knew that was to be expected with him living in London, but deep down I knew that we had drifted apart because we'd had sex, and he was still either ashamed or embarrassed about that, or probably both.

"Whatever," I mumbled and looked down to my untouched plate of food.

I pushed it away, sighing.

"Not hungry?" Lavender asked as she dug into the food before her.

I shook my head. "My stomach is still unsettled."

"I *told* you not to shoot sambuca," she said, clucking her tongue.

I growled. "I'm aware you told me not to, thanks."

Lavender smirked, clearly enjoying her sick form of torturing me.

"I'm just glad you didn't shoot Jack Daniel's when it was offered to you," she mused. "I'd probably have to carry you home every time we go out, otherwise."

I swallowed. "I'll never drink Jack Daniel's."

"Why not?" Layton asked. "It's not that bad. It's Kale's favourite drink."

"Exactly," I mumbled.

The smell and taste of Jack Daniel's reminded me all too much of my night with Kale, and Kale in general, so I steered well clear of it.

I was glad when Lavender's phone rang, putting the focus on her. She fumbled with the phone as she pulled it from her pocket.

"I'm sorry – I thought it was on silent. Uh, Lane, you're calling me?"

My eyebrows rose in surprise. "I'm not. My phone is in my bag upstairs."

Lavender turned her phone to face me, and I saw my name flashing across the screen. Without thinking, I took Lavender's phone, answered it and put it to my ear.

"Hello?" I asked.

"Lavender?" a male voice asked.

"No," I said. "This is Lane. Who are you, and how did you get my phone?"

The voice chuckled. "You left it in my apartment last night."

I drew a blank.

"Your apartment?" I questioned. "I wasn't in any apartment last night—"

"Yes," Lavender whispered. "You were."

I frowned at her. "Are you sure?"

"Yeah," she murmured. "Me, you, Daven and the hot lad you pulled went back to his place after the club closed for more drinks."

I thought back to last night and began to remember what Lavender was talking about.

"Shit," I mumbled, and moved the phone away from my mouth. "What was his name again?"

Lavender glanced in Kale's direction and said, "Jensen."

I could practically feel the glares of the males around the table, and I sensed the disappointment radiate from my mother in waves. I ignored them all and focused on my conversation with the lad on the phone.

"Can I have my phone back, Jensen?" I asked, politely.

He chuckled, again. "Of course, I was calling Lavender from your phone, because I didn't have her number, so I could return it to you."

That was . . . nice of him.

"What's your address and I'll—"

"Just text your info to Lavender's phone, and I'll get it later."

When I feel human again.

"Okay, babe," Jensen chirped.

I cringed. "Okay, bye."

"Bye."

I hung up and handed Lavender back her phone. She was looking at everyone in the room, and then looked at me like she thought they would kill me, which made me laugh.

"You think this is funny?" Lochlan growled. "You were with a lad last night, drunk off your head, you don't remember it and now you're laughing?"

I closed my mouth and just shrugged because I didn't know what else to do.

"Those are the actions of a dirty tramp," he scowled. "What the hell is wrong with you?"

"Mate," Kale glared. "Don't fucking talk to her like that!"

I shared a surprised look with Lavender because Kale looked like he was ready to jump my brother for saying what he did to me, but my attention was forced away when Layton bellowed, "Lochlan!"

Lochlan looked at our brother. "You condone this shit?"

"No," Layton growled, "but I'm not about to call her out in front of company. Don't be an arsehole, and keep your comments to yourself. She isn't a damn kid anymore."

Regret washed over Lochlan's features when Layton, as usual, got through to him. He was too stubborn to apologise to me, though, and while I appreciated my brother's support, I was still humiliated. I excused myself from the table and hurried up to my room. I tried to close the door behind me, but Lavender was quick to follow and stopped me from doing so.

"I'm okay," I whispered.

She didn't say a word, only hugged me as my tears fell.

"He didn't mean it," she said, and squeezed me tightly. "That was just not something a brother would ever want to know. He was angry, that's all."

I nodded. I didn't blame Lochlan for saying horrible things about me. I thought them about myself too.

"It's not like he's lying, though," I murmured.

Lavender pulled back and scowled at me. "You aren't dirty, and you aren't a bloody tramp. Do you understand me?"

"But—"

"No 'buts'," she said, cutting me off, her tone harsh. "No one is perfect. You've made some mistakes, but that doesn't make you a bad person."

I swallowed. "Thanks, Lav."

"I'm serious," she pressed. "Hear me clearly."

I sighed. "I do, but the mistakes you mentioned, I don't want to make them anymore."

"Then we'll cut off the source to those mistakes," she said with a firm nod.

I raised my brows. "And what is the source?"

"Alcohol," she said.

I blinked. "Yeah, nothing good has ever come from me drinking."

"You use it to drown your sorrows, but we'll find a new way for you to do that." Lavender kissed my cheek and gave me another hug. "We'll figure this out together. I'm right here with you; I'll help you up if you fall."

"I love you, Lav," I said, and held her tightly.

Lavender gave me a squeeze in return. "I love you too, even if you are a pain in my arse."

I laughed, and just like that, she eased the tension out of the room. She was right: I'd eventually find a new way to deal with getting over Kale, and this time it wouldn't be something to just help the pain for a few hours.

~

"Do you want me to come with you?" Lavender asked as she dropped me outside of the apartment complex that I vaguely remembered being in last night.

I shook my head. "I'm just getting my phone and then going home. I'm not sticking around to chat. I'm too hung over for speaking at any volume."

Lavender snorted. "Okay, I'll call you after I get off work."

We both worked part-time at my nanny's café to help us avoid dipping into our student loans until absolutely necessary. We already owed our lives to debt, and we didn't need our casual spending to be a problem for us, so we got jobs to give us some extra cash.

"Love you," she shouted.

I winced at the volume of her shout and mumbled, "I love you too."

I closed the door to Lavender's car and waved as she drove off. When she was out of sight, I turned to face the apartment complex, and without a second thought, I walked up the steps and searched the names next to the apartment numbers. When I spotted Jensen's, I pressed the button next to his name. A few seconds passed before a tired voice spoke through the intercom.

"Hello?" the voice grumbled.

I cleared my throat. "Hi, it's, uh, Lane Edwards. I'm here to pick up my phone from Jensen."

"Yeah, I'm Jensen – come on up." The voice had suddenly perked up. "I'm on the third floor in apartment three-zero-three."

I had a bad feeling as soon as the door to the apartment building opened, but I shook it off and walked inside. I had to get my phone, and that meant I had to go inside to do that.

Suck it up, I told myself.

I took the stairs to the third floor instead of taking the elevator; it was really small and made a weird noise when the doors opened. I envisioned getting stuck in it, and that thought alone had me walking up the stairs of the building not five seconds later.

When I reached the third floor and found apartment three-zero-three, I knocked on the door and waited. The door opened pretty fast, and the lad to open it smiled at me like he was very happy to see me. I inwardly cringed because I knew why.

I had flashes of my body rolling around with his during the early hours of the morning, and it made me feel sick with myself.

"Hey," I said, forcing a smile. "Can I get my phone from you real quick? I'm late for work."

I wasn't on shift today, but Jensen didn't need to know that.

He nodded and gestured me into the apartment.

"Yeah, of course," he smiled. "Come on in. I'll go get it for you."

I hesitated for a second or two, but against my better judgement, I stepped into Jensen's apartment and allowed him to close his apartment door behind me.

"Do you want a cup of tea?" he asked as he walked down a hallway that I knew led to his bedroom.

I shuddered. "No, thank you."

I just want my phone so I can leave.

"Here we are," Jensen announced a minute or two later.

I looked in his direction and exhaled a relieved breath when I saw he did in fact have my phone in his hand. I reached for it when he neared me, but I frowned when he held it up in the air, out of my reach.

"I have to get to work, Jensen – give me my phone," I said flatly.

"Can you not give work a miss?" he asked, sounding hopeful.

Was he joking?

I snorted. "No, I can't, sorry."

His brows furrowed. "But you had fun last night."

I was sure I did, but it didn't mean I was sticking around for round two.

I felt my cheeks flush. "I can only remember bits of last night. I was pretty wasted."

He stepped towards me, a grin playing on his lips. "I'll happily remind you of what you can't remember."

Alarm bells began to sound in my head.

"No, thank you," I said, and looked towards the front door.

Jensen laughed at me like we were playing a game of cat and mouse, and I'd definitely got stuck with being the mouse.

"Come on," he teased. "I want to hear you cry out when I make you come again."

I swallowed bile, not liking hearing someone I barely knew talk about me in such a way.

"I'm leaving," I said firmly.

He moved fast, and before I could get to the door, he blocked it with his body.

"Jensen," I said in a warning tone, even though fear was seeping into my pores. "I would like to leave, please."

He raised an eyebrow and said, "Why are you being so shy? You weren't last night when my cock was in your mouth." He winked then. "Best head I've ever gotten, by the way."

My stomach lurched as I tried to push by him.

"Keep the fucking phone," I spat. "I'm leaving."

I ran for the front door, but Jensen roughly pushed me back by the shoulders. I fell backwards and landed on the floor with a loud thud. I yelped in pain, but fear drove my body to instantly put itself back up into a standing position. Jensen was on me before I got fully upright, though, and he brought me back down to the floor like a pile of tumbling bricks.

"Get off me!" I bellowed, and swung my hand, connecting my fist with his face.

Jensen's face jerked to the right, and it caused him to curse out loud.

"Fucking bitch!" he shouted, and fisted his hand in my hair, forcing my mouth to his. "Just give me one kiss," he growled, and pressed his lips to mine. "Just like last night."

I reacted with my teeth and bit him, causing him to tear his mouth from me and roar, "You fucking cunt!"

I saw the movement of his hand too late but felt the moment it connected with my face. I cried out, and white dots spotted my vision as pain erupted. I lifted my hands to protect my face because biting Jensen sent him into a frenzy of throwing punch after punch at me.

I tried to defend myself, but he landed every hit he threw.

The tang of metal attacked my taste buds, and blood filled my mouth.

I tried to scream, but all that sounded was a disgusting gurgle as blood gushed from my nose and ran down my throat. I noticed then that Jensen had stopped hitting me, but it was only because I heard him telling me to do something.

"Open your legs or I'll cut you," he growled.

Cut me?

I felt light-headed, and his voice sounded like it was coming from all directions. I looked up at him, and I could see him as plain as day, hovering over me, his breathing rapid as the sweat beaded his forehead. It confused me, because my face, arms and chest were throbbing like he was still hitting me.

The pain was immense.

"Please," I spluttered. "Please . . . don't."

He shook his head. "It's too fucking late for that now. All you had to do was kiss me! You made me hit you, you *made* me!"

I watched as he began to unbutton his jeans, and I saw he had an erection. It scared me enough to scream bloody murder.

"Help me!" I screamed as loud as I could and fought against Jensen when he tried to cover my mouth with his hands.

I heard a female voice shout outside of the apartment, and hope filled me.

"Help me!" I cried out once more. "Help!"

"Shut the fuck up!" Jensen bellowed, but he jolted with fright when a large bang sounded on the front door. Once, twice, then on the third bang a crunching noise filled the apartment as the door was kicked open.

I couldn't see who it was, but I heard a female voice scream when a body rushed at Jensen. I felt the weight of his body lift off me, and I was so thankful for it.

"Oh, my God," the female voice screamed. "Is she dead?"

I made a noise to show her I wasn't because I didn't want her to leave me. I felt the woman drop to her knees beside me and push my hair out of my face. She placed something against my forehead that caused me to cry out in pain when she applied pressure.

"I have to stop the bl-bleeding," she stuttered, then repeated, "Oh, my God" over and over again.

"Drew," a male voice snapped. "Call an ambulance right now."

Drew? I tried to open my eyes but found I couldn't.

"Drew?" I rasped.

She was silent for a second as a piece of fabric was rubbed over my face, and then I heard a strangled gasp.

"Lane?" she cried. "Oh, my God! Lane, what has he done to you?"

I wanted to answer her, but I couldn't seem to do a bloody thing with my vocal cords.

"You know her?" the male voice asked.

Drew whimpered, "She's my boyfriend's best friend."

I was his best friend when it suited him. At the thought of Kale, I forced my mouth to open and my voice to work.

"Don't," I rasped.

She grabbed hold of my hand and said, "Don't you close your eyes. Do you hear me, Lane?"

I heard her, but my body didn't want to listen to her. It wanted to sleep.

I blinked a couple of times. "Drew, don't tell Kale."

I didn't know why, but I didn't want him to know what had happened to me.

She ignored me and rattled off information to the person she was talking to on the phone. She got mad and told this person to stop asking so many questions and to send police and an ambulance because she thought I was dying.

I felt like I was floating, so I had no clue why she was thinking something so ridiculous.

Her tone changed then, and I heard her cry, "Kale!"

I don't know how, but I heard his raised and panicked voice through my cloud of light-headedness.

"I'm fine," she cried. "It's Lane. Oh, God, Kale, there is so much blood."

Kale was practically screaming through the receiver of the phone.

"Jensen Sanders," Drew cried. "He was beating her, but we got to her in time to stop him before – before anything *really* bad happened. She's hurt, and I can't stop her head from bleeding."

I exhaled a deep breath in defeat as Drew told Kale everything I didn't want her to. I closed my eyes because I was going to need my rest to face Kale and my family when it came time for me to explain what happened. I ignored Drew's pleas for me to stay awake and drifted into a surprisingly peaceful slumber.

~

When I awoke, there was so much activity and noise that it hurt my already throbbing head.

"Lane?" an unfamiliar voice called out.

I groaned.

Go away, a voice in my head hissed.

"Can you hear me, Lane?" There was a man talking to me, and he was really bloody loud.

"Stop shouting," I said, causing a huge sigh of relief to echo.

"Thank God," a familiar voice whispered.

I blinked my eyes, but only my left eye would open, which freaked me out.

"My eye," I gasped.

Why can't I open my right eye?

I felt gentle hands press against my shoulders, and with my good eye I squinted and saw there was a man with dark skin leaning over me. He smiled brightly at me, which surprisingly relaxed me.

"What is your name, sweetheart?" he asked, his voice deep and soothing to my ears.

I winced in pain but said, "Lane Edwards."

He nodded, still smiling. "What is your date of birth?"

I had to think about that for a second, but I remembered the correct date and said, "The fifth of February, nineteen-ninety."

"Last question," the smiling man said. "Who is our prime minister?"

I grimaced. "David Cameron, unfortunately."

"That's really good, Lane," he said, laughing.

"Where am I?" I asked, bewildered.

"My name is Jacob, and I'm your paramedic," Jacob said clearly. "You're in my ambulance, and we're en route to York Hospital to have you assessed and admitted by a doctor. You gave us a scare there for a minute, but you seem to be doing better. You're awake and talking, and that is what I like to see."

What the hell does that mean?

"What happened?" I asked.

Jacob frowned down at me. "Can you remember anything, Lane?"

I closed my eye and thought hard about what could have happened to me that had me in the back of an ambulance and on the way to the hospital. For a minute or two I drew a blank, and then, like the impact of a train, it all came flooding back.

"Jensen," I shouted. "He hurt me, he tried to – he tried to—"

"Shhh," Jacob soothed. "It's okay. He was arrested at the scene and cannot hurt you anymore. Hear me clearly, love, he cannot hurt you."

I continued to panic, and Jacob looked distraught.

"I have your friend Drew here," he said, and that got my attention.

"Drew?" I called out.

I heard movement, and then suddenly she was hovering over me.

"I'm here," she breathed.

Her eyes were red and bloodshot, obviously from crying.

I swallowed. "My family . . . Kale . . ."

"They'll meet us at the hospital."

I closed my eyes and swallowed.

"I had to call them, Lane," Drew sniffled. "You have to understand how scary it was seeing you like that . . . like this."

I tried to nod, but the neck brace around my neck and shoulders prevented that.

"I know," I acknowledged. "Thanks, Drew. You . . . you saved me."

Her eyes glazed over. "I heard you scream. I didn't know it was you, but I knew whoever was screaming was in trouble."

Thank God she heard me when she did.

"Why were you in that building?" I asked.

"My friend Carey lives on the third floor," she explained. "I was leaving her apartment when I heard screaming coming from Jensen's, so I called for Jack, Carey's boyfriend, and he kicked the door open."

My throat clogged up with emotion, so I blinked in acknowledgement that I'd heard her.

"Drew," Jacob said, "can you retake your seat, please?"

Drew disappeared, and I yelped when the ambulance ride got bumpy.

"Sorry, Lane," Jacob called out. "We're just pulling into the emergency bay now. We'll have you in the hospital in a minute or two."

I winced and cried in pain when the stretcher I was on was lifted out of the ambulance and then wheeled into the hospital. I stared up at the ceiling, watching light after light pass by. It got a little hard to stay awake then, so I closed my eyes to rest them for a few seconds.

"Room four with her, please," a female voice said to Jacob, who was pushing me in the direction of the room.

"This is where I take my leave, Lane," Jacob said when he leaned back over me. "You hang in there, love, okay?"

"I will," I said. "Thank you."

Jacob left to go outside to talk to the nurse he was leaving in charge of me, so Drew came to my side.

"Drew?" I heard my mother shout, her voice clearly distressed.

Drew exhaled a huge breath of relief and rushed outside into the hallway. I closed my eyes as she said, "She's okay. She's awake and talking."

"Lane," I heard my mother cry, closer this time, and then a shadow came over me. "Oh, my baby."

I felt her hands on me, and it upset her even more that I winced in pain when she pressed too hard.

"Oh, Christ." Lochlan's voice was strangled. *"Lane."*

"Lochlan," my father's voice shouted. "What room do they have her – Lane!"

"No," Lochlan shouted. "You don't want to see her like this."

"Get the hell out of my way!" my father bellowed, and I heard some grunting, then a male cry.

"Baby," my father whimpered. "Oh, my girl."

Wake up!

I forced my left eye open, and when my vision adjusted, my parents' distraught faces came into view.

"I'm . . . okay," I rasped.

This caused both of them to cry with what I think was relief.

"I'm okay," I repeated, louder.

My mother leaned down and kissed every part of my face that she could, and I let her, even though it hurt like hell.

"My eye," I said to her. "I can't open it."

Tears were streaming down her cheeks.

"It's swollen shut," she cried.

It is?

"Better than losing it," I chuckled, trying to stop her tears, but I winced in pain when laughing made my chest hurt. "It hurts," I said to my mother, tears welling in my eyes.

She called for a doctor, or anyone, to come in and help me then. I closed my eyes because the room I was in was bright, and my eyelids were very heavy.

"Lane," a new male voice called out. "Lane, can you hear me?"

I was really tired, and I groaned in response to the voice.

"Lane, can you open your eyes for me?" the man asked.

I opened my left eye, but only for a second before it fell shut again.

"Is she okay?" my father's voice asked. "Why can't she stay awake?"

"I've only got partials on what happened – we're still gathering information – but she has quite clearly received a lot of brute blunt-force trauma to her head. I'm hoping it is mostly cosmetic and her brain wasn't affected. We will run an MRI and other tests after she is cleaned up and her wounds are stitched closed."

I need stitches? I wanted to ask the question on my mind, but I could only groan instead.

"I know you're hurting, Lane," the man, who I guessed to be my doctor, said. "A nurse will set up an IV line and administer morphine to help get you somewhat comfortable."

That sounded brilliant.

I heard the different voices of my family as they spoke to me and asked the doctor questions, but one voice stuck out, one pretty loud voice.

"Lochlan?" I heard Kale call.

"She's down here," Lochlan shouted.

"Quiet, please," a voice chastised.

"I got here as fast as I could – oh, my God," Kale breathed. "Lane. Oh, sweetheart."

I'm here, I thought.

"I'm going to fucking kill the prick," he growled.

"Drew," my father said. "What happened?"

My brain chose that moment to fade into darkness, and I was thankful for it because listening to Drew explain what she saw wasn't something I wanted to hear. Experiencing it was more than enough.

~

Four days later, I was still in hospital, but I was awake and fully alert to my surroundings. The first three days after I was brought to hospital, I was in the ICU because I didn't regain consciousness after I conked out in the emergency room. My doctor assured my family it was due to some very minor swelling on my brain and that the rest would only do my body good as it began the process of healing. The MRI scan and other tests the doctors ran came back clear, which was good news. All of my injuries were simple flesh wounds and a couple of bruised ribs – which I thought was the sorest thing I had ever experienced. It hurt to breathe.

My right eye was still swollen shut, and I had a pretty nasty cut through my right eyebrow that took six stitches to close, and one on my left cheekbone that needed three stitches. All in all, I was expected to make a full recovery, with only a small scar or two to show for it. So the doctor said anyway. But he was wrong. What Jensen had done ran deeper than physical scars. What he'd done would stay with me for life.

"Lane?"

I looked to my nanny when she called my name.

"Hmm?" I murmured.

She frowned at me. "I asked if you were okay, sweetheart?"

"I'm okay, Nanny," I assured her, then looked to the doorway as my uncle suddenly barrelled into the room, looking the worse for wear. This was the first time I had seen him in three weeks. He'd been on a business trip in Asia and wasn't due home for another week at the earliest.

He took one look at me, and his face turned red.

"I'll kill him," he snarled.

My brothers, father and Kale, who were in the room with me, my mother and my nanny, grunted in agreement. I had never seen my uncle look so angry before, so I raised my eyebrows at him and just stared. He quickly came over to my side and let out a puff of breath at what he was seeing.

"Darlin'." He swallowed.

I winked with my good eye. "I'm okay; you should see the other guy."

My uncle appreciated my jab at humour, and he chuckled, but nobody else in the room did. They hadn't cracked so much as a smile since I'd woken up this morning. It was starting to grate on my nerves. I knew what had happened to me was very serious, and I definitely knew it wasn't a laughing matter, but I was okay. I was going to recover from my injuries, and the piece of scum who caused them in the first place was in police custody.

Jacob was right when he said Jensen couldn't hurt me anymore.

"Have you spoken to the police?" my uncle asked after he kissed my forehead.

I nodded. "They were here a few hours ago. They came after I woke up."

Drew and her friend Jack had already given their eyewitness report of what they'd encountered a few days ago in Jensen's apartment. Early in the afternoon I gave my statement. It was embarrassing and shameful, but I had to tell them how I knew Jensen in the first place. My father feared Jensen's defence would play on that and somehow get him off the hook, but the officers assured us that he was tied up by the balls with the eyewitness reports and the condition I was found in.

They informed us that he was being charged with assault, attempted rape and attempted murder. He was refused bail and wouldn't even get a formal trial because the evidence against him was too great – that and the fact that he was caught red-handed. Drew's friend Jack had subdued Jensen until the police arrived and they took over. The most Jensen would see of a courtroom was the day he'd be taken for sentencing.

He couldn't deny what he did – well, he *could*, but that wouldn't help him. He would get locked up for what he did to me, and the sentence wouldn't be light.

I was very happy about that.

My father filled my uncle in on what happened with the police, and Uncle Harry was delighted that justice would come to Jensen, though he was gutted he wouldn't have a chance to break every limb on his body before he was sent to prison – his words, not mine.

"How was your trip?" I asked, changing the topic to something that didn't turn everyone's stomach.

My uncle smiled. "It was great, but it will be my last. I'm getting too old for those long-haul flights."

I nodded in agreement. "I don't know how you've done so much travelling. I can barely sit still long enough to watch a television show."

That made the room laugh and relieved me greatly. Their sense of humour hadn't died off after all!

"Have you had many visitors?" my uncle asked as he sat next to me.

I nodded. "Kale's parents came to see me today. So did Lavender and her boyfriend, Daven. She blames herself for what happened because she dropped me off at his apartment, but I told her that was stupid. If she'd come in with me, God only knows what he would have done to both of us."

The males in the room seethed in anger. I adjusted my position on the bed and groaned as pain spread down the left side of my ribcage.

"Shit, shit, shit," I whimpered.

My mother and nanny were on their feet and on either side of me, helping me lie back. Their faces twisted with emotion when tears fell from my eyes. I tried my hardest not to cry, but the pain was too powerful.

"Mum," I whimpered.

She leaned over and kissed me. "I'll press your morphine button, and it will give you instant relief, okay?"

Yes.

"Yeah, do that," I hissed in pain.

My mother pressed the button the nurse had shown her how to use earlier, and not ten seconds later the pain began to seep away, replaced by bliss.

"You should try some of this medicine, Uncle Harry," I slurred as my good eye grew heavy. "It'd stop you complaining about your back pain all the time."

"Cheeky mare," my uncle said, laughing.

My lip quirked at the laughter of my family and then, without warning, I fell into a deeply medicated sleep that felt really bloody good.

Morphine was the shit.

It had been six weeks since Jensen had attacked me and put me in the hospital, and three weeks since he had been tried and sentenced to life in prison without the possibility of parole.

I was more than ready to put Jensen and the attack behind me. I was so overtired of hearing people talk about it and reading about it in the papers.

I wouldn't give him the power to hold fear over me. For the first couple of weeks after I got out of the hospital, I was scared to be on my own, scared to leave my house, scared to do anything because of him, but not anymore. I would never let myself be controlled by him. Ever.

It was why, when my Uncle Harry's birthday came around and my mother suggested we throw him a small house party, I jumped at the opportunity. I wouldn't be drinking, but I would be around family, friends and talking, and people having fun.

We held the party on a Friday night, and as predicted, it went off without a hitch, and I felt alive for the first time in weeks. Since my face and body had healed from the damage Jensen inflicted on me, no one – apart from my parents – brought it up, and I was chuffed about it.

I was having a ball until Kale showed up, Drew on his arm.

I was doing well – kind of – when it came to getting over him, but it still hurt seeing him with Drew.

They looked really happy together.

"Lane!" Kale smiled when he spotted me in the parlour.

I smiled too and got up to hug him, and then I hugged Drew in greeting because it was the polite thing to do.

"How are you?" she asked.

I nodded. "Fine, and you?"

She beamed. "I'm better than ever."

She shared a secret look with Kale and grinned at him, while he seemed uncomfortable as he kept flicking his eyes in my direction. He cleared his throat and called out to Lochlan when he spotted him. He looked relieved that he didn't have to stand with Drew and me any longer.

I excused myself and moved to the back of the room, my mood turning sour. I wished I had Lavender to hang out with, but she had left the party half an hour ago so she could get home to Daven, who lived with her in our old apartment. After the attack, I'd moved home and considered dropping out of university.

I didn't want everyone on campus staring at me, whispering behind my back or, worst of all, pitying me. My father and uncle met with the chancellor of my university, and I was granted permission to attend class online, which meant I could finish my remaining two years and get my degree. I must have hugged my father and uncle every time I saw them for a week straight after I got the good news.

"Lane?"

I turned when my uncle's voice called me.

I walked over to him and smiled. "Yes, birthday boy?"

He snorted. "You don't look very happy – is everything okay?"

I didn't want to put a downer on his night, so I smiled and said, "It is, but I'm just really tired. I don't think I'm able to keep up with you old-timers."

My uncle cracked up before getting pulled into another conversation, which I was thankful for.

I turned and my eyes, as usual, found Kale. He had his arms around Drew, and his head was tipped back as he laughed. I didn't want to look at them so I headed up to my room, where I changed into pyjamas. I went into the bathroom to clean my face, and tied my hair up in a bun.

When I exited the bathroom, I came face-to-face with Drew Summers.

"I want to talk to you," she said firmly.

Uh.

"Can it wait?" I asked. "I was just about to go to sleep."

"It can't wait," she said. "I want to talk to you now."

I gestured her into my bedroom. I closed the door behind me and folded my arms across my chest, standing across from her.

"What's up?" I asked.

"You hate me," she said confidently.

I blinked. "I beg your pardon?"

She grunted. "You. Hate. Me. I know you do."

I scratched the healed cut above my eyebrow. "I don't understand what is happening here."

"I saw you downstairs, watching Kale with me, and you looked angry."

I was more sad than angry, but I tried to downplay it and said, "I'm just tired—"

"Don't lie," she said, cutting me off. "You hate me. Admit it."

She wants to have this talk? my mind hissed. *Fine.*

"I don't hate you," I grumbled, "but I don't like you either."

That was a white lie. I did kind of hate her.

"Why?" she pressed. "I've never done anything to you."

She was right; she hadn't.

"I know you haven't, Drew," I sighed.

"Then why don't you like me?" she asked. "Is it because I rang Kale after you were attacked?"

"No, I know you were trying to help that day, Drew," I sighed. "But part of me wishes you hadn't told him."

"Why not?" Drew asked, exasperated.

"I didn't want Kale, or anyone else, to look at or treat me differently, but now they do. Everyone treats me like a china doll."

It pissed me off.

Drew frowned and folded her arms across her chest. "Would you rather Jensen had gotten away with it? He didn't get to rape you, but what about the next girl who might not have been so lucky?"

The lump that formed in my throat kept me from replying.

"Once you have time to think on it, you'll see having Jensen sent to prison was the right thing."

"I *know* it was the right thing to do, and I'm over it," I said. "You were right to do what you did."

She frowned. "Then why do you hate me? Is it because of Kale?"

She must have read something in my expression because her face turned murderous.

"I *knew* it!" she snapped. "I knew you liked him. I have always had a suspicion, but Kale assured me you were just best friends."

"We *are* just best friends," I confirmed.

Drew's gaze didn't stray from mine. "But you want to be more?"

I rubbed my suddenly throbbing temples. "What does it matter? He's dating you, not me. *You.*"

Her jaw set. "I don't want you around him anymore. I refuse to let you ruin us."

I blinked. "You've *got* to be fucking joking me. I'm not going to do anything to ruin your relationship. If that were the case, I'd have done it years ago. I'm not *that* fucking bitter."

"Are you sure about that?" she questioned, her eyebrows raised.

I scowled. "Yeah, I'm sure."

"Well, I'm not sure," she stated. "I don't trust you around him."

Oh, for God's sake.

"You're the human version of Monday morning in my everyday life – I hope you know that."

Drew blinked at me. "Flat out saying you hate me would have been less bloody hurtful."

I hated that she was so nice. This was the first time she had ever been angry with me, and even then she wasn't being *half* as mad as I would be if our roles were reversed.

"Sorry," I said with a roll of my eyes.

I knew I was being horrible, but I just couldn't help it. My feelings for Drew were petty, childish and completely out of order because she was quite possibly the nicest human being on the planet, but it was what it was.

She'd saved my life; any good person would be extremely nice to her, but I was a miserable twit who couldn't get past her being Kale's girlfriend.

I was acting bitter and plain pathetic, and knowing that only made me feel even worse.

"Stay away from Kale, do you hear me, Lane?" Drew said, the venom in her voice not going amiss.

I reared back. "Or what?"

"You don't want to know what I'll do," she said through gritted teeth.

Well, shit, Drew actually looked like she was going to kick my arse if I gave her reason to.

"Whatever," I said, not really confident that she wouldn't come at me if I said something to challenge her.

She glared at me hard before she turned and stormed out of my room, pulling my door closed behind her. I shook my head clear and turned off my light, then climbed into bed. I lay staring up at the stickers on my ceiling for an unknown amount of time. Eventually, I heard more voices join the party downstairs, and they were loud as hell.

"Bloody hell," I groaned to myself, and turned on my side, putting my pillow over my head.

My night certainly didn't turn out how I wanted it to, I silently grumbled.

I must have fallen asleep, because I awoke to a clicking noise that startled me awake. I sat upright on my bed and rubbed the sleep from my eyes. I squinted into the darkness but almost jumped out of my skin at a loud clank that sounded against my window.

I tiptoed over to my bedroom window and looked out to find someone in our front garden, directly under my window. For a few seconds, I got really scared, but then I squinted and realised who the person was.

I opened my window and hissed, "Kale, what are you doing?"

He put his hands up to his mouth and said, "I want to talk to youuuu."

He was drunk.

"Damn it, Kale," I said in a low growl. "It's the middle of the night."

"It'll take two seconds," he said, and held up five fingers.

My God.

I shook my head. "Wait there. I'll be right down."

I closed my window and carefully crept out of my bedroom and down the stairs, where I turned off the house alarm before unlocking the front door. I shivered and carefully walked out to the front garden in my bare feet.

"I'm going to kill you for this," I warned Kale in a harsh whisper as I came to a stop in front of him.

I rubbed my hands up and down my bare arms to generate some heat.

"Okay," Kale chuckled. "You're mad, but this is very important."

I'm sure it is.

I sighed. "So talk."

He opened his mouth to do just that, but his gaze flicked to my eyebrow, then to my left cheek at the purple scars that marred my face. I knew what he was thinking, and it annoyed the hell out of me.

"I'm. Fine," I said through gritted teeth. "Please *stop* treating me like a victim. He didn't rape me. He just smacked me around."

"Lane," he murmured.

"He didn't rape me, Kale," I said, trying my best to be strong. "He tried to, but I fought. I promise I did."

His arms came around me.

"I know you did, Laney Baby," Kale whispered in my ear. "You did good, babe. So bloody good."

I wrapped my arms around his waist. "I'm sorry. I should have brought you or one of my brothers with me—"

"Don't do that." Kale cut me off and pulled back out of the hug, keeping me at arm's reach as he looked at me through his bloodshot eyes. "Don't place the blame on yourself. Jensen is a piece of shit who wanted to hurt you and did, and that's not on you. It's on him."

He sounded furious.

I nodded. "I know, but I still feel like I should have known better."

"Repeat in that beautiful head of yours that you are *not*, and will *never* be, responsible for someone else's actions. People make their own decisions, no matter what the situation. If they do something, it's because they *choose* to do it. This. Is. Not. Your. Fault."

I pressed my face into the crook of his neck.

"I've got you, Lane," he breathed into my hair. "I've got you."

I smelled whisky on him, and it was strong. The scent caused my senses to come alive and my body to awaken for the first time in weeks.

"You shouldn't be here," I mumbled, trying to force away the urge to let the scent consume me. "Drew will kill me."

He grunted. "She told me what she said to you, and you better ignore her. She won't touch you. She was just in a bad mood."

Uh-huh.

"Have you had much to drink?" I asked, pulling back from him.

He nodded, his eyes bloodshot. "To celebrate your uncle's birthday I had some Jack – or a lot of Jack."

I needed him to leave. "Everyone is asleep, so maybe you should go on home—"

"I love you," he interrupted.

I blinked. "Excuse me?"

"I said," he chuckled, "I *love* you. I love you so much."

"Stop it." I frowned at him. "You are *drunk*. You say and do stuff you don't mean when you're drunk."

"No, I don't," he slurred.

"Yeah," I argued. "You do."

And I have the broken heart to prove it.

"I've been thinking a lot tonight," he said, smiling.

"You thinking?" I questioned. "That's always a dangerous thing."

Kale snorted. "Ha ha ha."

I shook my head at him, smiling.

"Kale, go home. You need to go to sleep."

"No," he stated. "What I need to do is talk to you."

I couldn't deal with him when he was like this. "Okay, talk really quick because I don't want my parents to come down here and see you drunk in the front garden."

Kale lifted his finger to his mouth and whispered, "I'll be quiet."

Why does he have to be so bloody adorable?

I bit down on my lower lip. "Okay, talk, but still be quiet."

"Okay," he exhaled, then shook his head like he was trying to stay awake, "what I wanted to talk to you was about us having sex—"

"Whoa, Kale." I cut him off, feeling my face flush with heat. "It's best if we don't speak about that, okay?"

It was less gut-wrenching not to voice it aloud. Just thinking about it hurt enough.

"Why not?" he asked, tilting his head and almost falling in the same direction, until I grabbed hold of him.

He was wasted.

I grunted in annoyance. "Just because."

"Okay." He frowned, blinking very slowly. "I won't talk about it, but I want to talk about what it meant—"

"Kale," I groaned. "Please, I can't do this with you. I really can't."

"Will you let me finish?" He scowled, swaying on his feet.

I rolled my eyes and waved him on.

"I'm trying to tell you that" – *hiccup* – "I've thought hard" – *hiccup* – "and long, and I want you to" – *hiccup* – "be with me, please and thank you." He thought about what he'd just said and then laughed at himself, hard.

I stared at him in disbelief. "What, Kale?"

"I love you a lot," he slurred. "Be with me."

"Do you *hear* yourself?" I snapped, anger surging through my veins.

He shoved his finger in my face and said, "No, but I know what you're saying, or what I'm saying."

He was hurting my head.

"Love you." He beamed. "Be mine."

"No," I snapped, and pushed his hand away. "No, you don't love me – you love *Drew*."

Pain and awareness flashed across his face.

"I love both of you."

I laughed humourlessly. "Aren't you lucky having two girls on the go?"

Kale scowled at me, stumbling to the left. "Stop that. Don't be hurtful."

"You're being hurtful!" I retorted. "This is evil what you're doing, I'm *not* doing this with you."

"I love you," he repeated as if I'd never spoken. "Be with me."

He'll wake up sober tomorrow and regret saying any of this, just like he did after we had sex.

I swallowed. "No, Kale."

He stared at me, his eyes inflamed. "No?"

I nodded. "No."

He swallowed, and I saw the muscle in his jaw roll back and forth.

"Okay," he said, his voice low. "Okay."

I was doing this to protect my own heart, and to protect him from having to talk his way out of this tomorrow morning, but it didn't make saying what I did any easier.

"We're best friends," I whispered. "I'm like your sister."

That word was like vinegar in my mouth.

Kale almost glared at me as he nodded. "Okay." He stretched the word out.

I stepped towards him, but he stumbled away from me.

"I'm going to my parents' house," he said. "See you later, Lane."

He turned and walked away from me then, and with every step he took, my legs threatened to run after him, but I forced myself to turn around and go back into my parents' house. I halted at the top of the stairs and stared at my bedroom door.

I didn't want to sleep on my own – not tonight. Not after what had just happened. Without much thought, I walked towards my parents' room and opened the door.

"Mum?" I whispered.

She shot upright in her bed. "I'm awake – are you okay?"

I hesitated in speaking for a moment and then shook my head.

"Can I sleep with you?" I whispered.

"I'll go into your room," my father's voice said as he got out of bed. "Get in beside your mother, darling."

He stood out of my way as I walked around to his side of the bed and crawled into it and wrapped my arms around my mother. I hated what I was doing to them. I had slept with my mother a lot after I came home from the hospital, because I was having nightmares, and I knew they both had trouble sleeping because they were so worried about me.

"I feel broken," I muttered against my mother's chest.

"It will be okay, baby," she whispered, and kissed my head. "I promise."

My father left the room, and I heard a loud bang seconds later as if he'd hit something.

"Do you want to talk to me, or to someone, about what happened?" she asked.

I blinked in the darkness.

She thought I was in her arms because of what Jensen had tried to do to me, but I wasn't. I was still in a state of shock over that, but I felt like the only damage from that night was the small physical marks he left, and once they were gone, he had no hold over me. He'd scared me straight; I would never again behave the way I did to get myself into a situation like that.

I swore it to myself.

What my mother didn't know was that it was the person she considered a son who had me so torn up and vulnerable. She didn't know that he was the reason I used to drink and got lost in different lads. She didn't know I gave him my virginity and that he didn't remember a single thing about it. She didn't know I had been in love with him since I was ten years old, and she definitely didn't know I'd give up everything to be his.

My mother didn't know she had raised a complete idiot, and she wouldn't if I had anything do with it. I was going to change. *Everything* was going to change.

CHAPTER THIRTEEN

Day four in York

"Lane, are you ready?"

I jumped with fright when Layton's voice called my name.

"Sorry," he said, laughing from behind me. "Didn't mean to scare you."

I got up from the kitchen table and turned to face him.

"You didn't scare me."

My brother grinned. "Aye, that's why you almost jumped out of your skin then?"

I scrunched up my nose, making him laugh.

"Are we good to go?" I asked.

He nodded. "Nanny is just using the loo, and then we're heading out."

I nodded. "Come in and close the door then; I want to speak to you."

Layton eyed me warily. "About what?"

I didn't exactly know. I just knew I needed to speak to him to make sure we were okay. I was cool with my nanny, Lochlan, my parents, and that left Layton and Kale for me to square away any spot of bother that lingered.

"Sit down, you big girl's blouse, and I'll tell you," I chuckled.

Layton didn't appreciate the teasing, but he did as I asked and sat across from me at the kitchen table.

"You're okay, aren't you?" he asked, his concern for me obvious.

His gaze lingered on my right eyebrow, then my left cheek, a little longer than necessary, and for a split second, I wondered if he thought back to that time that I'd received the faint scars. I hoped not, because I didn't, and I didn't want him to either.

I smiled. "Yeah, I just want to make sure we're okay."

Layton raised his eyebrows. "Why wouldn't we be?"

"Because the only times we have spoken over the last few years were when I called at Christmas and on your and Lochlan's birthday. I don't blame you if you hate me."

"Hold the phone," he said abruptly. "I have never, and will never, hate you, Lane. You're my baby sister: I love you to death."

My throat got tight with emotion. "I guess . . . I guess I just figured you would feel some sort of way towards me because things ended badly with us before I left, and we never spoke."

"I'm just as much to blame for us not speaking." Layton sighed. "I just hate the thought of you living so far away. Something awful happened to you just down the road, Lane. What if something bad happened to you over in America, and you were without us? I didn't accept or agree with your decision and just closed myself off. I hated your decision, not you."

"I'm sorry, Lay. It was really shitty of me to move so far away. I just didn't think about anything like that at the time."

He nodded. "I know, but I thought about it a lot. So did Dad, Lochlan, Kale and even Uncle Harry, God rest him."

I swallowed. "I'm so sorry."

Layton leaned forward. "I know you still have your troubles with Kale, but will you not consider moving home, or somewhere close by?"

The fact that I was definitely considering it spoke volumes about what I had to do.

I nervously nodded to my brother. "It's become more and more clear that living in New York isn't helping me. It's not fixing me, but maybe coming home will in some way."

Layton's eyes lit up. "You have made me so bloody happy, sis."

I laughed as he pulled me into a standing hug and almost squeezed the breath straight out of me. "It's not decided yet, but it's an option. Just keep this between us for now. I have to figure out a lot of stuff in my head."

My brother pulled back and winked. "You got it."

I relaxed. "I had a talk like this with Lochlan, and he sprung upon me that he was in a relationship with Ally Day. Are you going to tell me you're dating Anna O'Leary?"

Layton laughed merrily. "No, I'm not dating anyone, but I'm trying my luck with Samantha Wright. You met her, kind of, when you came home on Friday. I like her, and we went on a date just before Uncle Harry died. I'm hoping we can go out on another one soon. She's pretty great."

I smiled. "I'm happy for you, Lay. I'll have to get to know her."

"You will," he said, and smiled.

I hugged him again, bursting with joy that things were really okay between us.

"Layton? Lane?" Lochlan called out. "Come on, we're leaving."

We were heading to the family solicitor's office to hear my uncle's will. We hadn't been to my uncle's house yet to start organising it and clearing things out, and we couldn't until we heard the will. He might have wanted his belongings donated someplace or items sold and the money donated to charity. Our hands were tied until we heard what he wanted for the future of his possessions.

I drove with Lochlan and Layton into town, and we got there the same time as our parents and nanny. We were expected and didn't have to hang around the waiting room, so we all filed into the solicitor's main office. My brothers and father gave us women the chairs, and they sat on the windowsill behind us.

"Nice to see you again, Jeffery," my father said to the solicitor when he entered the office.

We each shook hands and introduced ourselves. He already knew everyone but me.

"Thank you all for coming. In light of recent events, I want to offer my deepest condolences to your family. Harry . . . he was more than a client; he was a friend, and I'll miss him greatly. I hope that after today you can find a sense of peace."

Jeffery looked directly at me when he finished speaking, and I couldn't respond, so my nanny did in my place.

"Thank you, Mr Twomey," she said, smiling warmly. "We're still in a state of shock and are somewhat beside ourselves, but we greatly appreciate your kind words."

Jeffery bowed his head and smiled before he moved around his desk and seated himself behind it. He lifted up a thin brown folder that had my uncle's name stamped onto the cover in thick black ink.

"Harry's will is very simple," he began. "The simplest will I have ever drawn up for a client."

I blinked. "That's good, right? Less paperwork for us to comb through."

Jeffery chuckled. "I believe he used similar words when we were in talks for his will."

I grinned. "That's my Uncle Harry for you."

Jeffery opened the folder. "I know it was a trip to come into town to see me, but this will be a very quick meeting. The contents of the will for Mr Harry Larson are as follows: his house and all of his belongings, everything in his possession and name, has been left to Miss Lane Edwards, his niece."

He rattled off my address and other legally accurate information, but my mind stopped working after he said my name. I looked up at Jeffery, my eyebrows raised in shock. "I'm sorry; I think I misheard you. Can you repeat that, please?"

Jeffery clasped his hands together. "Everything that Harry owned has been left in your name, Lane. His money, his house, his entire estate, but only on one condition."

I blinked my eyes and tried to process the information.

"What is the condition?" I questioned.

Jeffery smiled. "He wrote it in a letter addressed to you."

I nodded because I didn't know what else to do or say.

"It is also side-noted in the terms that if any family member contests the will, or Lane fails to keep to the condition, the entire contents of the will would be liquidated for a cash sum and then donated to the fan club of the Liverpool Football Club."

Everyone in the room gasped in horror.

We were a family that bled red for Manchester United, and any mention of Liverpool Football Club was banned in our house. It was punishable by being disowned, or perhaps even death.

Uncle Harry wasn't messing around.

"The evil bastard!" Nanny suddenly bellowed, breaking the veil of silence that fell upon the room.

I looked at my nanny and saw that steam was practically pouring from her ears. Her hands were clenched into fists, and her lip curled in anger. I stared at her for a few more moments, then laughed. I covered my mouth with my hands and cackled until she whacked my arm.

"This isn't funny!" she snapped. "What did he think he was playin' at? He should burn in hell for even thinkin' of doin' such a thing for that *disgrace* of a club."

That was it. My parents and my brothers burst into uncontrollable laughter, and damn it if it didn't feel good to laugh, and to laugh with them.

"He was ensuring his condition was met." Jeffery smiled, looking like he could barely contain his own laughter. "That's all."

My uncle was a bloody gem.

I shook my head, smiling. "I'm not even surprised that he's done something like this."

"He was very careful when we drew it up." Jeffery nodded, grinning. "He got a kick out of the threat when he thought of your reactions."

My mother grumbled to herself, "The bloody git."

I chuckled, and so did my brothers.

"We can discuss things in detail before you choose whether or not to abide by the condition, Lane," Jeffery said. "It is a little complex as Harry said I would have to take your word and trust you when you reply to my question."

I didn't even have to think about the next words that left my mouth. "I'll abide by the condition. My uncle was a smart man, and I know whatever he wants me to do will be the right thing. I trust him."

Jeffery beamed. "Fantastic. I'll start the paperwork to have you named as the new property owner of Harry's home, and you can decide what to do with the contents. I will need your bank information so I can transfer your inheritance from your uncle to you."

This was surreal.

"I'll have to email that information to you."

"No problem," Jeffery said, and smiled.

I zoned out for a minute or two, enough time to allow myself to comprehend the magnitude of what I'd inherited. I came back to the present just as Jeffery, who was speaking to my nanny, said, ". . . had me draw this up after he found out about his heart condition."

"Wait a second," I suddenly gasped. "What do you mean by 'heart condition'?"

I looked from Jeffery to the faces of my family members.

"He didn't tell you?" My mother seemed surprised.

I stared at her. "You think I would have stayed away if I knew he'd had a heart condition? Really, Mum? Do you think that little of me to ever believe I'd be so dismissive of someone I love so much?"

My mother shook her head. "No, of course not. I just can't believe this. How could he *not* have told you?"

She looked at my father as if he had the answer.

We all looked to Lochlan when he spoke. "Isn't it obvious?"

"Not to me," I quipped.

"Why didn't Kale allow anyone to tell you about Kaden when he died?" my brother asked.

I swallowed. "Because he didn't want me to come unless it was my decision to."

Lochlan nodded. "Uncle Harry obviously thought the same as Kale. He knew you better than anyone, and he knew that you weren't ready to come home, so he kept the heart condition away from you."

I was furious.

"Why does everyone think they know what's best for me?" I snapped.

My father sighed. "Because *you* don't know what's best for you, darling. If we step on your toes, it's because we want to help you."

I knew that was true, but it didn't make it any less frustrating.

"What was wrong with him?" I asked, my heart pounding in my chest.

My mother answered me. “He had coronary artery disease.”

I sucked in a pained breath. “Did . . . did you all know he would die?”

If they said yes and still had never contacted me to tell me, I didn’t know what I would do.

“No,” Layton said. “We didn’t. We all only found out about it a few months ago because he had some chest pains here and there. He changed his diet, took on different medication in order to lower the risk of a heart attack, but none of it worked. He refused a procedure to try and remove some plaque because he didn’t want to be stuck up in a hospital. You know how much he hated them.”

“I can’t believe this,” I murmured. “I had no idea.”

“This is a lot to process for you, Lane. Take a minute,” Layton said.

My nanny placed her hand on mine. “The will is done with. You said you’d abide by the condition to keep everything. You don’t have to stress about that; we can get in and clear everything out at any given time. There’s no rush on it.”

“Unless,” Lochlan murmured, “you plan on selling and moving back to America.”

He wasn’t being rude; he was just stating one of my options.

“Do you all think New York is the best place for me?” I asked, my eyes pleading for honesty. I needed some guidance, and the usual two people I sought it from – my best friend and uncle – were gone from this earth.

“No, I don’t think it is,” my mother answered. “I’m not just saying this because I want you to come home, but you’ve been there for six years, and I saw the moment that you looked at Kale in the parlour the night you came home that nothing had changed for you. Whatever you thought would be solved by moving to America hasn’t changed. You still love him.”

She's right, I thought. *I do still love him.*

"I'm really confused, and I don't know what to do," I admitted. "You're right, Mum: I do still love Kale, but things are even worse than they were before. He lost Kaden and Drew, and in a lot of ways he lost me too. I've changed, and so has he. I don't want to cause any more hurt. What if being here makes everything worse?"

"What if it doesn't?" Layton questioned.

My shoulders sagged. "That's a pretty big 'if', Lay."

He nodded. "It is, but what do you have to lose?"

"Nothing," I replied.

"Exactly," he stated. "If nothing comes of you and Kale, at least we will all be here for you. You won't be alone again, and you'll never have to go to bed questioning if you've done the right thing. You tried being away, and it didn't help. It's time to be here and see what happens."

Layton was right. But could I handle coming home and going back to being just friends with Kale? I didn't have the answer.

"I'm scared," I whispered.

My father hunkered down in front of me and pushed loose strands of hair out of my face. "You have to be brave, kid."

I nodded.

"Can you really see yourself goin' back ta New York knowin' everythin' ye now know?" Nanny asked me.

I envisioned myself going back to New York and falling back into my usual routine while knowing Kale was back home, needing support. I thought about how I'd never receive a phone call, email or Skype invite from my uncle again, and how I'd be on my own whenever I missed him. I wondered if I could deal with only speaking to my family on the phone or over Skype when I felt so loved and supported in their presence. I asked myself one very important question: *Can you go back to feeling hollow and numb?*

"No," I said aloud, answering Nanny's question, and my own.

My family looked at me, and I saw the hope in their eyes.

"What are you saying, Lane?" my father asked. "Be blunt."

"I can't go back – I don't *want* to go back," I said, and I knew that when I spoke those words, I truly meant them.

"Lane," my mother whispered, tears filling her aqua-blue eyes.

I pressed on before the emotion of my decision hit me. "I'm staying here," I said, and felt the weight of the world fall off my shoulders. "Harry's house will be my house. I'm moving back here for good. I'm done with being away from you all. Uncle Harry's passing has shown me that this is where I belong. With you all. I belong at home."

Multiple arms came around me, and I heard little whimpers of joy and relief that I knew came from my mother. I made sure to hug each of my family members and assured them I was dead serious. I was moving back home.

Holy. Shit.

Roman. His handsome face was the first to enter my mind. I didn't know why the urge to speak to him was so great, but it was. There was so much that I had to tell him, and I suddenly couldn't wait to talk to him.

"Roman," I breathed when my family released me. "This is all a lot to take in, and I want to talk to my friend."

"You can use the office next door," Jeffery offered as he stood up from his desk.

I thanked Jeffery and walked into a large adjoining room that had a few boxes stacked on top of one another. I wasted no time in taking out my phone and dialling Roman's number.

He answered on the fifth ring.

"Hello?" His voice sounded huskier than usual, and it was then that I remembered it was very early in New York City.

"Sorry, Ro." I winced. "I forgot about the time difference. I didn't mean to wake you."

"It's fine," he assured me after a long yawn. "I'm glad you called. Are you okay?" I was about to answer, when he suddenly inhaled sharply. "Shit, sorry," he breathed. "You just buried your uncle. Of *course* you aren't okay."

I sat on a lone chair next to the window across the room. "I'm as well as can be expected, but I didn't call you to talk about that because I'll just cry, and I'm so fed up with crying."

"What did you call about then?" he quizzed.

"I don't know where to begin," I said on a groan.

"From the beginning?" Roman suggested. "That's as good a place as any to start."

"Kale's son, Kaden," I blurted out. "He died when he was ten months old, from cancer."

"Oh, my *God*."

"I know." I swallowed a lump that had formed in my throat. "And Kale made sure I didn't know about it because he didn't want me to come home unless it was my choice."

"Holy shit!"

"Right?" I breathed. "*And* I just found out that my uncle died of a heart condition that he hid from me. I just found out about it. Like Kale, he didn't want me coming home unless it was my choice."

"Lane, fucking hell, that is *insane*!" Roman stated. "I thought my family was the only one with deep dark secrets, but yours takes the cake."

I nodded in agreement. "But on a lighter note . . ."

"Girl, what?" Roman gushed.

"Lochlan is *engaged*!"

Roman sucked in a huge amount of air. "I'm fucking devastated!"

I couldn't help but giggle. Roman announced his attraction to my brothers when he saw a photo of them on my phone and declared he was only my friend so he could one day meet them.

"The plot thickens," I said, "because he is engaged to *Ally Day*."

Silence.

"*Please* tell me there is more than one Ally Day in your town."

I snorted. "Not that I know of."

"Dude!"

"I know, I bloody *know*," I said with a shake of my head. "She told me she was sorry for every mean thing she had ever said to me. I forgave her, but it will be a long time before I can shoot the shit with her, you know?"

"Totally," Roman quickly said. "I'm proud of you for forgiving her in the first place. I know how much she and that Anna bitch messed with your self-esteem."

"I'm just happy Layton isn't secretly dating Anna. I would have exploded altogether."

Roman laughed, which made me smile. "Are things okay with your family?" he asked.

"They are. I sorted things with my family. We're all very good."

"I'm so happy to hear that, babe. I know how much they mean to you and how much it hurt that you rarely spoke."

"Yeah," I agreed. "That sucked arse."

Roman chuckled, then said, "Are things with Kale any better?"

My shoulders sagged. "Yes and no."

"Bitch, explain that," Roman demanded. "I want to know *everything*."

"He doesn't hate me like I feared. He has spoken to me, joked with me, and he took care of me on the day of my uncle's funeral.

He was, as usual, his perfect caring self, but there is an emptiness in him, Ro. I see it in his eyes. I know that sounds crazy, but I can see the difference in them."

"His son died. I don't think that kind of pain will ever go away; it will just get easier to bear over time."

I rubbed my face with my free hand.

"It feels like I've been home years instead of just four days." I exhaled. "I've learned so much, and it's draining."

"Do you feel any better with your newfound knowledge?" Roman asked.

"Yes and no. It hurt to learn about Kaden and my uncle's condition, but if I hadn't been left in the dark, I don't think I'd have made the decision I did."

"What decision?" Roman quizzed.

Tell him, my mind urged.

"I'm staying, Ro," I whispered.

He cleared his throat. "I had a feeling you would."

I pulled the phone away from my ear and stared at it for a moment. Roman had never given me any inkling that he thought I would ever return to York, so his admission stunned me a little.

"Can you repeat that?" I asked, my eyes wide, when I placed the phone back against my ear.

Roman chuckled. "You've been away from home for six years, and while you think you're pretty good at hiding your feelings, I can *see* how much you miss your family when you talk about them. Throw in your uncle dying and finding out your best friend's kid died . . . there's no way you're leaving your family – or Kale. You're home."

My throat was tight with emotion.

"I just want you to know that I'd have been lost without you. I love you with all of my heart – well, with what's left of it anyway."

Roman sniffled. "Shut up. Stop talking like we're never going to see each other again. We'll talk all the time on the phone and Skype."

I nodded even though he couldn't see me.

"Will you stay in your parents' house?" Roman asked.

Uncle Harry's will, I reminded myself.

"Actually," I chuckled, "my uncle has sorted my living arrangements for me."

Roman gasped almost instantly. "You got his house?"

"He left me *everything*," I emphasised. "His house, his money, his possessions. Everything."

"Oh, my God," Roman breathed. "I love your uncle so much for taking care of you."

I swallowed. "He is still looking out for me."

"He always will," Roman stated.

I smiled. "He is sneaky, though. I inherit everything on a condition written in a letter he left me. I haven't read it yet, but I can only imagine what he wants me to do."

"Lane, you've been in York for four fucking days! How could all this have happened in four days?"

"You know what, Ro?" I laughed. "I've been asking myself that exact same question."

Roman and I laughed and talked for a few more minutes. He assured me he would pack up my apartment and reminded me to email my landlord about my moving out. When it came time to say goodbye, I felt so much better about everything. Roman was a true friend and would be the only thing I would miss about New York.

When we hung up, I re-entered Jeffery's office. My family and Jeffery were chatting, but when my father spotted me, he crossed the room and stood before me.

"Are you okay?" he asked.

I nodded and gave him a hug. "I'm good, thanks, Dad."

I pulled back from my father and looked to Jeffery when he called my name. He had a brown envelope extended in my direction. "Here is the letter from your uncle."

With a shaking hand, I took the letter and thanked Jeffery. I stared down at the envelope and then excused myself from the room so I could go to the bathroom. I suddenly felt a little nauseated – the excitement had got to my nerves – and wanted to be near a toilet in case I threw up. After I splashed my face with water and took a few deep breaths, I entered an empty stall and sat on the closed toilet seat. With quivering hands, I opened the letter my uncle had written to me. I took a couple more deep breaths before I began to read.

Lane,

If you're reading this letter, it means I'm with my Teresa. Please don't be sad for me. Know that I'm out of pain and with my love. I'm happy. I'm sorry I never told you about my condition. I didn't want you to worry or come home out of concern for me. I don't know exactly when I'm going to kick it, but if the signs my body is showing are anything to go by, I think it will be soon.

Being thousands of miles away hasn't fixed anything. You need to come home and get some closure. I know that you're stubborn, though, and only something drastic will bring you home. I think it will be my funeral.

I've watched Kale over the last few years, and I'm just going to say it: that man loves you, kid. His face lights up when I talk about you and what you've been up to in New York. You make his day, even when you're not here. I know very well that you still love him too; you wouldn't be running away if you didn't.

No more excuses from you, sweetheart. I've made sure that when I'm gone you'll want for nothing. You'll just have to come home and fix things with Kale. I don't know what the outcome will be, I don't know if things will turn out the way you both want them to, but you need to talk. You know what talk I mean.

Take care of yourself, trust yourself, love yourself as much as I love you and be happy. You deserve it, darling. I'll see you later.

All my love,
Uncle Harry xx

Tears blurred my vision as I reread my uncle's letter over and over. I missed him so much it hurt, but I also wanted to whack him around the head for being such a sneaky shite. I laughed as I cried.

I folded his letter up and put it into my bag for safekeeping. After I exited the stall, I splashed some more cold water onto my face. I dried myself off as I glanced at myself in the mirror. As I stared at the woman looking back at me, I was happy to find that I was starting to recognise her again. I wasn't a stranger to myself anymore.

I left the bathroom feeling drained, but good. My uncle had single-handedly secured my financial future and given me a beautiful home in the process. I was truly blessed.

I re-entered Jeffery's office to find that my family had left. I signed the papers to start the process of my inheritance.

"Hey," Lochlan called out to me when I walked down the hallway of the office building in the direction of the exit. "Everyone has gone back to Mum and Dad's. I told them I'd bring you home. Are you okay?"

I nodded. "I am – I just feel very overwhelmed. He's left everything to me with the condition that Kale and I talk."

"He did?" Lochlan laughed. "That sneaky son of a bitch."

I guffawed. "You can say that again."

"Are you ready to go?" my brother asked me.

I nodded but placed my hand on his arm. "Can you drop me off somewhere first?"

Lochlan raised an eyebrow. "Sure, where do you want to go?"

"I need to go and clear my head. This is a lot to process."

My brother frowned and gave my shoulder a squeeze. "Where will you go to do that?"

I smiled and looked up at the sky when we walked out of the solicitor's office. "To see Lavender, of course."

CHAPTER FOURTEEN

Six years ago (twenty years old)

Lane," my father shouted up the stairs, "can you come down here for a minute?"

I sighed and looked up to the ceiling.

"Can it wait?" I asked, irritated that he was interrupting me. "I'm meeting Lavender at the cinema in twenty minutes, and I'm not ready yet. She'll kill me if I'm late."

I think she knew I'd be late; it's probably why she was ignoring my calls and texts. She wanted to tell me off in person. I snorted to myself but stopped when my father replied.

"We need to talk. Right now."

Something was wrong, I could hear it in the tone of his voice. Without a second thought, I walked out of my room and headed downstairs and into the sitting room, where I found my parents. I was surprised to see my brothers and Kale there too. Everyone was on their feet, staring at me, and trepidation filled the room.

"Is it Nanny?" I asked, my heart in my throat.

My mother shook her head. "No, darling."

"Uncle Harry?" I pressed, noticing he wasn't in the room either.

My mother shook her head once more, but this time her eyes glazed over with tears.

"Tell me," I almost shouted with panic.

My mother burst into tears and couldn't speak around her sobs, so I looked to my father, who was frowning deeply at me. "Sit down, honey."

"I don't want to sit down," I argued.

Kale, who was standing behind my father, came to my side and put his hand on my back, nudging my body to move towards the sofa, where I caved and sat down.

"Okay, I'm sitting down. Now tell me what's wrong."

My father blew out a saddened breath. "It's Lavender," he said, his eyes locked on mine.

My mind went blank then, and any logical form of thinking went out the window. "What's Lavender?" I asked dumbly.

My father looked positively gutted. "She was driving home from work today," he said on a sorrowful sigh, "and got into an accident."

I felt my stomach churn.

"Lavender was in a car accident?" I asked, sounding surprisingly calm.

I felt as if my voice was on a speakerphone, because it suddenly sounded robotic and slowed down, like I was tripping on something and was hearing things.

"Yes, sweetheart, she was," my father replied, his eyes, and everyone else's, watching me with intent.

I heard my heartbeat as it thudded away. "We have to go to the hospital," I said, and tried to stand up, but Kale, who was still next to me, placed his hand on my knee, halting my movements.

I looked down to his hand, my eyes drilling holes into it. It was the first time since we had been together that he had touched me in a way that wasn't a friendly hug or nudge. It made me look at him with fear of what he was going to say next. The despair I saw in his eyes cut me in half.

"No," I said to him, almost glaring. "She's okay."

The muscles in his jaw rolled back and forth, and he stared at me. "I'm so sorry."

"No!" I said louder. "She's okay, she's just in the hospital—"

"Her dad rang your mum, Lane." Kale cut me off, the hurt he felt for me plastered over his face.

I became aware of everything.

My heartbeat.

The churning in my stomach.

The sweat gathering in the palms of my hands.

"Laney Baby," he murmured, and lifted his hand to my face. "I'm *so* sorry."

Shut up, my mind screamed.

I shook my head. "It's not true."

"She died, kid," he whispered. "Her injuries were too much for her to overcome."

I gripped onto my stomach when it lurched. "I'm going to be sick," I muttered.

I felt his arms come around me. One second I was in the sitting room with my family, and the next I was running up the stairs with Kale right on my heels. I made it into the bathroom just in time to vomit into the toilet. Kale was holding my hair back for me with one hand and rubbing my back with the other.

When I was finished, I sat back on my heels and took the tissue Kale offered me. I wiped my mouth, threw the tissue in the toilet and flushed it. I went still then and just repeated what Kale had said about Lavender over and over in my mind.

She died, kid.

"I have to go to the hospital," I said to Kale without looking at him. "I have to see Lavender."

Kale helped me to my feet and held onto my arm tightly as we descended the stairs. I walked straight to the front door and opened it, causing a stir behind me.

"Where is she going?" my mother asked, her voice rising an octave.

Kale sighed. "She wants to go to the hospital."

My mother began to cry again, and I didn't know why, but it was annoying me, so I walked out of the house and waited by my brother's car. Lochlan came outside and unlocked the doors, so I got inside and sat in the back seat, buckling my seatbelt.

Both my brother and Kale got into the car, and neither of them spoke to each other, or to me, as Lochlan backed out of the garden and drove to the hospital. It was the longest car journey of my life, but in reality it was only a few minutes. When we got there, Kale came into the hospital with me and did the talking at reception when I just stared at the lady who was asking me stupid questions.

He got permission for us to go to the family room at the back of the hospital near the morgue, and we walked together in silence.

"Say something, Lane," he pleaded.

I swallowed. "I have to see Lavender."

We came to a door with "Family Room" printed very clearly on it, and Kale lightly knocked. A few seconds later, a man opened the door, a man with bloodshot, swollen eyes, a man who was Lavender's father.

"Mr Grey," I whispered when I walked into the family room.

Mrs Grey, who was sitting in the middle of the room, surrounded by some other women, looked up when I entered the room, and when she saw me, she burst into tears and got to her feet. I instantly walked to her and encased her in my arms, holding her body to mine.

"She's gone, Lane," she cried into my chest.

My heart squeezed with pain, but for some reason, no tears came.

Not even one.

"I'm so sorry," I whispered, and gently swayed her from side to side.

I sat down next to Mrs Grey and her other family members while Kale hovered by the doorway, watching me with a sad expression. I turned my focus from him to Lavender's family, and I listened as they spoke about what happened to her.

She was driving home from her shift at work, and a drunk driver ran a red light and slammed into the driver's side of her car, causing a blow to her temple that killed her instantly. My stomach threatened to revolt as I listened to the details that the police passed on to Lavender's family, so I tried to block them out.

"Mrs Grey," I said.

She looked at me.

"May I see her?" I asked, praying she wouldn't deny me.

Her lower lip wobbled as she nodded. "We've seen her already, she doesn't look injured at all."

I stood up and asked, "Where do I go?"

Kale cleared his throat. "I'll bring you. I saw a sign pointing to the morgue."

I hugged Lavender's parents, said goodbye to her family, then left the room with Kale. We followed signs to the morgue, and when we reached it, I told the man outside the double doors that I had permission to see Lavender.

I gave him her full name, and he passed the information on to a staff member inside. He told me to wait a few minutes, and then I'd be allowed in when they were ready to show her. I thanked the man and lingered outside with Kale.

"Are you sure you want to do this?" he asked me.

I was never surer of anything in my life.

"I have to see her," I replied.

He was quiet for a minute or two, and just as he was about to speak, the double doors to the morgue opened, and I was told I could go see Lavender.

"Wait," Kale said as I began to walk forward.

He grabbed hold of my hand and said, "You don't want to see her like that, Lane. You think you do, but you don't."

I pulled my hand from his. "You don't know a thing about what I want, Kale. You never have."

I turned away from him and walked through the doors that led to the morgue. I nodded to the man who allowed me entry, and I followed a different man wearing a long white coat into a very cold room. I hesitated for a few seconds at the entryway of the room, but I walked through the doors. When the sight of my friend lying on a steel bed came into view, I placed my hand against my stomach in silent prayer for it not to spill.

I walked slowly over to Lavender, keeping my eyes on her beautiful face, and not on the white sheet covering her body. When I was next to her I reached out and placed the back of my fingers against her cheek, my heart squeezing with pain when I felt how cold she was. She had died only a few hours ago, but already her body was drained of heat, and it was hard to bear because I knew how much she hated being cold.

"How did you get here, Lav?" I whispered to her.

When she didn't reply, my lower lip trembled.

I could see the point on her temple where she had been struck. It was discoloured and looked a little dented, like something had crushed into the side of her skull. It was comforting knowing she had felt no pain, and she looked like she was sleeping, but my heart knew otherwise. Her cold skin was paler than I had ever seen, and her lips weren't pink anymore; they were a pasty white colour.

The bruising on her forehead and the rest of her face didn't look that bad, but logically I knew it was because she was dead, and that meant her body wasn't working anymore. Her heart wasn't pumping blood to give a distinct colour to her skin any longer.

I didn't know how long I stayed with her, but when I kissed her and left the room, I was shivering with the cold. Kale, who was sitting on the floor where I'd left him outside of the morgue, jumped to his feet when he saw me return.

"Are you okay?" he asked.

I shook my head but said nothing.

"Darling," he murmured.

"She's really dead," I whispered. "I touched her. She is really cold, her skin is sickly pale and she has no heartbeat. She's not moving, she's so still . . . just lying there with a little white sheet over her body."

"Lane," Kale sighed, and put his arms around my body, hugging me to him.

It was a weird thought, but I wondered what Drew would do if she knew Kale was with me. She'd probably lay me up in the morgue right next to Lavender.

"Sweetheart," he murmured, "you're scaring me. I've never seen you so withdrawn before."

I blinked up at Kale and said, "I don't feel anything. What's wrong with me?"

He frowned. "It's shock, that's all."

I felt numb, and I didn't like not feeling anything. I looked up at Kale then and decided I needed to feel something. Without warning, I lifted my face to his and brushed my lips against his. For a moment he applied a sliver of pressure, but then he broke away.

"I can't, Lane," he whispered as he pulled back from me. "I'm with Drew."

I felt like I'd been kicked in the stomach, and my chest ached. I got what I wanted. I didn't feel numb anymore.

"I know." I looked down, realising it was a shitty thing I'd just tried to do knowing good and well that he was taken. "I'm sorry."

"It's okay," he said, his voice low. "Do you want to go home?"

I shook my head. "I want to go see my uncle."

Kale nodded and exited the hospital with me. He called Lochlan on the way out to come and pick us up. We waited outside in complete silence. Kale turned to speak to me a couple of times but never got the words out. It got on my last nerve, so after the sixth time he did it, I said, "Just bloody say whatever it is you have to say."

"Drew, she's . . . she's pregnant," he blurted out.

I stopped breathing.

"She's having my baby." He swallowed audibly. "I'm going to be a dad, Lane."

I felt the blood drain from my face, and in that moment I was thankful I'd already puked today, because otherwise vomit would be covering Kale's polished-up shoes.

"Lane?" he prompted. "Say something, please?"

I only knew one thing to say that was acceptable.

"Congratulations," I whispered.

Kale took a step closer to me. "I didn't want to tell you today of all days, but . . . but with what happened back there between us, I felt like you should know."

I let that sink in, then after a moment, I looked up at Kale's face.

"How long have you known Drew is pregnant?" I asked.

Kale paled. "A few weeks now."

I took a step away from him. "A few weeks?"

He tried to close the space between us, but I held my hand up in front of his chest.

"Don't," I said, my voice almost a snarl. "Don't touch me."

"I'm so sorry. I know how you feel about me, or felt about me, so I know this isn't what you want to hear," he divulged. "Hurting you is the last thing I ever want to do."

I felt like I should be crying, but the tears wouldn't come. A fresh feeling of numbness rooted itself within me.

"All you seem to do is hurt me, Kale," I said solemnly.

"I don't mean to," he whispered.

I lowered my gaze to the floor. "I need to leave."

"Lane, please—"

"Kale," – I cut him off, my voice dropping an octave – "I need to leave. I don't want to be around you right now, so please, just let me go."

"I can't let you go," he replied, his voice strained.

I didn't know how to take that, but in that moment, I didn't care about Kale – or what he had to say.

"Congratulate Drew for me, will you?"

Kale's breathing picked up. "Lane, please, let me explain—"

"There is nothing to explain," I said honestly. "You and Drew are dating, you have on and off for years, so it's not a surprise that you would eventually get together for good and start a family."

It shouldn't have been a surprise, but it bloody well was.

"It wasn't planned," Kale blurted out.

That didn't matter. Drew was carrying Kale's baby whether it was what they wanted or not, and that was absolute fact. Another fact was that I needed to get away. I needed to get far, far away.

"I'm going to walk to my uncle's house," I said, turning away from him. "I need to walk."

"Lane!" Kale called out, the pain in his voice audible as I walked away from him.

Thankfully he didn't follow me, but I felt eyes on me as I walked from the hospital to my uncle's house, and I knew Kale and Lochlan were following in the car to make sure I got to my uncle's house safely. It didn't surprise me.

Lavender is dead, a cruel voice in my head reminded me.

My best friend, and the only person who knew every single one of my secrets, was gone. My confidante and partner in crime was no more. She was the one person in the entire world I could talk to about *anything.* I could act any kind of way around her, and she'd never judge me; she'd just laugh and join in with whatever craziness I was doing.

I never knew how much I loved her until I saw her lifeless body on that steel bed. I didn't even know if she knew how much I loved and appreciated her, and that without her I would have gone off the rails even more than I had already.

I took my phone out of my pocket, and I didn't know why, but I dialled her number and placed it to my ear. It didn't ring out; instead it went straight to her voicemail.

"This is Lavender, and there is a great chance that I saw your call but let it go to voicemail because I hate talking over the phone. What you should do now is text me. None of that leave your name and number bullshit – just shoot me a text and I'll hit you up. Latersss!"

I laughed as a beep sounded, indicating my message was recording.

"I swear your voicemail is *still* the stupidest thing I have ever heard, but I love it, and I love you, Lav." I swallowed. "Do you know where I just was? In the morgue, looking at you on a bed in a cold room. I'm really hoping you're going to text me and tell me that you just pulled off the most epic and evilest prank of all time. I really hope you do that because I don't want you to be gone. You can't be gone, do you hear me? We have too much to do. We have to finish college and go to Ibiza, do you remember? We said we were going to go there and have fun after we were done with school. So you can't be gone, we made plans and you can't break plans like those. You just can't . . . Please text me, Lav. I won't even be angry at such a horrible prank. I swear on my life I won't shout at you. I *promise*."

I neared my uncle's house and frowned as I squeezed my phone.

"Text me later, I love you."

I hung up just as I arrived at my uncle's house, and used a key he gave me years ago to let myself in. I stood in the hallway of his house, and even though something horrible had just happened, I felt safe.

"Uncle Harry?" I called out.

"In the kitchen, darling," came his reply.

I walked into the kitchen and found him at the kitchen table, a cup of fresh tea in front of him, and one on a coaster for me. "Your brother called ahead," my uncle said, answering my unspoken question.

I nodded and sat at the kitchen table, and took a sip of my tea.

"I'm so sorry about Lavender, Lane."

I didn't reply to him for a long time, but when I did, I felt like dying myself. "I've never had someone close to me die," I whispered to my uncle. "I know Aunt Teresa died, and I'm sad she is gone, but I was only twelve when that happened. I didn't understand then, but I understand now. Lavender is really gone, Uncle Harry, and she isn't coming back."

I broke down when my uncle's arms came around me. I cried the tears that hadn't come in the hospital when I saw Lavender or her family, or when Kale told me Drew was pregnant with his baby.

"Kale," I sniffled. "He is going to be a dad. He and Drew are having a baby."

I heard my uncle mumble, "Fuck."

It mirrored exactly what I was thinking.

"What are you thinking?" my uncle asked me.

"I want to leave here," I whispered.

My uncle frowned down at me. "Darling, I don't think leaving is the best thing for you—"

"My best friend just died, and Kale and Drew are having a baby," I said, cutting him off. "I can't be here to watch him have a family with someone else. I don't have Lavender to help me get though that. I need to get away from here, from him. I think it will help me finally get over him."

"Lane—"

"I can't be here anymore, Uncle Harry," I cried. "I can't do it anymore."

I felt my uncle's gaze on me. "Do you really want to move away?" he asked.

I nodded. "It hurts too much being here; it's killing me."

"Then do what you feel is right for you, sweetheart," he said after a lengthy silence.

I wasn't surprised by his support; I knew he'd give it to me.

I sniffled. "I'm scared."

"It's something new and unknown; of course it's scary, but that doesn't mean it'll be impossible. People move all the time. You aren't the first and you won't be the last."

I wiped my face with the back of my hands.

"Everyone will think I'm crazy."

My uncle sighed. "They'll be hurt and will probably say things they don't mean out of worry for you, but they won't hate you. You're precious to all of us, Lane."

I hoped he was right.

"I don't know where to start or how to start the process of moving."

My uncle asked, "Where are you thinking of going?"

Far, far away.

"I've been to New York with Mum and Nanny. I thought it was great there."

My uncle just stared at me. "America, Lane? Really?"

"I need distance," I whispered. "I *need* it."

He nodded his head and hugged me once more.

We got down to it then. With the help of my uncle, I found somewhere in New York to rent that, from the pictures, looked to be a complete dive for a price I could afford. I could finish my online classes from anywhere in the world, so that was in my corner.

I tried to refuse money from my uncle, but he gave me enough for my first six months' rent, and he also bought me a one-way ticket to New York. He made me promise to start accepting editorial work because even though I wasn't qualified to call myself an editor yet, he said I was good enough to edit anything that was given to me. He said he'd always known I'd work somewhere in the literary field because of my love for books and that I'd be damn good at my job. He even promised to set up a website for me because he said freelance editors needed to have something professional to engage clients. Once I agreed, he applied for an ESTA visa for me; it meant I could stay in the States for ninety days before I had to leave. As soon as I got over there, though, I would apply right away for a work visa to extend my stay.

In the space of three hours after I cemented my decision to move away, we arranged everything, and it was set that I would fly out after Lavender's funeral. I overheard in the hospital waiting room that her funeral was in four days' time, so it left me virtually no time to break the news to my family that I was leaving. I knew the conversation would be bad, but my mind was made up. I had to leave. Staying in York just wasn't something I could do.

I was about to tell my family that I was moving away, and even though I had my uncle in my corner, I was still scared shitless. I leaned against the kitchen counter while my family sat around the table. My uncle was leaning against the wall opposite me, with his arms folded across his chest. They all waited for me to speak.

"Lavender's gone and she is never going to come back to me." I sat, looking down at the floor. "And I haven't even begun to fully comprehend that yet. She only died three days ago, and nothing feels real to me. I'm expecting her to text me or walk into my room."

"Darlin'," my nanny murmured.

I bit down on my lower lip. "I want you all to listen to me clearly when I say what I have to say. It's important, okay?"

I looked up and found each person nodding.

"I love Kale," I breathed.

My brothers shared a look, and so did my parents before their gaze refocused on me.

"You love Kale?" My father blinked.

"I always have," I said, nodding.

My mother played with her fingers. "Are you *in* love with him?" she asked.

"Yes," I replied.

My father set his jaw. "And him? Does he love you?"

I shook my head. "Not in that way. He doesn't even know that I love him. I've never told him."

"Why not?" Layton asked.

Where to begin? my mind grumbled.

"Because everyone has gone on and on about how much of a brother and sister we are to one another, when I've never thought of him like that. Not since I was little."

My mother paled. "I didn't . . . I didn't know it was love," she blurted out. "I thought it was a crush."

I frowned at her. "It's not your fault, Mum. I've kept how I felt about Kale to myself. Only Lavender and Uncle Harry knew how I felt about him, but they were both sworn to secrecy by me."

My father cut his eyes to my uncle and glared at him, hard. It surprised me because I had never even seen my dad and uncle argue.

"Stop, Dad," I chastised. "I made him swear not to tell."

My father cut his eyes to mine. "Something is going on here, something bigger than Lavender and Kale. What is it? Tell me. Now."

Bloody hell, I thought. *Does anything get by him?*

I rubbed my face with my hands. "I can't be here anymore," I said, swallowing nervously. "Lavender is gone, and Kale . . . he and Drew are having a baby."

"What?" my brothers gasped in unison.

"Drew is *pregnant*?" Lochlan asked.

I nodded.

"Oh, honey," my nanny frowned.

"I can't stay here and watch them have a family. I can't stay here without Lavender. I need to get away."

My father set his jaw. "Like on a holiday?"

I shook my head. "No, Dad, not like a holiday."

Things were silent for a moment until Layton said, "You want to move away?"

I nodded.

"To where?" he asked.

It's now or never, I told myself.

"To New York."

Silence.

"Can you repeat that?" my father said, his voice dangerously low.

I swallowed. "I'm moving to New York."

My father's face turned a shade of red I had never seen before. He flicked his eyes to where my uncle stood, and he glared. "What the fuck is this?" he asked.

My uncle's shoulders sagged. "She can't be here anymore, Tom. She needs to get away and clear her head."

"So go down to the country for a spa weekend or something," my father bellowed when he looked back to me. "You are *not* moving to America. No fucking way."

I pinched the bridge of my nose. "I'm twenty, Dad. I don't need your permission."

"Don't throw that in his face," Layton snapped at me. "You aren't thinking clearly; you can't—"

I cut my brother off: "I can't *ever* think clearly here, Layton. I need to leave and figure myself out."

"Have you forgotten what happened to you last year?" he raged. "You could have died, and now you want to up and leave the country on your own? That's fucking selfish of you. You can't do that to us."

I pushed my hair out of my face. "I'm not trying to hurt anyone, Layton, but this is my decision."

"It's a shitty fucking one!" he bellowed, surprising all of us.

Layton was not one to fight; he was usually the peacekeeper, but not today. Today he was furious, and I was his target.

"I'm sorry you feel that way," I said calmly.

Lochlan growled. "You aren't moving to America."

I set my jaw. "Yes, I am. It's all arranged."

"What?" my mother whispered.

I looked at her and hated that I saw tears in her eyes. "I'm leaving tomorrow afternoon after Lavender's funeral."

"What?" everyone screamed.

I jumped and tried to think of something to calm everyone, but there was nothing I could say that would change the situation.

"Lane," Nanny shouted, getting my attention. "You cannot up and leave the country. You're distraught over losin' Lavender and about Kale startin' a family, but this isn't the right move, sweetheart."

"Staying here isn't an option," I replied. "I need distance. I need space. I need time."

"Are you hearing this bullshit?" Lochlan snapped at our uncle. "How can you stand there and be so calm when she is talking about leaving the country on her fucking *own* when she is in this state of mind?"

My uncle locked eyes with Lochlan. "Talking her out of it was the first thing I intended to do when she mentioned it, but I saw in her eyes that she was leaving here whether we wanted her to or not. It's be on board and help her or—"

"Or nothing!" Lochlan snapped. "If she leaves, I'm fucking done. I refuse to worry myself sick over her. I've done it all my life."

"Are you kidding me?" I said to my brother. "I never once asked you to bother yourself with worrying about me. I never asked for anyone to do that, but you all did it, and I know it's because you love me, but you can't protect me from everything. I have to do this."

"Why?" my father shouted. "*Why* do you have to leave?"

My shoulders slumped. "It's too hard."

"You will get over your crush on Kale—"

"It's not a crush. I love him!" I shouted.

My father narrowed his eyes. "You're twenty and you've never had a relationship. What do you know about love?"

My father's words cut me deeply.

"I know that watching him be with someone else is *killing* me, do you understand that?" I asked, my voice tight with emotion. "It. Is. Killing. Me."

"She's in a state over Lavender and—"

"Nanny, stop," I said, cutting her off. "I'm not blinded. I'm seeing clearly and I need to leave here."

"If you leave here, Lane," my father said coldly, "don't come bloody back!"

With that said, he left the room, leaving me staring after him with fear swirling around in my stomach. I looked to Lochlan and Layton when they stood up.

"Please," I pleaded. "I don't want to leave and be fighting."

"Then stay and there won't be a problem," Layton bit out.

I shook my head. "I can't."

"Then I have nothing else to say to you." Layton walked out, and I looked from him to Lochlan, who was staring at me with a pain in his eyes that I didn't understand.

"If you leave here, and you cause a rift between all of us, then I am done. Fucking *done*."

My lower lip wobbled when my mother and grandmother stood and left the room without a word in my direction. Not a curse word, not a farewell. Nothing.

"Oh, my God," I breathed. "They hate me."

I felt my uncle's arms come around me. "They don't hate you. They're hurt and scared for you. I told you, you're precious to us all."

I hugged my uncle tightly. "They don't understand me."

"They will, just give them time."

I nodded and breathed my uncle's scent in, remembering everything about him in that moment because I didn't know when I would next be able to hold him like this.

~

Do I have everything? I thought to myself as I scanned my parents' sitting room for the millionth time. I was flying out to America today to start a new life, and I was a nervous wreck. I was so emotional. Breaking the news to my family had been an utter disaster. I couldn't lie: it hurt that they didn't even want to say goodbye to me, but I knew how upset and worried they were for me. They just couldn't get on board, and the Edwards stubborn trait reared its ugly head when I wouldn't change my mind for them.

It didn't help that I had buried my sweet Lavender only a few short hours ago and was experiencing a pain that I had never known until they lowered her six feet below the earth. My trip was a great distraction, though, and I immersed myself in it instead of thinking about my friend.

"Money," I mumbled to myself, and checked my personal belongings once more.

My Uncle Harry would be by soon to bring me to the airport, and he would run through a checklist with me. He had travelled hundreds of times and would catch something if I forgot it.

"Lane?" Kale's voice suddenly called out.

Oh, bollocks. I paled. *What the fuck was he doing here?*

I turned and looked at Kale with wide eyes when he walked into the sitting room. His eyes went directly from me to the two large suitcases that were next to me. He stared at them, hard, before he lifted his gaze to mine.

"What are they for?" he asked, frowning.

Please, I silently pleaded, *go away.*

"What are you doing here?" I asked, dodging his question.

He blinked his whisky-coloured eyes that I loved so much. "Lochlan called me and told me you needed to talk to me and I had to come over right now."

Anger surged through me. "Lochlan is a fucking bastard!" I growled.

How fucking dare he, my mind raged.

Kale refocused on my suitcases. "Lane, what are they for?"

Fuck.

"I . . . I have to leave."

Kale didn't move an inch. "I don't understand," he said after a few moments. "I mean, I get what this looks like, what it is, but *why*?"

I looked away from him. "You know why."

He sucked in a breath. "Please don't tell me this is because of *us*?"

Was there ever an "us" to begin with? my mind taunted.

"I'm leaving because I need space, a lot of space, to clear my head. It's been clouded with you for years, and I just need to get you out of my system. Lavender is gone too, and I just can't be here without her. I buried her today and it's hitting me that she is gone. I need to get out of here."

The muscle in Kale's jaw rolled back and forth as I spoke. "Where will you go?" he asked.

"New York," I swallowed. "I found an apartment with cheap rent in a good neighbourhood."

I watched as Kale let my words sink in. "America?" he whispered. "You're leaving for *America*?"

I nodded. "I'm sorry, but I have to leave."

"And I only find out now?" he angrily snapped. "Right before you walk out the door to up and move out of the country, you decide to fucking tell me?"

Anger was good; I could fight it with my own.

"Yeah, like how you knew Drew was pregnant for weeks and never told me until a few hours *after* I found out my best friend was dead?"

Kale reeled back like I hit him. "That's different."

"How?" I snapped.

"Because I was figuring out a way to tell you without hurting you."

It was always going to hurt. Always.

"You're having a baby with someone else. How could that ever not hurt me?" I asked as my shoulders slumped.

Kale licked his lip, and instead of answering my question, he said, "This is so fucked up."

Finally, something I agreed with.

"Yeah," I nodded. "It is."

He remained silent in the doorway of the sitting room, blocking my exit. I pushed my glasses up the bridge of my nose and checked the watch on my wrist. When I saw the time, I cursed. "I'm not going to make my flight if I don't leave now," I said to Kale. "I have check-in and security to get through, and my gate opens in an hour."

He stood rooted to the spot.

"Kale," I said with impatience. "Move."

"No," he replied firmly. "I won't. We can figure this out. You don't have to leave the bloody country, Lane."

I didn't want to hear any of this, so I gripped my cases and tugged them over to the doorway and tried to get by his lean body. I angrily shoved at his chest when he wouldn't budge.

"Move!" I pleaded.

"Lane!" he shouted and grabbed hold of my arms. "What the hell do you want from me? Nothing I do is good enough for you. What the hell do you want? *Tell* me, because I don't fucking know."

I dropped my guard and unleashed the feelings I'd bundled deep down for years.

"You, Kale!" I bellowed. "I just want *you*!"

Kale stumbled back a step or two from me like my words hit him with the force of a train. When he balanced himself, he stood motionless as he stared at me. The silence between us was deafening, but I used it to get everything I had wanted to say all my life off my chest. I needed to tell him how I felt, even if it meant the end of everything.

"I've always wanted you, but I couldn't have you," I cried, breaking down as fat tears fell from the brim of my swollen eyes and rolled down my flushed cheeks. "I have to leave. It's ripping me apart watching you be happy with someone else. I want you to be happy, I swear I do, but it's hurting me that I'm not the woman making you smile. I'm so tired of being sad, Kale."

Kale didn't speak; he just continued to stare at me.

"I love you. I've always loved you . . . just not in the way you love me." I looked him in the eye. "I'm *in* love with you. I have been forever."

Kale opened his mouth to speak, but when nothing came out, he closed his lips.

I held my hand up. "You don't need to say anything – you don't even need to feel any type of way about this," I assured him. "This isn't your issue; it's mine."

Kale blinked his eyes a couple of times.

"You love me?" he whispered, his eyes wide and distant.

I swallowed. "Yes, I love you."

Kale blinked his eyes back into focus and trained his gaze on me. "But . . . but you told me it wasn't like that between us – you told me it wasn't. I asked you, and you told me no. You told me no."

My heart shattered once again.

"I was terrified what I felt was wrong. I tortured myself for years because I thought I was dirty for loving a person who everyone considered my brother." I cast my eyes downward to try and gain control of my tears; if I didn't look at him maybe I wouldn't hurt as bad.

"We have been around each other since the day I was born. You were the first man that wasn't my father to hold me. I know you were little too, and at that time it was friendship that sparked, but it changed for me, Kale. I've loved you since that night when I was ten years old and you slept outside my wardrobe all night with a baseball bat to keep the monsters away. I just didn't realise you keeping them away would awaken new ones within me."

I could tell by the look on his face that he was in shock. He couldn't begin to think about the weight of my words until he had time to process what I was telling him. He needed space, and I was going to give it to him.

"You told me no," he whispered.

I sobbed when his eyes filled with water.

"You told me no. I wanted you, and you told me no. I hurt when you refused me your heart, God knows." He wiped his tears as they fell onto his cheeks. "I hurt so bad, Lane, but I learned to live with it. I learned that there was never going to be a Kale and Lane together in the way I wanted. I learned to love you without needing you. I learned to move on from you."

I didn't think I could hurt more than I already did, but hearing the words "move on" come from Kale broke me into a million pieces. I wanted the floor to open up and swallow me whole.

"I'm with Drew, and I love her. She is an amazing woman, and she's stood by me for as long as I can remember." I looked up as he spoke, even though it was killing me. "I'm going to have a baby with her, I'm going to marry her one day. But I don't think I'll ever be able to look at her and feel the way you made me feel."

"Made", not "make". Past tense.

"Kale, I'm so sorry," I whispered, and gripped onto the arm of the sofa next to me to keep from falling to my knees.

"I'm sorry too," he replied. "You have no idea how much."

He took a step backwards, then another, until he was out in the hallway.

"Take care of yourself, okay?" He swallowed. "I'll always be here if you need me."

He turned then and walked out of my life, destroying what was left of my heart in the process. Before the hall door clicked shut, I heard him say three words that would haunt my dreams every night for the next six years.

"Goodbye, Laney Baby."

CHAPTER FIFTEEN

Day four in York

"Hey, Lav," I said, smiling down at the picture of my old friend on the front of her beautiful grey marble headstone.

I reached out and brushed my thumb over the image, then sat down on the cold grass of her grave and criss-crossed my legs. I placed the bouquet of lilies I brought her in front of the cute little ornaments on her grave and sat, simply staring at her picture.

"I'm sorry this is only my second time to come and visit you," I began, then frowned, guilt gripping me. "After your funeral things kind of went to hell."

I could practically hear her voice in my head say, *"No shit, Sherlock,"* and it made me smile.

"Things with Kale went really bad, Lav, and then they went even worse with my family when I packed up and high-tailed it out of here." I swallowed and looked down at my hands. "I ran away and stayed away for six long years."

I sighed and shook my head.

"I was so heartbroken when I found out you died, and then I found out that very day that Drew was pregnant with Kale's baby. It was all too much, and I figured if I was thousands of miles away, it would somehow help, but it didn't. My mind is my own worst enemy. Even though I couldn't see Kale, I would envision him and Drew together with their baby all the time, and it killed me." I frowned deeply. "When I wasn't thinking about them, I was thinking about you and what would have happened if you hadn't died. I don't think you would have let me leave . . . I don't think leaving would have even been an option if you had still been here. Losing you pushed me over the edge, Lav."

I licked my dry lips and looked back up to Lavender's headstone.

"Everything ended up being a nightmare, though. Things panned out worse than I ever could have imagined. Kale's poor baby boy died, and now he is alone. I can sense the change in him. I see it in his eyes. He's like me, just existing, and I hate that. I don't want him to feel like that because I know how empty and cold it is."

I picked a few blades of grass from the ground and broke them up with my fingers.

"I think about you all the time too, Lav," I said, just in case she thought I didn't. "You'd know what to do if you were here; you always had the best advice."

I glanced around me then, checking whether anyone was close to me. I was glad when I saw there was no one around; it made me feel better knowing my conversation with Lavender was private. Talking to her made me feel better. Even if she didn't reply back to me, I knew she was listening.

I could feel her.

"Are you with my uncle?" I asked in a whisper. "If you are, can you tell him that I really miss him?" I smiled as a cool breeze swirled around me. "I think I'm still in a state of shock, because I have moments where I completely forget that he is gone, then I realise he is, and my heart breaks all over again."

I rubbed my nose with the back of my hand. "I thought burying you was the hardest thing I ever had to do, but my Uncle Harry's death hurts on a whole other level. He was all I had from home after I left, and now he is gone."

I rubbed my eyes.

"I made things right with my family again. Being away from them, from here, was solving nothing. It was only causing more unnecessary heartache. And after all that shit that went down with Jensen when I was a kid, I really shouldn't have upped and left the country in the first place. Layton told me how much they would worry for me, but I didn't listen. I'm home now, though, and I've made things better."

I sighed and pushed loose strands of hair out of my face.

"I've yet to have my proper talk with Kale, and I'm honestly quite scared about it. I have absolutely no idea what will happen after we do talk, and the not knowing is terrifying, but no matter what happens, we need to clear the air. He needs to know how I still feel about him, and he needs to know why I couldn't be here anymore."

I was silent for a long time after I finished speaking. I just sat there as still as a statue while the magnitude of loss swept over me. It was a part of life, but it sucked. I was grateful to finally be seeing the light at the end of the tunnel. I needed my family now – I saw that clearly. Their love and concern wasn't overbearing anymore. It was comforting.

I wasn't staying to please anyone else, I was doing it for myself, and I couldn't help but smile because of my uncle's sneaky hand in it. I'd do right by him. I'd talk to Kale because I needed to speak to him for *me*, not for an inheritance. At the thought of Kale, I looked in the direction of Kaden's grave, and I froze when I saw who was standing before it.

Drew.

I watched her for a moment, and before I knew it, I was on my feet and walking towards her. I had no idea what I was going to say to her, but I needed to say something. Anything.

I approached her with the gravel crunching under my feet. I stood a few feet from her and exhaled a deep breath. "Hey, Drew," I said softly.

I startled her, because she jumped and looked at me with surprised eyes. "Lane?" she breathed, and placed a hand on her chest. "You scared me."

"I'm sorry." I frowned. "I thought you heard me walking up."

She shook her head. "I was in a world of my own."

I shoved my hands into my coat pockets. "I was visiting Lavender and saw you down here. I wanted to come and say hello."

She flicked her eyes over my shoulder before sliding her eyes back to mine. "I never got a chance to say it, but I'm sorry about your friend. Kale told me how devastated you were when she died. He said he lost you that day in the hospital."

I stared at her, surprised she'd revealed that to me.

"He said that?" I questioned.

Drew nodded. "He used to have nightmares about it. He'd sit up in the middle of the night apologising to you and trying to console you, but then he'd wake up and realise you weren't there."

My stomach churned because I knew that he had been trying to make amends and comfort me because that was when he had told me he and Drew were going to have a baby together.

"I'm sorry," I said.

Drew blinked. "What for?"

"For being on his mind when he was with you."

Drew smiled then, and I couldn't help but notice how pretty she was. She was older now, but she was also still the nine-year-old girl I'd first met in the school playground all those years ago.

"Lane, you were always on Kale's mind. He'd talk about you without realising what he was doing. We'd be watching a film or having a random conversation, and you'd pop into his head, and everything would become about you."

Shame filled me.

"I'm so sorry."

She laughed. "Why are you sorry? You couldn't help that he thought about you."

I knew that, but I felt guilty all the same. "I owe you a massive apology, Drew," I said, keeping my gaze on hers.

She blinked her emerald-green eyes. "What for?"

I swallowed. "For how I treated you growing up when you were nothing but sweet to me. I was petty, childish and plain horrible to you for no other reason than you had Kale. I was out of order to ever be rude to you, and I should have known better. I'm so sorry; I hope you can forgive me."

Drew stared at me for a moment, and then the corners of her eyes creased as she smiled. "You don't have to be sorry."

My mouth fell open, and it caused her to laugh.

"What do you mean?" I asked. "Of course I do. I was awful to you."

"I forgave you years ago." She shrugged. "You were heartbroken, and I now know that people do things beyond their control when they are heartbroken."

I looked at Kaden's picture.

"He was a little stunner, Drew. You and Kale created someone incredible, and I'm so sorry that he died."

"He's still with us." Drew looked from me to Kaden's picture on his headstone, and she smiled. "He was a hoot – you'd have loved him."

"I would have," I said quickly.

She sighed. "I miss him every day. He'd have been nearly six if he were alive now."

"Six," I whispered.

"He was a mini Kale," she mused.

I smiled. "Kale showed me videos and pictures, and I said Kaden was the double of him, but he was adamant that he looked like you."

That made Drew chuckle, and then a long stretch of silence unfolded before Drew looked at me and said, "You need to help him."

I blinked. "I'm sorry?"

"Kale," she said. "You have to help him. I've tried for years to help him find peace about losing Kaden, but he is trapped in time. Every day it's like he relives the day our son died. It took time, but I now relive the other memories we shared with our boy. I remember the good times. When I think of him, happiness fills me, but I know when Kale thinks of him, he's filled with sadness."

"I don't know how to help him," I admitted. "He isn't the same Kale I knew. Too much has changed between us."

To my surprise, Drew touched my shoulder and said, "The pair of you are two sides to the same mirror. You're the same but reflect different things. You *know* him, Lane, better than anyone. If anyone can help him, it's you."

I didn't know if her faith in me was well placed.

"I'll always love Kale, Lane," she continued, "but he was never mine."

My hands began to shake. "Of course he was."

She shook her head. "He was yours. He just didn't know it. I knew it, though, and I fought tooth and nail to have him when I knew I should have let him go to be with you. He chose you over me, and I know that if I'd never gotten pregnant with Kaden, he wouldn't have stayed with me as long as he did. Kaden bonded us together, but our son was never going to *keep* us together. We loved each other, but he loved you more."

"Drew—"

"The night of your uncle's birthday party, when I threatened you to leave him alone, I followed him back to your house, and I heard him tell you he loved you and that he wanted to be with you."

Shock tore through me.

"You did?" I whispered.

She nodded. "Instead of being mad at him, I started to hate you like you hated me. I hated you because you had his heart and I could never get it, and you hated me because I had his body and attention."

I didn't know what to say so I stared at Kaden's headstone.

"I can't believe things have wound up this way," I said after a few minutes of silence.

Drew chortled. "Trust me, I've thought that for *years*."

"I'm glad we're talking about this, though," I said to her. "I ran away to America to escape these kinds of conversations."

"How did that work out for you?" she asked, sarcasm laced throughout her tone.

I laughed. "Not good. I still feel the same as I did six years ago."

"*Tell* Kale that then, Lane," she pressed. "Don't leave anything to chance. You don't know what's around the corner for anyone. You could be here one minute and gone the next."

I nodded. "I thoroughly believe that."

"I'm sorry about your uncle," Drew said, as if she sensed me thinking of Harry. "He was a sweetheart and was great with Kaden when Kale brought him around."

I smiled. "I've no doubt. He was brilliant with me and my brothers when we were little. I think that he spoiled us because he never had any kids of his own."

Drew linked her arm through mine. "I want to be your friend. I want to get to know the Lane that Kale always went on about, because she sounded pretty cool. A little crazy, but still pretty cool."

I laughed as I turned to her and gave her a tight hug. When we separated, Drew walked up to Kaden's headstone and kissed his picture. "See you later, sweetheart." She turned to me and winked. "Don't be a stranger."

I nodded. "I won't. You'll see more of me, I promise."

Drew left then, and I could have collapsed with the weight that lifted off my chest. Never in a million years would I have thought a conversation with her could turn out that way, but I thank God that it did, because I didn't realise how much I needed to resolve things with her.

I looked at Kaden's sweet picture once more before I turned and walked back up to Lavender's grave, where I retook my seated position on the grass.

"Dude," I breathed, "I just made up with Drew Summers." I shook my head in disbelief. "She wants to be my friend and wants to get to know me. She wants me to help Kale too – can you *believe* that?"

I exhaled a deep breath because *I* still couldn't quite believe it.

"Lane, is that you?"

I looked over my shoulder when a man called my name. I pushed myself to my feet and brushed my clothes down when I saw a familiar face walking towards me.

"It *is* you," he said, smiling wide, his eyes gleaming.

I gaped at him in utter shock. The moment he smiled, I knew exactly who he was. There was only one person, besides Kale, whose smile I thought was stunning, and this man was rocking it.

"Daven?" I gasped. "Daven Eanes?"

He gestured to himself with the large bouquet of flowers he had in his hand.

"The one and only," he chuckled.

It was the strangest thing, but I felt like I needed to hug him, so that was exactly what I did. I moved to him, threw my arms around him and hugged him tightly. For a few moments he did nothing, but he eventually hugged me back, and laughed when I stepped away from him with wide eyes.

"You look like you've seen a ghost," he mused.

I blinked. "I feel like I have, I haven't seen you since . . ."

I stopped talking and frowned.

Daven gave me a small smile. "Since our girl's funeral?"

Our girl. That made me smile.

"Yeah, since then," I nodded. "It's been so long. How have you been? You look great."

He really did. He'd been a slim twenty-year-old boy when I left, but now he was a twenty-six-year-old lean man.

"Thanks, you're looking pretty good yourself," he said, winking playfully. "I'm doing great. I've got myself a beautiful wife, and we have two kids – twin boys. My wife is working on our third."

I gasped. "You have a *family*?"

Laughter rumbled from him. "You seem quite surprised."

Shit.

"It just seems so grown up." I chuckled, hoping I didn't offend him.

He smiled wide, taking my shock in his stride. "I did a lot of growing up after I lost Lavender. After she died, I did a lot of reflecting, and

I didn't like the person I was. I was an all-round arsehole, and I didn't treat Lavender the way she deserved. Thank God she put up with my shit all those years; I treasure every one of them that I had with her."

My heart warmed.

"She loved you," I said with a smile. "Trust me when I say I argued the case of how much of an arsehole you were better than anyone, but she knew you deep down, and she loved who she saw."

"Thanks, Lane," he said, his voice holding some sort of emotion that he chased away with a clearing of his throat.

I nodded. "It's the truth – she loved you greatly."

"I know," he said, smiling sadly. "I love her too. I always will."

Present tense. He was still in love with my wonderful friend, and I didn't blame him. She was one heck of a girl. "I love her too." I smiled, sorrowfully. "I miss her every day; I still can't quite believe that she is gone. It doesn't feel real, and I don't think it ever will."

Daven nodded in agreement, then turned and looked down at her grave for a moment before he placed the beautiful bouquet next to the flowers I'd brought her. He had a small smile on his face, and leaning down, he kissed her picture and murmured, "Hello, babygirl."

It choked me up.

"You want to know something?" I muttered to him.

He stood upright and looked at me. "What?"

My tears fell. "I've cried myself into dehydration multiple times since I got here on Friday."

Daven laughed at me and dug out a Kleenex packet from his back pocket. He took a piece of tissue out of the packet and handed it to me. I accepted it with a raised brow, and it caused him to laugh. "I've two kids, I need tissues and wet wipes on me at all times."

I laughed too and wiped my cheeks and under my eyes.

"So, you got home on Friday?" he asked.

I nodded. "Yeah, but it feels like I've been here a hell of a lot longer. I think it's the reason I'm back that has me so messed up."

"I'm sorry about your uncle, Lane," Daven said and gave my shoulder a squeeze. "I met him down the pub a few times after I got off work. He was a great guy. I went to his funeral, and I would have spoken to you, but you had a constant crowd of people around you that day. Kale was like your personal bodyguard; I didn't want to get too close. He isn't very fond of me for some reason."

I tearfully laughed as I wiped under my eyes once more. "He knew I didn't like you, so as my best friend, he automatically didn't like you either. It seems he hasn't grown out of it."

Daven snorted. "I'll say, sometimes when we're in the same shop or something, he'll glare at me until I'm sure he is going to kick my arse."

I laughed. "He would never hit you – he's not like that."

Or at least he used to be not like that.

"I hope you're right," Daven mused and dropped his arm from around my shoulder.

I smiled. "He's just protective I guess."

Daven's lip quirked. "After all these years, if he is still that way with you, then it seems like he has a thing for you."

I felt my cheeks heat up. "Give over."

Daven laughed at my embarrassment over his teasing. "Are you staying for long?" he asked, then winced. "Sorry, that was nosey. You don't have to answer; it's none of my business."

"Don't worry about it," I said, waving him off. "I am staying. I decided to move back."

Another stunning smile spread across Daven's face.

"You know what this means?" he asked.

I blinked. "What?"

"We'll have to hang out and become the proper friends Lavender always wanted us to be."

I smiled warmly. "She used to blow a fuse when we'd be at each other's throats."

Daven laughed and looked down at her picture. "She was perfect, wasn't she?"

I nodded. "She was; her heart was my favourite thing. She was just brilliant."

Daven smiled, then looked back to me. "You'll have to meet my wife and kids – they'll love you. They've heard about you from my stories about Lavender, so they'll want to meet you."

Daven worked his way into my heart with that one sentence.

"You told them about Lav?"

"Of course." He nodded. "My wife is the one who pulled me from my depression and helped me start living again. I love her with all of my heart, and I'm a lucky son of a bitch to have her. My boys have seen some pictures of Lavender, and they know of her as my good friend who is in heaven."

I placed a hand on my chest. "Daven, I might cry again. It touches my heart that you keep her memory alive when you don't have to."

He smiled sadly. "I acted foolish when I was younger, but I was so in love with her, Lane. She was my world, and when she died, I wanted to die too."

"Me too," I whispered.

Daven suddenly chuckled and wiped at his eyes. "She'd be laughing her arse off if she were here right now."

"Don't I know it." I chuckled and dried my face once more.

Daven looked up then and said, "There's your Kale, walking in the gate."

My Kale. I felt my face flush but didn't correct Daven. I looked up and saw he was right. Kale was walking up the left pathway that would lead him to the section where Kaden, my uncle and my aunt were buried.

"It's really sad what happened to his kid. I can't imagine what he must be going through."

I liked that he said "going" instead of "went". Daven knew that losing someone wasn't a particular feeling that lasted for a certain amount of time; it was something you had to live with for the rest of your life. I looked from Kale to Daven when he cleared his throat.

"Give me your number," he said, grinning, "so we can set up a playdate."

I laughed again and called out my number to him, watching as he saved it into the contacts on his phone. He winked at me and then gave Lavender's picture a kiss.

I heard him murmur, "Catch you later, babygirl."

When he stood up, he wiggled his phone at me. "Speak to you soon."

"I look forward to it," I said.

Daven left then; as he walked down the pathway towards the cemetery exit, I switched my gaze to Kale. I found him standing in front of Kaden's grave, his hands in his pockets as he stared down at the headstone. I wanted to go over to him, but I didn't want to intrude. Instead, I sat back down on Lavender's grave and smiled at her picture.

"You're taking care of Daven, I see." I shook my head. "I'm sorry I never saw what *you* did, but I'm seeing him now, and you were right: he is pretty fabulous."

I chuckled and then sat in silence for a while, picking blades of grass out of the ground and cutting them with my nails. I was about to talk some more to Lavender when a shadow fell over me. I looked up and Kale was standing over me.

"Hey," I said, smiling, and got to my feet, brushing my jeans down as I stood.

He nodded and joined me in looking down at Lavender's grave. I frowned as I stared at the picture of my beautiful friend who was taken far too soon.

"I saw Daven Eanes over here with you," Kale mentioned after a moment. "Did he give you any trouble? I know you never got on well with him."

I chuckled. "It was fine. I think we actually just became friends. He was visiting Lav and found me here instead."

"I see him here a lot," Kale commented. "He brings her fresh flowers every week. Sometimes his wife and kids are with him, and they keep her headstone clean and the area around it nice and tidy. He's pretty close to her parents too."

That brought me a great deal of comfort.

I exhaled. "It's insane to think he is married with kids. So many people that I went to school with are all moving forward and doing normal things people do when they grow up. They fall in love, get married and have kids. I feel stuck in time. Right now, I feel like I'm twenty again and just buried Lavender."

"I feel like that every day, kid," Kale sighed. "It's been five years since my Kaden died, and it still feels like I just lowered him into the ground."

My heart hurt for him.

"I hope it gets easier for you, Kale, I really do."

He didn't reply, but looked back to Lavender's picture.

"She was one of the greatest people ever," I said, smiling. "She came into my life right when I needed her; it was like she was my guardian angel. She helped save me from myself."

I shivered when Kale's arm slid around my waist.

"I'll be forever grateful to her for that," he murmured.

I looked up at him and sorrowfully smiled. "This hurts."

"I know, darling."

"Before anyone I knew had died, there was a time when I used to come here with my dad," I mused. "We'd take a shortcut through here to get to the playing field through the hedges, and I remember thinking, even though I was little, that I wouldn't like to say goodbye to anyone I loved. Now my aunt, uncle, friend and best friend's son are buried here. I still can't believe Lavender is gone, and I don't think I'll ever get over my uncle and Kaden."

Kale kissed the crown of my head.

"Life throws curve balls at you, Laney Baby. There will always be something unexpected. We just have to pick up the pieces the ball smashes and try to put them back together."

I frowned. "I'm not as strong as you, Kale."

He turned me to face him. "Are you joking?"

I shook my head. "I'm a coward."

He almost growled at me. "Don't you *ever* say anything like that about yourself again. After all the shit you've been through, you're still here, and that counts for something, Lane."

I stared up at him, mesmerised that I was finally seeing some emotion in him.

"I met Drew when she was on her way out," he commented. "She said you both spoke."

I nodded. "I apologised to her for how awful I used to be, but she was adamant that I had nothing to be sorry for. She's pretty great."

"Yeah," Kale agreed.

I glanced up at him. "She told me that you used to talk about me a lot, and that you used to have nightmares about—"

"The day I lost you."

I frowned. "Kale, don't do that to yourself."

He tried to smile, but his lips never did fully curve. "I can't help it."

"Hey," I murmured.

His whisky-coloured eyes roamed my face. "Yeah?"

I licked my dry lips and said, "I think it's time we had our talk."

CHAPTER SIXTEEN

Day four in York

Explain this to me one more time," Kale said as we entered his apartment. "Your uncle left you his entire estate, but under the condition that we . . . talk? Am I getting that correctly?"

Thank God it sounded just as insane to someone else.

I nodded. "Yeah, it was written in black and white. If we don't talk, and we both know what talk he means – he worded it exactly like that – then his estate will be liquidated into a lump sum and donated to . . . to the Liverpool Football Club."

A gasp of pure horror left Kale.

"That manipulative bastard," he said, scowling.

I couldn't help but laugh. Kale, like the rest of my family, was a hard-core Man United supporter.

"I just can't believe he had to take such drastic measures. I hate that I made him feel like he had no other option. He probably thought if he asked me to talk to you that I would have cut him off like I did everyone else."

My lower lip trembled as shame filled me.

"Hey now," Kale murmured as he moved closer to me and placed his hands on my shoulders. "He knew you loved him, but he also knew you needed to figure everything out for yourself. We all did. Your brothers and parents just took it harder because they were caught in the crossfire of losing you."

I nodded. "I know, but my decisions didn't help anything."

"Everyone makes mistakes, Lane. We learn from them and grow."

I glanced up at him. "When did you become so wise?"

His lip quirked, and for a second I thought I spotted the familiar glint that once dwelt in his beautiful eyes. "I've done a lot of thinking over the years."

I had no doubt about that. I had done a lot of thinking too.

There was a beautiful bookcase in the corner of the sitting room, and before I knew it, I found myself standing before it, brushing my fingers over the book spines in greeting. I loved books, and I loved that Kale still read them. I was about to turn away from the case when the name of an author caught my eye: K.T. Boone. She was an author I worked with. I scanned the other books and gasped.

"Kale," I breathed.

I felt him come up beside me.

"You . . . you bought every book I have ever edited," I whispered as my eyes scanned over the familiar titles.

Kale cleared his throat. "Like I wasn't going to follow your work. You're my best friend, and you have a kick-ass job. I've read them all. I had a book club in the making with your dad and Uncle Harry." He chuckled. "You're truly brilliant at what you do. I couldn't find a fault in any of them. I love reading the author's acknowledgements to you too. I'm so proud of you, kid."

Don't cry, I warned myself. *Don't you dare bloody cry.*

"This is so sweet, Kale," I said, clearing my throat when my voice dropped that octave.

"Speaking of sweet, you want a cup of tea?" Kale asked after a moment, and I appreciated the subject change.

I snorted. "Do you have to even ask?"

He grinned down at me and headed into the kitchen to put the kettle on. I followed him, and I glanced around as I walked, noticing how plain everything was. There were no pictures of Kaden anywhere, but I was too afraid to ask about it in case it upset Kale. I walked by him and moved to the large window over by his kitchen counter.

"Great view of the cathedral from here," I commented.

Kale chuckled. "Why do you think I bought the place? For the generous-sized rooms?"

I noted his sarcasm and grinned.

"I like it," I said. "It's cosy."

"It's nothing compared to your new house. Harry's place has five bedrooms." Kale whistled. "What will you do with all that space? It'll fetch a nice price for you, that's for sure."

I wasn't surprised that he assumed I would be selling my uncle's house; I'd been threatening to leave ever since I'd arrived.

"I'm not selling the house," I casually said as I continued to look out the window, admiring the beauty of the town.

I felt Kale's eyes on me. "What does that mean?" he asked in a low voice.

I shrugged. "It means I'm not selling. It's my house, and I don't want to sell it to someone else."

Kale swallowed. "Will you lease it out and be a landlord?" he asked, grabbing at straws. "You'd get decent monthly rent for it."

I shook my head. "No, if I did that I'd have to live in my parents' house forever, and while I love them dearly, I don't want that."

I felt hands on my shoulders, and then my body was turned.

"Don't play jokes on me," Kale warned, his eyes trained on me.

I looked up at him. "I'm not playing games. I'm telling the truth."

He blinked, his surprise evident. "You're . . . moving back—"

"Home," I finished for him. "I'm moving back home."

His eyes widened, and he didn't say a word, but just stared at me. I held back a gasp when the glint I thought I'd seen minutes ago flashed across his eyes, and this time it didn't leave.

My Kale, my mind whispered.

I glanced for something to distract me from doing something stupid. My eyes flicked around his empty walls, and I frowned. "Why don't you have any pictures up?"

Kale gnawed on his inner cheek. "Of Kaden?"

I nodded.

"Because they're a reminder that he is gone."

I tilted my head. "Couldn't they be a reminder that he was here? Even though it was for a short time?"

Kale looked away from me. "I don't know if I want to talk about him. It hurts."

"I know." I frowned. "I wish that one day we'd wake up and his passing would all just be a nightmare."

Kale gripped the counter, then took my hand in his and led me into the sitting room, where we sat on a very comfortable sofa. For minutes we sat in silence.

"I miss my son, Lane," he whispered. "I miss his laugh, his cry, his screams and even his serious conversations with his chubby toes. I miss everything about him."

I was silent as he spoke.

"Day by day it's ripping me apart because I know I'll never see him again. Never hold him again. It kills me that you'll never get to know him. I was robbed of you, and then I was robbed of him. God hates me. I hate me."

I got up and kneeled before him and put my hands on his face, forcing him to look at me.

"You're the bravest person that I have ever known. You're so strong, and sweetheart, you're a good fucking person. Horrible things have happened to you for no reason, because *no* reason is good enough for you to lose a child. The why can never be explained, and nothing will ease that pain you feel, but I truly believe that one day you won't feel sorrow or sadness when you think of Kaden. You will think of happiness and love, because I know in my heart that he was pure light. You *will* see him again."

Kale's whisky-coloured eyes were glazed over with tears, and when he blinked, they fell and splashed onto his cheeks. Without thought or hesitation, I leaned in and kissed the salty droplets away. I pressed my forehead against his and looked into his beautiful eyes.

"I wasn't there for you when you lost Kaden, but I will be here for you now and every moment after. I don't care what has happened between us in the past. Before you were my crush, you were my best friend. You're *still* my best friend, and I refuse to lose you again."

"You . . . you *really* aren't going back to America?" he asked, the hope in his voice almost breaking me.

I shook my head. "No, darling, no matter the outcome of this conversation, I'm not going anywhere. I'm staying right here where I belong, with my family, and with you in any capacity. You're my best friend. I'll give up everything before I lose that, lose *you,* again."

I barely finished speaking before he covered my mouth with his and kissed me.

"Kale, no," I said, and broke away from him. "You're kissing me because you're sad."

"No," he said, looking at me with searching eyes, "I'm kissing you because if I don't, I'll lose my fucking mind."

I sat back on my heels. "You don't know what you're—"

"Don't tell me what I'm feeling or what I'm thinking," he growled, cutting me off. "I'm sick of people thinking they know what's best for me. *I* know what's best for me."

I felt a moment of déjà vu as he echoed my earlier words to my family.

"And what's best for you?" I quizzed.

"You," he growled.

I was confused with his anger.

"You're mad at me," I said, stating the obvious.

"I'm not mad at you, Lane," Kale stated calmly. "I'm fucking *livid* with you."

I stood up as I sensed a fight brewing. Kale did too, because he was on his feet before I was. "Why're you angry?" I asked, confused.

"Because when I think about how things ended with us before you left me, it fucking infuriates me."

What the hell? I thought.

I pointed my finger at him. "You walked away from me, Kale."

"And you made damn sure of that, didn't you, sweetheart?" he bellowed, his tone taking me by surprise. "You told me everything I wanted to hear a year too fucking late."

"I never wanted you to look at me again the way you did the morning after we had sex, so when you told me you loved me, I lied and pushed you away to protect myself."

"Are you kidding me?" he screamed. "Are you *fucking kidding* me, Lane?"

I backed away from Kale's shaking form. He was fuming with rage.

"No!" he snarled, and shot forward into my personal space.

I wasn't planning on leaving, but he was making sure I couldn't even if I wanted to.

"You aren't running away anymore," he stated. "We're going to hash everything out right fucking now."

"I had to run away!" I screamed and shoved at his chest. "I couldn't sit by and watch you play happy families with her. I couldn't do it!"

"You didn't give me time after that admission," he snapped. "I realised the day after you left that I wanted you and not Drew, but you were gone, and I had a responsibility to step up with her."

"Exactly," I emphasised. "You had that – be thankful for it at least!"

"What the hell are you saying?" he shouted.

"If I'd told you I loved you, you wouldn't have had Kaden!"

Kale stumbled back like I'd punched him. "Don't you ever . . . don't fucking *ever* justify your walking out on me by using my son, do you hear me?"

"I'm not justifying anything, Kale," I said, my voice tight with emotion, "but it's true. If I'd told you I loved you, if I'd pressed you out of your comfort zone, then Kaden would have never existed."

Kale glared at me. "You don't know that."

"Yes," I said, nodding, "I do."

"How?" he growled.

"Because you would never have got back with Drew if you'd had me," I whispered. "I see that now."

Kale struggled to keep his composure. "So I'm supposed to be *happy* you left me? I'm supposed to be happy that I was robbed of six years with you?"

I shook my head. "No, you should be happy that I made a decision that led you to having Kaden, even if it was just for a short time, because I'm learning that having someone that special in your life is worth every second you have with them. Focus on that, focus on the time you had with Kaden, and you will be happy that you had him."

My own words triggered something my dad had said to me the night before my uncle's funeral. He'd said, *"You can find yourself again, and possibly help Kale find peace in the process."*

"I'm realising that for myself too, Kale," I said after a moment of laboured breathing. "It's killing me that my uncle is gone, but I cherish all the time I had with him, every memory, every laugh and even every fight. Lavender too. I wouldn't be the person I am today without her, and I miss her every day, but it's only because I loved her so much."

I looked up at Kale's glassy eyes. "I cherish every moment of our friendship before I left and lost you." I swallowed. "But even though things hurt, Kale, if we focus on the good times, the love we have for our loved ones will outweigh the heartache we feel when we think of them. I thoroughly believe that."

"Do you really think I can get to a point where I can be happy when I think of Kaden?" Kale asked me, his body still tensed.

"I do, and I'll help you *every* step of the way, I promise." My shoulders slumped. "You should be happy I didn't get in the way of Kaden, Kale."

Kale blinked at me. "You get in the way of everything, Lane."

I frowned. "I don't understand."

"I can't see past you," he said, and shook his head. "I've never been able to see past you."

I waited for him to explain.

"When Kaden was born, all I wanted was for you to be his mum so you could experience how brilliant he was right along with me. How horrible of a person does that make me? Wishing Drew was you? When I lost him, I wanted you there to make losing him easier. When I had Drew, I wanted *her* to be *you*. Every decision I make, no matter how small or stupid, is always accompanied with the thought of you. I incorporate you into everything without even meaning to do it. You're my life. You always have been."

Kale carefully watched me from across the room as I processed what he said.

"Want or wanted?" I whispered.

He raised his eyebrows at me. "Wh-What?"

"You wanted me, or you want me?" I asked, sucking up every ounce of courage within my body.

Kale pushed himself away from the wall he was leaning against. "Don't ask me that unless—"

"Unless *what*?" I interrupted.

"Unless you're fully prepared for my answer."

CHAPTER SEVENTEEN

Day one of forever

Worry filled me, but I didn't care, I needed the answer.

I stood up straight as I said, "Kale, you wanted me, or you want me? I'm not running away from you anymore. I'm not running away from anything ever again, no matter how scared I am."

He began to stalk towards me.

"Which one is it?" I asked with my head held high. "Because when it comes to you, it's always been want for me."

"I don't want you, Lane," Kale growled as he neared me. "I fucking *need* you."

He rushed at me and collided into me with his massive, sculpted body. I almost whimpered as the touch I so desperately craved invaded my senses. Kale took possession of my lips and kissed me so hard that it almost hurt. His hands were on my cheeks, holding me in place, and his forehead was against mine as he kissed me with a hunger that I eagerly matched.

I felt the passion he was showing me deep in my bones.

I gasped into his mouth when his hands slid down my body, around my waist and down to my behind where he squeezed. He bent his knees a little, then without warning he lifted me up into the air.

"Wrap your legs around me," he urged before taking my lips back as I became his willing captive.

I did as he asked and wrapped my legs around Kale's hips and my arms around his neck. I hummed into his mouth as we kissed. I rolled my pelvis into him, and he growled into my mouth, causing a surge of excitement to shoot through me. I knotted my hands in his hair and tugged on it, making him hiss as we kissed.

I grinned into his mouth, and he contracted his hands on my bottom, making me whimper a little as stinging pain hit me. It was Kale's turn to grin then, and I quickly found that whatever I did to him, he would do back to me tenfold.

That might not be so bad, my mind purred.

"Bedroom," I panted against his lips. "Now. I need you right *now*."

I needed him more than I needed my next breath.

With me still in his arms, he walked out of the sitting room and headed down a hallway. Down at the end of the hallway, he pushed open the door into his room and stepped inside.

I screamed when my mouth was torn from Kale's as I fell back through the air, only to land on a soft mattress. I gripped my chest and felt my heart slamming inside it. At Kale's laughter, I shook my head.

"You bastard," I said, laughing. "You frightened the life out of me."

I leaned on my elbows as Kale gripped his T-shirt from behind his neck and pulled it off his body, throwing it behind him. I stared at his body in awe.

"Holy shit," I breathed. "Kale, you have abs, and that V thing that is making me forget my own name."

"Oblique muscles, they're called oblique muscles." He snorted and crawled onto the bed, nudging his way between my thighs.

"I worked out a lot while you were away," he said, then brought his mouth down to my neck.

I placed my hands on his chiselled back, and the muscles beneath my hands moved. The pulse between my thighs was becoming unbearably achy, for which I blamed Kale's stunning body.

"You're so hot," I breathed.

Kale spoke in a low, guttural voice, "That'd be you."

I felt my cheeks heat up. "I'm not the size I was when I left here. I've probably gained between fifteen and twenty pounds and look like I've aged forty years while you've gone and got yourself ripped and become even *more* gorgeous. That's a shitty trade-off for you."

Kale pulled back from kissing my neck and glared down at me. "You. Are. Beautiful."

My heart thudded against my chest.

"Thank you," I whispered.

His gaze was still hard as he stared down at me. "Do you remember when you were fifteen, and I stood behind you while we looked at you in the mirror, and I listed everything I thought was beautiful about you?"

I'd never forget it.

I nodded, my breathing turning rapid.

"All of those things I listed back then have multiplied by a thousand now," he said and smiled down at me. "You're perfect, Laney Baby. Simply perfect."

My voice was tight with emotion, but I refused to cry.

"Take me," I pleaded. "Right now."

Kale's eyes flashed with fire as he reached down and pulled me into a sitting position. In the space of a few seconds, he rid me of my jumper, T-shirt and bra, throwing them God knows where. I lay back and fisted the sheets around me as he kissed his way down my stomach and used his teeth to pop the button on my jeans.

"Oh, God," I breathed when he lowered my zipper and I felt his hot breath on my skin.

My boots, jeans and socks were next to go. Kale gripped the hem of my underwear and slowly inched it down until I almost screamed at him to tear it from my body.

"Please," I panted.

He flung my underwear over his shoulder and brought his mouth down to my centre and inhaled. His hands gripped my thighs and he groaned.

"Fuck," he said, his voice strangled. "You smell better than I remember."

Crimson. That was the colour I was certain my face and neck were.

"Kale," I pleaded. "Inside me. Now."

"What if I want to take my time with you?" he asked, his voice low and husky.

I whimpered. "I'll fucking die, that's what."

I screamed when Kale suddenly buried his face between my thighs and flattened his tongue against me, lapping at me like I was his favourite treat. I thrashed about, and like our first time, he hooked his arms around my legs and clasped his hands together atop my mound. He held me in place while he licked and suckled on my slick bundle of nerves.

"So close," I cried out when I felt the delicious heat of bliss lick at my core, igniting a fire within me that I thought had burnt out long ago.

Right there, my mind screamed. *Right. There.*

"Kale!" I shrieked.

I sucked in a deep breath and held it as the first pulse of heaven slammed into me, followed by another and another. Each throb of pleasure spread to my every nerve ending, and sensation became me. I greedily sucked air into my lungs when they began to burn, a reminder that I wasn't breathing.

"I can't wait," Kale's voice growled, breaking through my clouded high.

I blinked my eyes into focus just in time to catch him rid his body of clothing and climb over me, his hardened length thick and purple as it jumped with anticipation.

"Later," he swore. "Later I'll take my time with you, later I'll explore every inch of you, but right now, I need you hard and fast."

I needed that too.

"Yes," I pleaded. "Yes, please."

Kale gripped the base of his length and rubbed the head up my glistening slit, causing my body to jerk at the sensation. He lowered the head to my entrance and slowly, painfully slowly, he pushed inside me. I cried out as I felt my inner walls stretch to accommodate Kale's thickness.

"Christ," he shuddered, his face looking almost pained. "You feel . . . it's impossible. You aren't a virgin. How are you this tight?"

"I haven't been with anyone in six years," I panted. "I wanted you, needed you. Never anyone else."

Kale lowered himself to his elbows as he buried himself to the hilt. I opened my mouth when he pressed his lips to mine, groaning when he nipped at my lower lip with his teeth.

"What you do to me, Laney Baby," he growled and began to thrust in and out of me as if the Devil himself were on his heels. "It's been years . . . so long, I won't last."

I cried out into Kale's mouth, and he took my cry and swallowed it down. He moved his hands until they were buried in my hair, and tugged on it, as he loved my body with his. I felt my insides tighten as Kale picked up his pace and slammed into me, dominating my body and heart with each thrust.

"I'm gonna come," he moaned. "You feel too good."

"Let me feel you lose control," I begged.

I dug my nails into his back, which caused him to hiss before he threw his head back and roared my name as he came, his hips jerking forward as his body sought its much-needed release. When he was spent, he fell forward and pressed his face into the crook of my neck. I panted as Kale lay sprawled out over my chest. His breathing was rapid, matching my own. I mustered up all the energy I had left in my body and tapped him on the back.

He hummed in response.

"If you fall asleep on me again," I teasingly warned, "I'll bite your dick off."

Kale winced, then vibrated with laughter. "I'll fall asleep next to you, cuddling this sexy little body of yours. How does that sound?"

I shivered as he pulled out of me and rolled onto his side; I snuggled closer to him, using his bicep as a pillow. "That was amazing," I whispered, smiling.

Kale lazily smiled. "That it was, darling."

I smiled back, but then quickly cringed. "We didn't use a condom. Again."

Kale widened his eyes, then closed them and cursed himself. "I'm sorry, Lane. I didn't even think. I don't seem to do that often around you."

I couldn't help but chuckle. "It's okay. I'm just mad because I didn't think of using one either, but don't worry. I'm on the pill, and I'm clean. We're good."

Kale nodded. "I'm clean too, and that's a relief that you're on the pill. I want you to myself for a long while before you get pregnant."

I felt my heart drop to my stomach.

"Kale," I whispered, "don't play like that."

He stared at me with happy puppy-dog eyes and said, "Do I look like I'm playing?"

He bloody did *not*.

I gaped at him. "You want us to have a *baby*?"

"I want us to have everything," he instantly replied.

Is this real?

I didn't trust myself to speak, so the only thing I could do was press myself as close as I could to Kale to show him that some day, I wanted everything with him too. I closed my eyes, promising myself to rest for just a moment and catch my breath. I heard Kale call my name a few times a few minutes later, but he sounded as if he was far off in the distance. When I didn't respond, I felt him look down at me and heard him laugh.

"Who is falling asleep on who now, kid?" I heard him chuckle as he covered us with a blanket and wrapped his body around mine.

I hummed with contentment, and just before I fell into the most peaceful sleep I'd had in years, my last thought echoed through my mind.

Please, I prayed, *don't let this turn into another nightmare.*

~

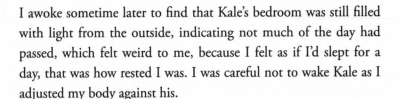

I awoke sometime later to find that Kale's bedroom was still filled with light from the outside, indicating not much of the day had passed, which felt weird to me, because I felt as if I'd slept for a day, that was how rested I was. I was careful not to wake Kale as I adjusted my body against his.

I lay watching him sleep for an hour or more, memorising every inch of him. I could have stayed and watched him forever, but when my stomach rumbled, I silently slipped out of Kale's bed and pulled on his plain white T-shirt, smiling when it fell to my mid-thigh.

I tiptoed out of his room, down the hall and made a stop into a room I discovered to be the bathroom. I cleaned myself up and went into the kitchen and put the kettle on, helping myself to the contents of his fridge. I set out making us sandwiches. I knew he would be hungry when he woke up, and I wanted to do something nice for him, so feeding him was my chosen deed.

"Lane!"

I jumped at Kale's roar and dropped the knife I'd used to cut our sandwiches in half. Then I automatically ran for his room when I heard a loud bang. I bolted into the hallway and ran for his bedroom door, reaching for the handle, but the door was pulled open before I got a chance to open it, and I ran straight into Kale's bare chest.

"What?" I asked, panicked. "What is it?"

Kale sucked in a breath and placed his hands on either side of my face, pressing his forehead to mine. "You were gone," he said, panicked. "I woke up and you were gone. I thought . . . I thought—"

"Shhh, sweetheart," I soothed, and wrapped my arms around his body.

I knew exactly what he thought; he thought I'd run away from him again.

"I'm here, Kale," I breathed, and kissed his chest. "I'm never going to leave you, I promise."

He hugged me so tightly I thought I might pass out. He released me after a minute, then held me out and his eyes scanned my body, before pulling me back into him, moulding my body against his.

"I feel like there is a monster in me, muttering in my ear that this isn't real."

I rubbed my hands up and down his back. "We all have monsters telling us lies that we can't have what's right in front of us. Mine told me the same thing about you, but for now, our monsters seem to get along."

He kissed the crown of my head. "It appears so."

I hugged him. "I was hungry, and I figured you would be too when you woke up, so I was making us sandwiches."

He exhaled. "I'm sorry, darling. I just reacted when I didn't find you next to me."

My stomach burst with butterflies.

I leaned back and smiled up at him. "I'll get right back into your bed next to you as soon as we eat."

"Sounds good to me," he said, lips curved upwards.

He kissed my nose, turned my body away from him, then slapped my behind, forcing me into a walk. I yelped, and Kale laughed.

"My clothes look good on you," he murmured as I walked in front of him and took the turn into the kitchen.

I chuckled. "You're just saying that because I've nothing underneath it."

Arms came around my waist as I continued to prepare our sandwiches, and through the material of Kale's T-shirt, he palmed my breasts, causing me to moan as my nipples hardened.

"You won't wear anything else when you're here," he murmured in my ear. "That's *my* condition."

I snorted. "Does everyone have a condition for me to abide by around here?"

Kale laughed and kissed the back of my head, lowering his hands to my hips. "It looks that way."

I leaned my head back against his chest and smiled. "Luckily, these conditions are something I can tolerate."

Kale's chuckle was a low rumble that caused his chest to vibrate. A comfortable silence fell between us as we ate our sandwiches and leaned against the kitchen counter, Kale holding me with one arm and his sandwich with the other.

"Do you feel like we've said everything that needs to be said?" I questioned when we finished eating.

Kale shook his head as he sat at the kitchen table. "You explained to me why you did what you did, and while I'm not happy over it,

I understand it. I know you need me to explain my part in all this, but first I want you to hear something that I truly mean from the bottom of my heart."

I licked my lips. "Okay."

"Laney Baby," he whispered as I sat on his lap and put my arms around his neck, "I've never said this to you while sober, but I am in love with you. I have been for a very long time, and I'm sorry for not telling you sooner."

The words I had dreamt of him saying for so long suddenly felt too hard to hear.

"Pup," I murmured, my lower lip trembling.

"Be mine," he pressed. "Be my girlfriend, my fiancée, my wife. Please, say you'll be my everything because you already are."

He's proposing to me? My head swayed as emotion, and utter disbelief, filled me.

"Isn't this too soon?" I asked, feeling like I was having an out-of-body experience. "We've only been back in each other's lives for *four* days—"

"It's long overdue, darling," Kale interrupted. "I should have asked you to marry me years ago."

I swallowed. "I don't want to rush into anything you'll regret."

He placed his hands on either side of my face and said, "I have *never* and will *never* regret anything about you. You're the love of my life, and I'm sorry I didn't realise it sooner. I'm sorry I let you think I regretted you; it was the only way I could think at the time to scare you away from me."

I almost fell off of his lap, causing his grip on me to tighten and keep me in place.

"What do you mean?" I asked, my heart pounding.

He brushed my hair out of my face and searched my eyes with his.

"I remember everything about the night you gave yourself to me," he said, shocking the hell out of me. "You were right: I wasn't *that* drunk. The drink just gave me the courage to be with you in the way I wanted to be. I was harsh and blunt with you to make you mad at me, so you wouldn't want anything to do with me in that way. I wanted you to believe I regretted making love to you."

I blinked as a veil of confusion fell over me. "I don't understand?"

Does he really not regret us being together?

"I was afraid of . . . of what your parents, my parents, your uncle and your brothers would think of me." He angrily shook his head. "I didn't want to lose your family from my life, and I thought they'd hate me if we got together. You told me you thought you were dirty for having romantic feelings about me because we were so close, and I felt the exact same way. I felt like I was taking advantage of your crush."

My crush.

"It wasn't a crush, Kale," I whispered. "I loved you."

He swallowed. "Is that still past tense?"

Tell him.

I shook my head. "I've never stopped loving you. You're embedded deep in my bones. I'd never love anyone as much as I love you in the *way* I love you."

"What way do you love me?" he asked, nervously biting his lower lip.

My lip twitched. "Not like a brother."

He glanced at our bodies, relaxed from lovemaking, and laughed. The sound warmed my heart.

"Marry me, Lane," he almost begged. "I promise to love, cherish and care for you until my last breath. Please, be mine."

He stared at me as if I had to even think about it.

"Yes," I nodded, my body trembling. "Yes, I'll marry you."

We kissed then, and I broke it off with a laugh.

"What's funny?" Kale asked, amused.

I shook my head. "I'm just wondering what my brothers and everyone else will think about this. Hey, guess what? Kale and I are getting married – surprise!"

Not that I cared what reactions we'd get, but I was still intrigued.

"Lane," – Kale chuckled – "your brothers have known I have loved you for *years*."

My jaw fell open.

"Yeah," he said, smiling at my expression, "I told them a few months after Kaden died. I told them what happened between us; I told them what I said to you, what I did to hurt you in order to turn you off me."

"What did they say?" I asked, completely taken back.

Kale snorted. "They told me I was a fucking idiot, which I am, for thinking that they would turn their backs on me. They said they would give their left arms to ensure you ended up with someone like me because they knew I'd never treat you badly, and I'd love you more than life itself. They said they'd be happy for us to be together."

"They did? Wow."

Kale nodded. "Even though they knew I loved you, they were sure you wouldn't come home, so they tried to push me into dating again, but it didn't interest me."

I stared at him. "Are you telling me you haven't been with anyone since you and Drew broke up?"

That would be years if he said yes.

"Why?" I asked when he nodded.

"I decided to wait for you to come home," he murmured.

"Why?" I pressed.

Kale licked his very tempting lips. "So I could make my play for you and try to win your heart back because I'm its rightful owner."

He was undoing me. "I can't believe you're saying this."

He took my hands in his. "It's the truth, darling. I've been waiting for you for the last five years. I'd have waited fifty if that's what it took."

"I feel like this is a dream," I said with a shake of my head. "You're telling me everything I have always wanted to hear."

He smiled. "We can have everything we've always wanted together now."

I began to tremble.

"We're really doing this?" I asked as pure joy filled me. "We're really going to be together?"

"Until my dying breath," Kale vowed.

My heart didn't know what to do; it was feeling something other than heartbreak for once and was close to shutting down. I pressed my forehead against his.

"The day you left, it took me all of two seconds to realise I'd die for you," he murmured.

Oh.

With a shaky breath I said, "I've been dying slowly, waiting for you, and I mean this quite literally – I can't live without you."

"You won't," Kale swore, pressing his forehead against mine. "I'll be with you until the day my heart thumps its last beat. You're everything to me. Do you understand that? Every. Fucking. Thing."

Tears seeped from my eyes and splashed onto my cheeks.

"I love you so much."

Kale smiled wide. "I love you too, Laney Baby, and to think we have your uncle to thank for bringing us back together," he said as he nuzzled his nose to mine.

I smiled warmly. "I miss him dearly."

"I know you do, sweetheart, but we'll see him again. We'll see your Aunt Teresa, Lavender and Kaden too." He nudged his nose into my neck. "We have a lot to look forward to as we grow old, darling."

I was going to grow old with Kale.

My Kale.

I joyfully smiled. "We do."

"Things would have been so different if you'd never come home," he murmured, his arm tightening around me.

"I know," I said, nodding against him. "Things would have never changed."

"Until Harry?" Kale questioned, kissing my shoulder.

"Yeah," I smiled warmly, closing my eyes as I bathed in the love my future husband freely gave to me. "Until Harry."

We were silent as we basked in the touch of one another.

"You're my soon-to-be *Mrs Kale Hunt*," Kale murmured.

I didn't know why, but I burst into laughter as I thought back to the times I'd scribbled those exact words all over my school journals and notebooks, wishing that one day those words would come true. Little did I know that day would come. Getting to it wouldn't be easy, but it would come, and I would be happy. Nothing else, just really bloody happy.

And you know something? My Uncle Harry was right. I deserved it.

CHAPTER EIGHTEEN

Day one of forever

"Nanny?" I said when I walked up the pathway of York Cemetery later that blissful and life-changing day and found my grandmother standing in front of my aunt and uncle's grave.

She looked over her shoulder and smiled. "Hello, me darlin'."

I put my arm around her waist and gave her a squeeze before standing by her side. "Are you okay?" I asked her.

She shrugged. "I'm okay as I can be."

I leaned in and kissed her temple before resting my head against hers. We stayed that way for a few minutes until my nanny spoke. "Lane," she began. "I miss me son," she said sorrowfully, "and I am sad that he is gone, but I'm also very happy that ye have come home ta us. I know Harry would have been over the moon with your decision, sweetheart."

I gave her another squeeze. "I'm just so sorry that it took me so long. I don't have everything figured out yet, but I'm getting there. I wish things didn't take so long to come to pass, though. I'll forever be regretful for that."

My nanny turned me to face her. "Listen ta me, Lane Edwards: ye did what you needed ta do at the time for *you*. Ye aren't a machine – you're a human, and you're no better at figurin' life out than the rest of us are." She reached for my hands and rubbed her thumbs over my knuckles, instantly relaxing me.

"I am so sorry for how we all reacted when ye broke your news about leavin', and I wish we could take it back, but ye were meant ta leave, and we were meant ta fight ye over it. Everythin' that has happened, the good, the bad, and the downright horrible, has led ta this moment. It was meant ta be, darlin'. Fate is a funny thing, and ye have no control over it. Ye can't even explain it."

"You just ride the journey that is life out and see where it takes you?" I asked, quoting her.

A beautiful smile overtook her face. "Exactly, and the sooner we all get that, the sooner petty things take a back seat to what really matters. Family. Friends. The things nobody should live without. You don't know what life has in store for you, sweetheart. Harry is a prime example that you have to live in the now, and stop dwellin' in the past. People create their happiness, but they also create their destruction. Live the life you want."

"You think people have that much control over their lives?" I quizzed.

My nanny lightly shook her head. "No, no one has control over their life span – that's out of our hands. But we can get a rein on how we feel while we ride this journey out. You just have to want it enough, or else happiness will pass you by, your life right along with it.

"You have your family right behind you, willin' to help you every step of the way. You don't have to run anymore. You can stand still and face everythin' head on, with us right along with you."

You don't have to run anymore. I repeated that particular sentence over and over in my mind.

I always knew that when I moved away, I was really running away, but I wasn't strong enough to do anything else at the time. Staying wasn't an option for me after life went to hell with Kale, and to hell in general. My heart ached every time I saw him, and I figured if he was out of sight, he would be out of mind.

Man, I silently sighed, *how wrong I was.*

Out of everything that was sour in my life, I hated my uncle being dead the most, but I couldn't travel any further along the path of despair that I'd paved for myself. If I wanted to feel something other than numbness, and sometimes sadness, I had to take my nanny's earlier advice and create my own happiness. I had to be there for myself. I had to take care of myself. I had to be my own rock, my own drive.

Being with Kale and having everything I'd always wanted gave me purpose, but I refused to allow him, or our new relationship, to be my only drive in life. I couldn't become so dependent on other people; in the past it broke me when they went away.

I blinked and tore myself from my thoughts, and I found my nanny staring at me.

"You look like you've decided somethin'," she mused.

I swallowed. "I did. I decided to create my own happiness."

My nanny smiled brightly at me. "I knew you would."

I released a shaky breath. "A few minutes in your presence, Yoda, and you have already turned my life around."

"Turned your life around, you did," she said, doing her best Yoda impression, making my lips curl upward. "I just gave you the little kick up the arse that you needed."

I smiled. "I've always thought I wasn't strong, but I'm beginning to see what Uncle Harry and you all see in me. In my own way, I'm a fighter."

"Your uncle shared a lot about you with me. He told me about your therapist spell and other things you got up to in the city, and let me tell you, you are strong. *You* decided to take action when you had those thoughts. *You* got help. *You* decided to stop your partyin' ways after you were attacked. *You* made a decision to help you cope with losin' Lavender and Kale. And now *you* have made a decision to come home and face everythin' head on. You're the strongest person I have *ever* known, sweetheart."

I let my nanny's words sink in, and smiled when I understood she was echoing what Kale had said to me earlier. They were right. I was strong.

I. Was. Strong.

Without speaking, I looked to my aunt and uncle's grave but looked back to my nanny when she touched my arm and said, "Your father is coming to pick me up. We'll wait out in the car park for you. You take as much time as you need with your uncle. I imagine you have a few things to say to the sneaky fecker."

I chuckled as I watched my nanny walk away, before I returned my attention to the earth before me. "You knew this would pan out the way it did, didn't you, Uncle Harry?" I saw my uncle's smiling face in my mind, and it caused me to chuckle. "I owe everything to you," I said with a firm nod. "You changed my entire life, and I will forever be grateful to you."

My lower lip trembled then. "I won't lie; I'm hurt and angry with you for not telling me about your heart condition." I swiped away a stray tear as it fell from my eye. "I would have come home sooner. I would have helped you. I would have been here for you."

I sniffled. "I know that you had your reasons, and while I may not know them all or even understand them, I'm confident you felt it wasn't the time for me to come back here yet. You were always the wise one in the family, and with you gone we're all bound to make some pretty risky decisions, but I hope you'll stay with us and help guide us in the right direction whenever we need a little nudge."

I felt a cool breeze wrap around me, and it almost took my breath away.

"You're definitely one of the loves of my life, and I'll forever miss you." I smiled, saddened. "Wait for me up there, okay? Your face is the first I want to see when it's my time."

I felt at peace with my uncle at that moment, and it was one of the best feelings I had ever experienced. When I turned and walked away from my uncle's grave, I had a smile on my face. I loved and missed him more than I could handle, and while I would forever wish to hold him just one more time, I knew that I'd get the chance to do it again one day.

I glanced over my shoulder as I walked away, and what I saw couldn't logically be explained. Maybe it was my mind or heart playing tricks on me. I saw my uncle sitting on top of his gravestone, with his arms around the waist of my Aunt Teresa and her head thrown back against his shoulder as she laughed with glee. Behind my uncle, I saw Lavender, who was dancing around in the grass and flowers with a small child in her arms, a child that looked exactly like Kaden. He was laughing with delight as he was spun round and round.

I stopped and stared for a second, and when my uncle locked his eyes on mine, he winked, and it sent shivers up my spine. They faded away then, my Aunt Teresa, Kaden and then Lavender. My uncle hung around a little longer, as if to see me off safely, and it made me smile. I decided then that I didn't want to see him fade away, because I knew he'd never be truly gone; I'd carry him around in my heart forever.

I smiled at him once more, then turned around and began to walk away, each step making me feel lighter than the last. Making me feel complete.

"I'll see you later, Uncle Harry."

THE END

ACKNOWLEDGEMENTS

I can't believe I'm typing out the acknowledgements on yet another book, but this book – this is a story that is very special to me and holds a very dear place in my heart. I've laughed and cried while writing Lane's journey, and I hope to have done her, Kale and Uncle Harry the justice they deserve. I wouldn't have been able to do it without an important group of people who define the word "brilliant".

My daughter – I love you so much, and after writing this book I'll make sure to stare at you a little longer, hug you a little tighter and love you a lot harder. You are my world, babygirl.

My sister – what can I say about your crazy self? It's quite simple, really; I love the bones off you. I am closer to you than any other person in my life, and there is no one else I would rather have as a partner in crime.

Yessi Smith – I never thought, when we first spoke over Facebook, that two years later we would be the best of friends. We talk every day about anything and everything, and we always have each other's back. Your help on my stories is forever appreciated. Thank you for helping make my babies an even better read. You're so important to me and I love you dearly.

Mary Johnson – You started out as a fan of my books and have grown to become a friend that I could, quite literally, not live without. Your friendship and support for my work and me are second to none, and I'm so blessed to have you in my life. I love you.

Mark Gottlieb – Thank you for going out on a limb for me and my stories. I couldn't have asked for a better agent to stand by me in this crazy literary world.

Melody Guy – Working with you has been an incredible experience. Your knowledge and editing style have helped me grow as a writer. I've learned so much from you. Thank you for loving Lane, Kale and Uncle Harry as much as I do.

Sammia and the Montlake Publishing crew – Thank you for giving *Until Harry* a fighting chance. You read a forty-page rough draft and offered me a deal based on something I wrote without giving it much thought at the time. I'm so thankful and happy that you did.

You, the readers – I hope with everything in me that you enjoyed reading *Until Harry*. This book is completely different from anything I have ever written, and I hope you fall in love with a group of characters that rule my heart. Thank you for taking a gamble on me, and for making my passion my job. You're all bloody brilliant!

ABOUT THE AUTHOR

L.A. Casey is the *New York Times* and *USA Today* bestselling author of the Slater Brothers series. She juggles her time between her mini-me and her writing. She was born, raised and currently resides in Dublin, Ireland. She enjoys chatting with her readers, who love her humour and Irish accent as much as they love her books. You can visit her website at www.lacaseyauthor.com, find her on Facebook at www.facebook.com/LACaseyAuthor and on Twitter at @authorlacasey.